THE MURDER AT MANDEVILLE HALL

THE CASEBOOK OF BARNABY ADAIR: VOLUME 7

STEPHANIE LAURENS

THE MURDER AT MANDEVILLE HALL

THE CASEBOOK OF BARNABY ADAIR:
VOLUME 7

#1 NYT-bestselling author Stephanie Laurens brings you a tale of unexpected romance that blossoms against the backdrop of dastardly murder.

On discovering the lifeless body of an innocent ingénue, a peer attending a country house party joins forces with the lady-amazon sent to fetch the victim safely home in a race to expose the murderer before Stokes, assisted by Barnaby and Penelope, is forced to allow the guests, murderer included, to decamp.

Well-born rakehell and head of an ancient family, Alaric, Lord Carradale, has finally acknowledged reality and is preparing to find a bride. But loyalty to his childhood friend, Percy Mandeville, necessitates attending Percy's annual house party, held at neighboring Mandeville Hall. Yet despite deploying his legendary languid charm, by the second evening of the week-long event, Alaric is bored and restless.

Escaping from the soirée and the Hall, Alaric decides that as soon as he's free, he'll hie to London and find the mild-mannered, biddable lady he believes will ensure a peaceful life. But the following morning, on walking through the Mandeville Hall shrubbery on his way to join the other guests, he comes upon the corpse of a young lady-guest.

Constance Whittaker accepts that no gentleman will ever offer for her —she's too old, too tall, too buxom, too headstrong…too much in myriad ways. Now acting as her grandfather's agent, she arrives at Mandeville

Hall to extricate her young cousin, Glynis, who unwisely accepted an invitation to the reputedly licentious house party.

But Glynis cannot be found.

A search is instituted. Venturing into the shrubbery, Constance discovers an outrageously handsome aristocrat crouched beside Glynis's lifeless form. Unsurprisingly, Constance leaps to the obvious conclusion.

Luckily, once the gentleman explains that he'd only just arrived, commonsense reasserts itself. More, as matters unfold and she and Carradale have to battle to get Glynis's death properly investigated, Constance discovers Alaric to be a worthy ally.

Yet even after Inspector Stokes of Scotland Yard arrives and takes charge of the case, along with his consultants, the Honorable Barnaby Adair and his wife, Penelope, the murderer's identity remains shrouded in mystery, and learning why Glynis was killed—all in the few days before the house party's guests will insist on leaving—tests the resolve of all concerned. Flung into each other's company, fiercely independent though Constance is, unsusceptible though Alaric is, neither can deny the connection that grows between them.

Then Constance vanishes.

Can Alaric unearth the one fact that will point to the murderer before the villain rips from the world the lady Alaric now craves for his own?

A historical novel of 75,000 words interweaving romance, mystery, and murder.

PRAISE FOR THE WORKS OF STEPHANIE LAURENS

"Stephanie Laurens' heroines are marvelous tributes to Georgette Heyer: feisty and strong." *Cathy Kelly*

"Stephanie Laurens never fails to entertain and charm her readers with vibrant plots, snappy dialogue, and unforgettable characters." *Historical Romance Reviews*

"Stephanie Laurens plays into readers' fantasies like a master and claims their hearts time and again." *Romantic Times Magazine*

Praise for The Murder at Mandeville Hall

"Stephanie Laurens never fails to delight with her tales of romance, mystery, and adventure set against the elegant, glittering backdrop of British high society." *Irene S., Proofreader, Red Adept Editing*

"A shared passion for justice turns into a shared passion for much, much more in this clever whodunit from Stephanie Laurens." *Angela M., Line Editor, Red Adept Editing*

"(The investigators) must sort through layers of intrigue and family pride to find the killer. At posh and proper Mandeville Hall, even murderers mind their manners." *Kim H., Proofreader, Red Adept Editing*

OTHER TITLES BY STEPHANIE LAURENS

The Promise in a Kiss

By Winter's Light

Cynster Next Generation Novels

The Tempting of Thomas Carrick

A Match for Marcus Cynster

The Lady By His Side

An Irresistible Alliance

The Greatest Challenge of Them All

Lady Osbaldestone's Christmas Chronicles

Lady Osbaldestone's Christmas Goose

Lady Osbaldestone and the Missing Christmas Carols (October 18, 2018)

The Casebook of Barnaby Adair Novels

Where the Heart Leads

The Peculiar Case of Lord Finsbury's Diamonds

The Masterful Mr. Montague

The Curious Case of Lady Latimer's Shoes

Loving Rose: The Redemption of Malcolm Sinclair

The Confounding Case of the Carisbrook Emeralds

The Murder at Mandeville Hall

Bastion Club Novels

Captain Jack's Woman (Prequel)

The Lady Chosen

A Gentleman's Honor

A Lady of His Own

A Fine Passion

To Distraction

Beyond Seduction

The Edge of Desire

Mastered by Love

Black Cobra Quartet

The Untamed Bride

The Elusive Bride

The Brazen Bride

The Reckless Bride

The Adventurers Quartet

The Lady's Command

A Buccaneer at Heart

The Daredevil Snared

Lord of the Privateers

The Cavanaughs

The Designs of Lord Randolph Cavanaugh

Other Novels

The Lady Risks All

The Legend of Nimway Hall – 1750: Jacqueline

Medieval (As M.S.Laurens)

Desire's Prize

Novellas

Melting Ice – from the anthologies *Rough Around the Edges* and *Scandalous Brides*

Rose in Bloom – from the anthology *Scottish Brides*

Scandalous Lord Dere – from the anthology *Secrets of a Perfect Night*

Lost and Found – from the anthology *Hero, Come Back*

The Fall of Rogue Gerrard – from the anthology *It Happened One Night*

The Seduction of Sebastian Trantor – from the anthology *It Happened One Season*

Short Stories

The Wedding Planner – from the anthology *Royal Weddings*

A Return Engagement – from the anthology *Royal Bridesmaids*

UK-Style Regency Romances

Tangled Reins

Four in Hand

Impetuous Innocent

Fair Juno

The Reasons for Marriage

A Lady of Expectations An Unwilling Conquest

A Comfortable Wife

THE MURDER AT MANDEVILLE HALL

THE MURDER AT MANDEVILLE HALL

Copyright © 2018 by Savdek Management Proprietary Limited

ISBN: 978-1-925559-13-2

Cover design by Savdek Management Pty. Ltd.

Savdek Management Proprietary Limited, Melbourne, Australia.

www.stephanielaurens.com

Email: admin@stephanielaurens.com

The name Stephanie Laurens is a registered trademark of Savdek Management Proprietary Ltd.

❀ Created with Vellum

CAST OF CHARACTERS

At Mandeville Hall:
Percy Mandeville – host of the house party, an annual event
Mrs. Enid Fitzherbert – Percy and Edward's ancient aunt; a deaf dragon to lend countenance
Edward Mandeville – Percy's older cousin; an unexpected addition, rigid and stuffy

House party guests:
Miss Holly Weldon – a connection of the Mandevilles; a delightful young lady as yet unmarried, an acquaintance of Miss Johnson
Mrs. Fortuna Cripps – Miss Weldon's chaperon; retiring but eagle-eyed
Miss Glynis Johnson – another delightful unmarried young lady; an acquaintance of Miss Weldon
Mrs. Dillys Macomber – Miss Johnson's chaperon; kind-hearted but given to dithering
Mrs. Rosamund Cleary – a friend of Percy; an experienced widow
Mrs. Prudence Collard – a friend of Percy; a racy matron with a good heart
Mrs. Tilly Gibson – an acquaintance of Percy; a well-heeled widow with her eye on a prize
Mrs. Hetty Finlayson – an acquaintance of Percy; a matron with a wandering eye

Mrs. Mina Symonds – an acquaintance of Percy; another matron with a wandering eye

Alaric, Lord Carradale – childhood friend of Percy and nearest neighbor

Mr. Montague Radleigh – Carradale's heir and a longtime friend of Percy; confirmed bachelor

Mr. Henry Wynne – the Earl of Dorset's nephew and a friend of Percy; has his eye on Mrs. Cleary

The Honorable Mr. Guy Walker – nephew of Lady Islay and a friend of Percy; currently looking over the field

Mr. Robert Fletcher – heir to Viscount Margate and a friend of Percy; also looking over the field

Cyril, Viscount Hammond – a friend of Percy; intent on consorting with Mrs. Gibson

Mrs. Caroline Hammond – Cyril's sister-in-law; a matron testing the waters

Mr. William Coke – an acquaintance of Percy; intent on enjoying himself

Mrs. Margaret Coke – dutiful wife of William; bent on enjoying herself

Colonel Walter Humphries – an acquaintance of Percy; long past active duty

Mrs. Maude Humphries – dutiful wife to the colonel

Captain Freddy Collins – a friend of Percy; very taken with Miss Weldon

Arriving later:

Miss Constance Whittaker – a distant cousin of Miss Johnson; a lady Amazon sent by Miss Johnson's family to fetch her home

Pearl – Constance's maid; mature and knows what's what

Vine – Constance's groom; there in support of Pearl and his mistress

Staff: all locals and long established in their positions

Carnaby – the butler

Mrs. Carnaby – the housekeeper

Various footmen

Various maids

Mitzy – the tweeny

Hughes – the stableman

Gardeners and grooms

At Carradale Manor:

Alaric Radleigh, Lord Carradale – a sophisticated rakehell in search of the right wife

Staff:
Johns – manservant
Morecombe – the butler
Mrs. Morecombe – the housekeeper
Hilliard – the stableman

From Elsewhere:
Senior Inspector Basil Stokes – of Scotland Yard
The Honorable Barnaby Adair – longtime friend of Stokes, acting as consultant to the Yard
The Honorable Penelope Adair – Barnaby's wife, longtime friend of Stokes, not about to be left out of the investigation
Constable Philpott – one of Stokes's regular team, an efficient note taker
Constable Morgan – another of Stokes's regular team, baby faced and good with staff
Sir Godfrey Stonewall – local magistrate; thinks highly of himself
Peters – innkeeper of Tabard Inn in nearby village of Wildhern

CHAPTER 1

AUGUST 26, 1839. MANDEVILLE HALL, HAMPSHIRE

What am I doing here?

With practiced languor, Alaric Augustus Radleigh, ninth Baron Carradale, strolled among the guests in the Mandeville Hall drawing room and endeavored to conceal his impatience to be elsewhere. Around him, the twenty-plus acquaintances the Honorable Percy Mandeville had summoned to his annual weeklong summer house party smiled, chatted, flirted, and preened. As it was after dinner and nearing ten o'clock on the second night of the planned revelry, amid the laughter and unceasing chatter, invitations of an intimate nature were being issued, not with words but with arch inviting looks. Or by a gentleman gazing into a lady's eyes while holding her fingers in a possessive clasp—as Mr. Henry Wynne was presently doing with Mrs. Rosamund Cleary, a fashionable and racy widow.

Giving no indication he'd noticed the couple's intent interaction, Alaric smoothly skirted the pair and continued moving through the crowd. He was passingly acquainted with all those present; Captain Freddy Collins determinedly caught his eye, and perforce, Alaric paused to exchange opinions on the latest fancy—and to bestow upon Freddy's attractive companion, Mrs. Hetty Finlayson, the pleasant but distant smile he'd perfected as a means of conveying to lovely ladies that he was reluctantly, but definitely, otherwise engaged.

Mrs. Finlayson wasn't the only bored matron attempting to lure him, but with gentle ruthlessness, he refused all offers; he had no interest in any short-lived and inevitably unfulfilling liaison.

He'd had a surfeit of such affairs over the years. Admittedly in the past, he'd found such engagements mildly amusing and had indulged when the mood took him. This year, however…he'd changed.

For the past decade and more, he'd prowled the drawing rooms and ballrooms of the upper echelons of London society and, in short order, had been deemed one of the more dangerous wolves of the ton. That long-established reputation was well known to those gathered at Mandeville Hall; they assumed it was the reason he was there.

Of course, by "dangerous," the grandes dames had meant that he was likely to turn the heads of impressionable young ladies, leaving them smitten and dreaming of him rather than of the more attainable gentlemen their mamas and said grandes dames steered their way. He embodied a threat to the grandes dames' schemes that, courtesy of his birth and station, was largely beyond their control—and such ladies never approved of anyone they couldn't rein in.

If they could see him now…the grandes dames would cackle themselves into fits. The notion of him finally biting the bullet and seeking a suitable wife would have them grinning evilly; that was one of the reasons he was determined to make his choice quickly, efficiently, and with as little social noise as possible.

The other major reason was his sisters. One older and two younger, all were happily married and comfortably settled, and all three had long been of the oft-stated opinion that he should join their company. Well aware of his age and situation, lately they'd shown signs of growing restive. If they heard or saw enough to suspect he'd finally come to the point of selecting a bride, they'd be on his doorstep offering to help within the hour. In his mind's eye, he could see their faces alight with enthusiasm… He would never be able to harden his heart enough to dismiss, deny, and disappoint them. Better he avoided the necessity altogether.

His parents had died more than a decade ago, leaving him as head of his ancient house, with the associated title and estate. Consequently, marriage at some point had always been in his cards, not least because his current heir, Montague Radleigh, also present at the house party, was viewed by the entire Radleigh family—Monty included—as unfit to inherit.

Monty had strengths, but those strengths did not include the talents required to run an estate. Although Carradale Manor, the house, was relatively modest, the wealth that lay behind it courtesy of farms, woodland, and funds invested was significant. So significant the family made a point of keeping that reality close to their collective chest; no one wished to see Alaric hunted by matchmakers intent on snaring a wealthy gentleman for their charges.

Luckily, Alaric's intentionally well-founded reputation afforded him some protection, ensuring that matchmakers did not glance his way and never looked deeply enough to stumble on the family's wealth. However, now he'd finally decided it was time to select a suitable lady and propose, the instant he took a public step in furtherance of that aim, the matchmakers' eyes would narrow, and they would delve and find out...

He judged he would have not more than a week to cast his eyes over the likely candidates before he became a hunted man.

The advisability of learning all he could about suitable young ladies prior to returning to town in a few weeks when society regathered in the capital was weighing on his mind and making the hours he was wasting at Mandeville Hall all the more frustrating. Admittedly, there were two marriageable young ladies present, but neither fitted his bill; both were too young for his taste.

Given it was late summer, as was his habit, he was in residence at Carradale Manor, his ancestral home, located approximately half a mile away through the woods. He'd spent the past weeks ensuring his affairs were in order and the manor was in excellent repair so that his way would be clear to make an offer for his suitable young lady the instant he found her.

He'd yet to decide whether to secretly appeal to his older sister for assistance; he wasn't at all sure she would agree not to tell the other two, and then...

With his ineffably urbane smile firmly in place, he finally stepped free of the crowd and paused by the wall, turning and pretending to idly scan the throng.

"Enjoying yourself, old man?"

Alaric turned his head as Percy Mandeville—his host—lightly buffeted his arm.

Smiling genially, Percy settled shoulder to shoulder with Alaric and surveyed his guests. "A good bunch, this year. Everyone seems to be getting on with no unexpected tensions." After a second, Percy glanced sidelong at Alaric. "Sure you wouldn't rather stay over the nights? You have before, and you know you always have a room here."

Alaric's smile grew more sincere. He shook his head, then met Percy's brown eyes. "I know, but this year, I have business to attend to." Deciding on the right wife surely qualified. "I didn't want to miss your house party, but to justify attending during the days and evenings, I need to retreat to my library at night."

And he needed the escape—and the safety of his own house. There, he was in no danger of having an unwanted companion attempt to invite herself into his bed.

"There you are, Carradale!"

In time with the booming words, a bony finger jabbed his arm.

Alaric turned to find himself being minutely examined through an old-fashioned quizzing glass wielded by a crone swathed in diaphanous draperies; thankfully, there were too many layers to permit any sight of what lay beneath. A silk turban in a hideous shade of puce wobbled atop the old lady's head; steel-gray curls protruded beneath the turban's lower edge. Knowing what was expected of him, he swept the old lady an elegant bow. "Good evening, Mrs. Fitzherbert. I would inquire as to your health, but I can see you're in the pink."

"Ha!" Mrs. Fitzherbert, an ancient aunt Percy invariably invited to act as his hostess and lend his house party a veneer of respectability, lowered her quizzing glass and narrowed her eyes at Alaric. "You always did have the most honeyed of tongues." She wagged a gnarled finger at him. "'Never trust a man who knows which compliments will most disarm one' is a maxim no lady should forget."

Alaric grinned. "In your case, ma'am, I speak only the truth."

Mrs. Fitzherbert huffed, but then something caught her eye and her attention. She waved a vague dismissal and lumbered off.

Percy sighed. "She grows more eccentric every year."

"If one lives to be her age, one is doubtless entitled to whatever eccentricity one chooses to claim." When Percy said nothing more, Alaric glanced at the younger man. Percy's gaze was fixed on someone in the crowd, but Alaric, following Percy's gaze, couldn't see who Percy was watching so intently and with an expression Alaric couldn't interpret.

Although several years younger than Alaric's thirty-seven, the Honorable Percy Mandeville had been a constant in Alaric's life ever since Percy had been born. Alaric had only sisters, and with Percy's brother considerably older, from an early age, Alaric and Percy had gravitated into each other's company; they'd spent untold hours escaping from their nurses, tumbling through brambles, and falling into streams. Needless to say, Alaric—older, taller, stronger, and more confident—had always been the leader, while Percy, suffering from the tentativeness engendered by being a second and significantly younger son, had scampered in Alaric's wake, much like a puppy eager to please.

Truth be told, Alaric suspected that the annual Mandeville Hall house parties Percy had hosted for the past six years—the present event being the latest—were simply another example of Percy attempting to emulate Alaric and, at least in Percy's mind, copy Alaric's lifestyle. Not that Alaric had ever bothered to host a house party; instead, he'd attended more of them than he cared to count.

Mandeville Hall had been made over to Percy a few years after Alaric had succeeded his father at Carradale Manor. In Percy's case, it was his father who had inherited the title of Viscount Mandeville, after which Percy's parents had decamped to the viscounty's principal seat in Lincolnshire, and Percy's older brother, next in line for the title, and his family had elected to remain at their home in Leicestershire.

Refocusing on the shifting crowd—more than twenty people in the Mandeville Hall drawing room definitely constituted a crowd—Alaric noted again the overtly assessing and, indeed, inviting glances thrown his and Percy's way. They were both tall and built to make the most of the prevailing fashion; Alaric had broad shoulders and the lean, rangy build of a horseman, while Percy was two inches shorter and heavier through the chest. Percy possessed a mop of shining blond hair and a complexion that, as he aged, would doubtless turn ruddy, making him an excellent visual counterpoint to Alaric's more dramatic appearance—his near-black hair, aquiline features, and pale, faintly olive-toned skin. Percy had once declared himself a true Saxon, or perhaps a Dane, against Alaric's rather obvious Norman.

What am I doing here?

In truth, Alaric knew the answer. He was there in support of Percy, in acknowledgment of the long association between Carradale Manor and Mandeville Hall, between the Radleighs and the Mandevilles, and between him and Percy. He was there because Percy invariably invited him and he always came, and if he'd declined, Percy would have been hurt.

In Alaric's mind, Percy still featured as the younger boy following at Alaric's heels, eager for approval and encouragement.

Percy stirred. "I should circulate."

"We both should." Remaining stationary for too long would invite an approach and an invitation Alaric would have to skillfully decline without giving offence. "I'll see you before I head off."

With a nod, Percy made for a large knot of guests before the main doors. Alaric went the other way, toward the loose gathering of couples before the fireplace. He paused beside Guy Walker, a gentleman of similar reputation, who was chatting with Mrs. Tilly Gibson, who was attending sans husband, as were her contemporaries, Mrs. Prudence Collard and Mrs. Mina Symonds. All three ladies had been casting looks in Alaric's direction; he kept Guy between himself and Tilly and, after exchanging various inconsequential comments, moved on.

There were two married couples present—Mr. William Coke and his wife, Margaret, and Colonel Humphries and his wife, Maude—invited to bolster the respectability of the event, given the nine unmarried gentlemen in the company.

"I say." Monty Radleigh, Alaric's cousin and heir, hailed Alaric as he was about to step past.

Styling himself as something of a sartorial maven, tonight Monty was resplendent in a fine gray suit worn over a satin waistcoat in alternating stripes of a palette of grays. Shorter than Alaric by a good half head, with pleasant but undramatic features and a figure tending toward the rotund, Monty relied on the perfection of his appearance and his unparalleled knowledge of who was doing what in society to claim his place in the ton. Surveying the company, he opined, "A very pleasant gathering, what? Nice mix of people, don't you think?"

When Monty looked inquiringly at him, Alaric voiced a niggling observation for which he hadn't yet learned the reason. "The only surprise is the two young ladies—Miss Weldon and Miss Johnson." Finding Holly Weldon and her chaperon, Mrs. Fortuna Cripps, and Glynis Johnson and her chaperon, Mrs. Dillys Macomber, among the company had been distinctly unexpected. "I can't recall Percy previously inviting unmarried young ladies, complete with duennas."

Monty nodded. "I gather Miss Weldon is a connection of sorts, and her parents, perhaps not quite understanding the nature of Percy's event, pressed for her to be invited."

Alaric didn't doubt Monty's information; his cousin had an uncanny knack for unearthing such tidbits.

"Actually"—Monty shifted closer and lowered his voice—"I have to wonder if there isn't some on-the-quiet romance behind it. Freddy Collins seems much taken with Miss Weldon, and there's no doubt she's a bright young thing."

Alaric chuckled. "Beware, Monty—she might turn her sights on you."

Monty blinked. "No, no." Agitatedly, he waved aside the notion. "Not on the lookout for a wife. Everyone knows that." Monty cast a faintly harried glance around; quite aside from being Alaric's heir, courtesy of several inheritances from his mother's side, he was also independently wealthy enough to feature on the matchmakers' lists.

Alaric took pity on him. "As you say, it's common knowledge that you're a dyed-in-the-wool bachelor. But when a young lady attends an event such as this, one has to wonder why."

A gentleman approached, and both Alaric and Monty turned to meet him. It was Percy's older cousin, Edward Mandeville. After exchanging a nod with Edward, Monty promptly excused himself and went off to join some other guests, leaving Alaric with Edward, a situation with which Alaric wasn't all that thrilled.

"I must say, Carradale," Edward intoned, turning to stand beside Alaric and look over the guests, much as Percy had earlier, "I'm pleased you saw your way to attending. It eases my—and the family's—mind to know you're on hand to rein Percy back from any behavior that would constitute that one step too far." Pompously arrogant, Edward continued, "The family and I are well aware you are one of the few to whom my cousin will pay heed."

Meaning Percy wouldn't listen to Edward's frequent and insistent proselytizing on the paths of virtue, a reaction few would hold against Percy. Edward was the son of Percy's father's youngest brother, who had become a clergyman in the fire-and-brimstone vein. Following in his father's—and indeed, his religiously devoted mother's—footsteps, Edward had elected himself the moral guardian of the Mandeville clan.

Alaric had met Edward at various Mandeville events over the years but had endeavored to spend as little time in his orbit as possible. And in light of Edward's remark, it seemed that Alaric's reputation wasn't quite as widely known as he'd supposed; Percy's wildest and most licentious forays were but a pale imitation of Alaric's previous deeds. Or misdeeds, as the case frequently had been.

Of course, Alaric had long ago attained the age of wisdom; these days, any wild and licentious deeds on which he embarked were suitably cloaked in impenetrable discretion.

Now he thought of it, Alaric felt that Percy was also beyond the age of needing to be reined in by anyone, but convincing Edward of that—especially at Percy's house party with the inevitable undercurrent of seduction and suggestive hints of illicit interludes—would be a lost cause.

Alaric lightly shrugged. "I confess I was surprised to see you among Percy's guests." *Did he invite you?*

Edward humphed. "I heard from my aunt, the viscountess, that Percy was stubbornly persisting in hosting this yearly bacchanal." Edward's gaze fell on Freddy Collins, who had Caroline Hammond on his arm and was laughing uproariously at one of the lady's quips; Edward's lip all but curled with contempt. "I took it upon myself to journey down and represent the family's interests. While my uncle, naturally, has said nothing on the subject, I cannot imagine he is at all pleased by Percy's libertine tendencies. I thought it wise to have someone from the family on hand to ensure that nothing of an inexcusable nature occurred."

What would qualify as something of an inexcusable nature? Alaric was tempted to ask, but held himself back. He didn't need to encourage Edward—the man was stuffy and stiff enough, convinced of his own superiority, and haughty and condescending with it.

More, Alaric was well acquainted with Percy's parents. Percy was his mother's favorite, her youngest child, and consequently would have to blot his copybook in some fairly major way to earn even her displeasure, much less her censure. As for Viscount Mandeville, he'd always treated Percy's occasional lapses from grace as nothing more than the usual peccadilloes to be expected of a younger son of Percy's station. Alaric knew that was the viscount's opinion because Percy's father had told Alaric so.

Clearly, Edward's presence at the house party was nothing more than Edward being Edward. Self-important and self-aggrandizing.

Alaric felt compelled to state, "I doubt anything of any real moment will occur. As Monty and I were just remarking, Percy appears to have outdone himself in assembling a felicitous combination of guests."

Preparing to move on, Alaric glanced about—only to realize he'd remained stationary for too long. Miss Glynis Johnson and Prue Collard were advancing on him, with Robert Fletcher and Monty in tow. It was impossible to mistake the shy intent in Miss Johnson's eyes. Alaric knew many young ladies viewed him as an unattainable icon, one they'd all like to try their hands at attaching. Clearly, Miss Johnson was set on having her tilt at his windmill.

Inwardly resigning himself to the inevitable, he heard a suppressed snort and turned in time to note that Edward had grown even more rigid, his expression setting in stonily severe lines. Alaric had to wonder what Edward had heard about Prue Collard; it had to be she who had incited his disapprobation given Miss Johnson was, as far as Alaric had gathered, of pristine repute. Prue's reputation, on the other hand, was distinctly spotty.

"If you'll excuse me." Before the others reached them, Edward curtly bowed, turned on his heel, and stalked into the crowd.

Alaric watched Edward go—put to flight by Prue Collard—and decided he owed Prue his very best smile. He turned to greet her and bestowed his welcome with gracious languor, making Prue beam with genuine good humor.

"No need to dazzle me, Carradale." A good-natured, kind-hearted brassy blonde whom censorious souls might describe as being no better than she should be, Prue halted beside him, drawing Miss Johnson to face him. "As I was saying to Glynis here, you're not one to exert yourself over any lady."

"Nonsense." Alaric aimed an easy smile at Glynis Johnson; a slender, sweet-faced young lady with wheat-blond hair piled in a knot on the top of her head and pretty pale-cornflower-blue eyes, Glynis provided an unflattering contrast for Prue, confirming the older lady's good nature. "I refute Mrs. Collard's assertion utterly." Even though it was true.

With two quick comments, Alaric drew Monty and Robert into a glib, light-hearted exchange centering on the classic romantic pursuits.

"I always thought Romeo's address to the balcony was a trifle over-done," Robert stated, eliciting indignant if laughing protests from both ladies.

The five of them continued to entertain each other with similar nonsensical banter.

After ten minutes of easy repartee, Glynis Johnson laid a tentative hand on Alaric's sleeve. When he looked at her, she softly said, "I find I'm in need of some cooler air. I wonder, my lord, if you would stroll with me on the terrace—just for a few minutes." She glanced toward a grouping of three chairs set against the wall; on them sat Mrs. Fitzherbert and the two chaperons, Mrs. Macomber and Mrs. Cripps. "I can't imagine anyone will make anything of it."

Alaric agreed, although he doubted his reasoning was the same as Miss Johnson's; all those present knew his tastes did not run to seducing innocent young ladies.

He was more than experienced enough to have refused Glynis's request without giving offence, but he was, frankly, curious over why she'd chosen him as her escort. With a half bow, he said, "Of course. A few minutes on the terrace will doubtless refresh us both."

They excused themselves to the other three, none of whom evinced any notable reaction, but as he turned Glynis toward the long windows open to the moonlit terrace, Alaric caught a flash of satisfaction in Prue's eyes. As he guided the younger lady over the low step into the cool of the night, he deduced that—for some reason—Glynis Johnson had enlisted Prue's aid in approaching him, presumably so Glynis could have the next minutes alone with him.

Intrigued, he gave Glynis his arm, kept a gentle, unrevealing smile on his lips, steered her along the flagstones, and waited to see what she had in mind.

Artless chatter appeared to be the answer. Contrary to any expectations he might have entertained, Glynis seemed, if anything, relieved to be on his arm; she strolled, apparently carefree, beside him.

Amused, Alaric continued to wonder what she was about. He was too well versed in social exchanges to need to think to keep up his end of the undemanding conversation. For her part, Glynis prattled happily about events and people she'd met during her Season—the plays she'd seen, the exhibitions she'd attended.

She was animated and engaging, but naturally so, and while anyone glimpsing them through the drawing room windows might imagine she was flirting with him, Alaric sensed nothing of the sort. Even when her eyes met his, their expression was open, innocent of guile.

She wasn't trying to attract him or even to elicit any response from him, yet…

The night air was pleasantly fresh, and strolling with a pretty lady on his arm was no hardship. Her gown, fashioned in that year's style, was of pale-blue silk, a hue the moonlight rendered almost silver.

Alaric listened to Glynis Johnson's chatter, nodded and smiled when required, and continued to observe and assess.

After ten minutes had passed and he steered her back into the drawing room, he'd seen her dart two swift, almost-too-quick-to-be-caught glances at someone among the company.

Some gentleman?

It wouldn't be the first time Alaric had been used as a pawn to incite jealousy.

Not sure what his next move ought to be—he was far more experienced in house-party dynamics than she—he guided her to where Percy and Monty were standing in a group with Cyril, Viscount Hammond, his sister-in-law, Caroline, and Colonel Humphries.

Cyril and Caroline welcomed them eagerly. While the older Walter Humphries chewed Percy's and Monty's ears over some matter of military history, Alaric stood beside Glynis and chatted easily—waiting for his chance to depart.

He needed time alone in his library to consider his next steps, matrimonially speaking.

At last, a break in the conversations allowed him to catch Percy's eye. "I really must head back to the manor."

"Oh! But you'll be joining us tomorrow, won't you?" Caroline asked.

"Assuredly," Alaric returned with practiced charm. "I have no intention of missing the coming entertainments or the chance to spend time in such engaging company."

Caroline laughed. "Flatterer." Her smile said she was pleased.

Glynis appeared less certain, but when Alaric turned to her, she smiled sweetly and gave him her hand. "Thank you for a pleasant walk on the terrace, my lord."

Alaric bowed with elegant grace. "The interlude was entirely my pleasure, Miss Johnson." He smiled, taking in her expression—that of an ingénue. "I bid you a good night"—he lowered his voice to murmur, just for her—"and good luck."

She blinked at the latter words, her expression turning faintly perplexed.

Alaric smiled more definitely; clearly, she didn't realize how transparent she was—although, he had to admit, he as yet had no idea which gentleman she was truly interested in.

After exchanging nods with Percy, Monty, Cyril, and Walter, he made his way out of the room and into the front hall. There, he found Carnaby, Percy's butler.

"Leaving us, my lord?" Carnaby moved to open the front door.

"Indeed. However, as I assured your master and several others, I'll return tomorrow."

Carnaby hauled the door wide. "For breakfast, my lord?"

Pausing on the threshold, Alaric shook his head. "No. I'll come later."

"Very good, my lord."

Alaric stepped onto the front porch and looked up at the sky. The night was clear, with no clouds to shadow the black velvet in which myriad stars shone brilliant and bright.

Drawing in a deep breath, he inhaled the scent of the surrounding woodland—a scent he'd known from infancy—replacing the stale air of the drawing room and the cloying miasma of perfumes. Feeling rejuvenated, he started down the steps and heard the door close behind him. On reaching the gravel of the forecourt, he lengthened his stride and headed around the house, then diverted into the shrubbery, taking his customary shortcut to the stable.

There, he found Percy's stableman, Hughes, holding Alaric's horse, a huge gray hunter named Sultan, saddled and ready. "Didn't think you'd be much longer, my lord." Hughes ran his hand down Sultan's long neck. "This old fellow seemed to know—all but put his own nose in the bridle."

Alaric grinned, scratched Sultan between the ears, then took the reins Hughes offered; while Carradale Manor was within walking distance, to attend the house party's events, he'd elected to ride, taking the bridle path that connected the two properties, stable to stable. "Thank you, Hughes." Alaric swung up to the saddle, then raised a hand in salute. "I'll see you tomorrow."

"Ride safe, my lord." Hughes stepped back.

Alaric wheeled Sultan and set him trotting out of the stable yard, then picked up the bridle path and, allowing the big horse to choose his own pace, headed for the manor.

For home.

Two-thirds of the way along the path, on impulse, Alaric reined Sultan in. The horse stamped, then reluctantly settled. At that spot, a gap in the trees and a dip in the land afforded Alaric a view of Carradale Manor that he'd long considered his favorite vista. From where he sat, perched high on Sultan's back, the woodland fell away, and rolling fields —all part of the Carradale estate—lay gently illuminated by the faint light of the moon. And on the distant rise, his house—his home—Carradale Manor stood framed by woodland, a comfortable manor house in excellent condition, the windows of its three stories arranged in simple symmetry to either side of the front porch; in bucolic peace and untrammeled serenity, the manor overlooked the lands some long-ago ancestor had claimed, the house's pale-gray walls rising above the darker shadows of the lower-lying gardens.

It was a sight Alaric never tired of seeing, but it was rare to see it as it was at that moment, rendered in shades of gray and black by the lucent glow of the new moon.

Home.

Until recently—until he'd started thinking of a wife and of what was important in his life—he hadn't consciously acknowledged how much he loved the place, how it called to something deep in his soul.

How it anchored him.

Now he'd realized that, the house had, in a way, become a touchstone for him; any lady he took to wife would have to fit—to suit the place as well as suit him. Indeed, she couldn't do the latter if she didn't do the former.

Sultan had grown restless; he stamped and shifted.

Alaric loosened the reins, pressed his knees to the horse's flanks, and set him trotting once more. Generally speaking, riding deeply shadowed bridle paths at night was a foolish act, but he knew this path literally better than the back of his hand.

Not long after, Sultan clattered into the manor's stable yard. Hilliard, Alaric's groom, had heard their approach and was waiting to catch Sultan's bridle.

"A good evening, my lord?" Hilliard asked.

"Well enough." Alaric dismounted and handed over the reins. "I'll need him again tomorrow—about nine o'clock."

Hilliard stroked Sultan's nose. "Back to the Hall?"

"Indeed." Alaric started toward the manor's side door. "Only four more days to go, thank God!"

Hilliard chuckled; a local and longtime servitor, the grizzled stableman was aware that Alaric was attending Percy's house party more from a sense of duty and loyalty than from any real wish to indulge.

Alaric continued along the flagstone path; through the pervasive quiet, he heard Hilliard coo to Sultan and the heavy clop of the horse's hooves as he was led into the stable. Alaric reached the side door, opened it, and strode along the corridor that led to the front hall.

The lamps in the hall were still lit, but turned low. Through the dimness, Johns, Alaric's gentleman's gentleman, came hurrying from the rear of the house. "Do you require anything, my lord?"

Alaric paused to consider, then shook his head. "No—you can retire."

With a dip of his head, Johns retreated.

Standing at the base of the stairs, Alaric debated where best to think—in his bed or over a nightcap in the library?

The nightcap won. He walked on to the library and went in. No lamps were lit, but the heavy velvet curtains had been left open, and sufficient light streamed in through the tall windows for Alaric's purpose. He crossed to the tantalus and poured a measure of French brandy into a cut-crystal tumbler; the clink of the decanter against the lip of the glass produced a pure, clear note that hung in the silence.

Glass in hand, Alaric sank into his favorite armchair, angled before the cold hearth. Given the season, no fire burned in the grate, yet there was a certain comfort in the familiar position.

He sipped, and his gaze rose to rest on the coat of arms carved into the stone overmantel. It fell to him to marry and beget an heir so the long line of Radleighs could continue unbroken—from father to son down the generations. He'd always known that to be his duty, and now…it was time.

Everything was in readiness; there was nothing left to do—to prepare. All that remained was for him to choose.

So who was the lady who would be the right wife for him?

With his gaze locked on the empty hearth, he tapped the bottom of his glass against the chair's arm. "I have no clue who she might be, so perhaps I should define *what* she needs to be."

That seemed the most logical way forward.

He tried to conjure a vision of his paragon, imbuing her with the characteristics he required. She would, he assumed, be sweet faced and gentle, mild mannered and biddable—an elementally cheerful soul to balance his more cynical nature. Importantly, he required a lady unlikely to challenge, in any meaningful way, the direction in which he chose to steer their joint lives.

He knew himself well enough to admit that he never appreciated being countermanded, much less being directly opposed. He could and would hold his own in any confrontation, but he didn't like being forced to do so. Consequently, in order to guarantee a peaceful married life, his lady should be an acquiescent sort, one who would lean on his arm and leave it to him to guide them both.

On the thought, an image of Glynis Johnson as she'd looked up at him while on his arm and strolling the terrace blazed across his mind.

After a moment, he grimaced and drained his glass. "Obviously, my vision of my ideal wife requires further work." His hard edges and implacable will would frighten the Glynises of this world, and she—they —would bore him within a week.

And if a niggling inkling that a gentle, submissive wife might not be good for him—might exacerbate rather than ameliorate his tendency to hold aloof from the world—kept prodding at his brain, there was no denying that marrying such a lady would result in a more peaceful life.

Alaric snorted, rose, set the empty glass on a side table, and headed for the door.

As he climbed the stairs to his lonely bed, he reflected that that, at least, would shortly be rectified—just as soon as he found his ideal wife.

By the time Alaric rode into the Hall stable yard the next morning, the sun was well up, promising another warm summer's day.

After handing Sultan's reins to Hughes, Alaric, as usual, strode into and through the shrubbery. The area was extensive; the Mandeville Hall shrubbery consisted of five garden clearings of varying sizes, lined with high hedges and linked by grassed paths. The central clearing hosted a stone-lined rectangular pool with a small gazebo tucked away at the far end. The ivory water lilies floating on the surface of the pool had opened to the sun, and lazy droning drifted on the air as bees dipped into the cosmos nodding their bright flower heads along the pool's edge.

Fixing his gaze on the neatly clipped grass before his boots, Alaric strode briskly over the lawn bordering the pool. Another glorious day he was proposing to waste pretending to enjoy a type of entertainment that had palled and, in truth, now bored him to the depths of his soul.

I've outgrown this.

The next phase of his life hovered in the wings—waiting for him to give it his full attention.

But first, he had to weather the rest of Percy's house party.

Alaric's feet followed the route to the shrubbery's main entrance without the need for conscious direction. Turning in to the final avenue that led to the archway cut into the hedge bordering the side lawn, he glanced ahead—and saw a bundle of crumpled silk lying on the grass just inside the shrubbery entrance.

He blinked, stared, then understanding dawned, and his stride faltered. He recognized that particular shade of pale-blue silk.

He caught his breath and ran.

A second later, he stood looking down at Glynis Johnson. She lay discarded—thrown aside like a broken doll. Her pretty blue eyes stared sightless at the sky, her pale skin was discolored, and her tongue protruded between her once-lush lips. A ring of dark bruises circled her slender throat, an obscene marring of what had once been so lovely.

Alaric felt light-headed. He hauled his gaze up—away. Focusing on the green wall of the hedge, he forced himself to breathe...

Then he looked down again. Feeling battered by a rising tide of emotions—anger and fury foremost among them—he crouched and forced himself to look more closely, more impartially. To bear witness to the atrocity.

Who had dared to do this?

This, truly, was desecration of an innocent, and Alaric's true self—the inner man who was not nearly as far removed from his warrior ancestors as his elegant sophistication led others to believe—was already reaching for his sword.

Why he felt so strongly over a girl he'd barely known, he didn't know, but this shouldn't have happened.

Not here. Not now.

Not ever.

His faculties slowly emerging through the fog of shock, he reached out and gently drew down Glynis's lids. There was no point checking for a pulse; she'd passed beyond reach long ago. The dew had dampened her gown, enough to make it cling, converting the ball gown into a chilling shroud.

He stared, committing the sight to memory; there was something— some point, some earlier observation—niggling at the back of his brain, but he couldn't seem to catch it and haul it forward.

Registering the coldness of the skin beneath his fingertips, gently he grasped and lifted one outflung arm. The limb was slightly stiff—stiffen- ing. Although it was summer, the night had been clear, the air cool.

He heard the brisk rustle of skirts, then Monty's voice piped, "This is the shrubbery."

Before Alaric could react—could find his tongue and call a warning —an Amazon swept through the archway in the hedge.

The Amazon's gaze fell on him, still crouched by the body. The woman—the lady—froze.

Garbed in a green carriage dress and with a hat perched atop glossy brown hair, the lady was tall, curvaceous, and statuesque, and with just that one glance, Alaric knew she possessed a commanding, forthright, and forceful nature; a peaches-and-cream complexion notwithstanding, her character was there, displayed in her face for all to see. And to take warning.

With her, nothing was hidden; she made not the slightest attempt to veil the power of her personality.

Then her wide green eyes shifted and locked on the body itself...

On the periphery of his awareness, Alaric registered that Monty had followed the Amazon past the hedge and, goggling, stopped to one side and a pace behind her.

Also stumbling into view on the Amazon's other side was Mrs. Macomber, Glynis's chaperon. She peered at the body and went as white as a sheet. "Oh no!" came out in a thin wail.

The sound pricked the Amazon to life.

She swayed, then her gaze snapped to Alaric, and gold blazed in the green. "What have you done?"

Constance struggled to breathe. Glynis—that was Glynis lying there dead! And this man...

Her eyes took him in as he slowly rose, straightening to a height she didn't want to be impressed by. His face was of the sort she'd heard described as that of a fallen angel—a term she'd always associated with Lucifer and evil. The black hair that fell in thick locks, one sweeping over his broad forehead, added to the image, as did his clothes—a superbly cut gray coat over buff breeches and top boots.

Light-headedness threatened, but she thrust the sensation aside.

She was a second away from accusing the man of murder when he said, "I just found her."

His voice—deep, but strangely flat—held undertones of sadness and respect for Glynis and, buried beneath that, if Constance wasn't mistaken, a shock to rival hers.

He looked at the body, then drew in a breath, one that shuddered slightly. He glanced at Constance, then waved toward the woods. "I live in the neighboring manor house. I just rode in—this is the shortcut I always take to the house."

His gaze returned to the body. "I found her like this."

Mrs. Macomber's wail had devolved into ugly gulping, racking sobs.

"Of course you did." The dapper gentleman Constance had been introduced to and who'd volunteered to come with her to search for Glynis—Montague Radleigh—was chalk white and having difficulty catching a decent breath, but he waved at the other gentleman and gabbled, "He's Carradale. Lord Carradale. M'cousin, you know."

The name meant nothing to Constance, but the evidence of her eyes did. Despite his current pallor, despite his evident shock, Carradale was instantly recognizable as a dangerous sort. He doubtless possessed a languid façade, but the circumstances had stripped that away, revealing the unforgivingly hard angles of his face and the innate power beneath his surface.

A hedonistic rake he might be, yet by all the signs—his dry and pristine attire, the dampness of Glynis's gown and the sheen that dewed her skin, plus his shock and total lack of guilt—she'd been wrong to imagine he had any hand in Glynis's death.

Glynis is dead.

The realization was difficult to assimilate, even with the dead body before her. As for her emotions—the stunned shock, pending sorrow, and the underlying anger—she would deal with them as she always did, by giving vent to them through action.

She dragged in a breath, then looked directly at the gentleman—at Carradale; his gaze had returned to Glynis's body. "I apologize for leaping to an unjustified conclusion."

He glanced at her, then faintly frowned and waved one hand dismissively before his gaze again fell to the body.

Oh yes, the languid hauteur was there, albeit currently largely in abeyance.

She followed his gaze, forcing herself to catalog the horror that had been visited on her innocent relative. From the way Glynis was lying, with her knees and legs together, wrapped in the tangle of her skirts, which still covered her calves, it seemed unlikely she'd been ravished; at least, she'd been spared that.

But death at a man's hands should not be for the likes of Glynis, who had always been a sunny, unthreatening soul.

After a moment of dwelling on that—and the urge for vengeance that was steadily building—she cleared her throat. "How long ago do you think she was…killed?"

He didn't look up, just drew breath and said, "Sometime in the small hours." He nodded at the body. "That's the gown she wore for the soirée yesterday evening."

Constance frowned. "I thought you lived next door?"

Alaric finally looked up and met the Amazon's green eyes. "I do, but I'm an old friend of Mandeville's and always attend his house party. This year, I elected to ride back and forth." He paused, then added, "My people and Mandeville's can confirm I wasn't here through the night, and when I left, Miss Johnson was very much alive and the soirée was still going."

"S'right." Monty tugged at his collar as if it was the reason he couldn't breathe properly. "As far as I recall, she was there to the end. And that was an hour or so after you left."

Alaric focused on the Amazon; he couldn't go on labeling her that. "Having established my bona fides, who are you?"

She blinked, and faint color returned to cheeks that shock had rendered over-pale. Her face was striking, not pretty. Dramatically winged brows lay otherwise straight, angled over her large, well-set eyes —possibly her best feature. Her nose was too strong for feminine beauty, and her chin gave clear warning of her stalwart character. Her mouth was too wide, but combined with lips rosy and firm was of the sort to make men fantasize.

As he stared, those fascinating lips thinned, then parted on "My name is Miss Constance Whittaker. I'm Glynis's distant cousin." Miss Whittaker looked down at the body—and again, she swayed fractionally. Immediately, she stiffened her spine, then she drew in another breath and, in an uninflected tone, declared, "Glynis's mother sent me to fetch her home."

That information seemed to penetrate Mrs. Macomber's awareness. She stopped sobbing, stared at Miss Whittaker in something close to horror, then Mrs. Macomber gulped and gulped and dissolved into a fresh bout of racking sobs that sounded halfway to outright hysteria.

Apparently, Miss Whittaker thought similarly. She swung to Monty. "Mr. Radleigh, could I ask you to take Mrs. Macomber back to the house and place her in the care of the housekeeper?"

"Yes. Of course." Monty tugged down his waistcoat, advanced gently on Mrs. Macomber, and solicitously took the older woman by the arm.

"And if you would also inform Mr. Mandeville that we've found…my cousin?" Miss Whittaker's voice wavered, spurring Monty to shoot a helpless look at Alaric.

"Miss Whittaker arrived as we were finishing breakfast," Monty rushed to say. "When she asked after Glynis, we realized that she— Glynis—hadn't come down. We'd assumed she was sleeping in—some of the other ladies had—but when we checked, it seemed Glynis had vanished, and Percy organized a search." His voice higher than usual, Monty waved. "There are groups of us searching all over. I offered to go with Miss Whittaker, and we came this way…"

Curtly, Alaric nodded. "Tell Carnaby what's happened and ask him to send footmen with a stretcher—a ladder, door, or a gate will do. We need to carry Miss Johnson inside."

"Will do." Monty backed away, drawing the copiously weeping Mrs. Macomber with him.

Alaric transferred his gaze to Miss Constance Whittaker. She'd straightened and reassembled her composure, although to his mind, in the circumstances, a momentary weakness was hardly to be wondered at.

Nevertheless, she watched Monty and the chaperon depart, and when Monty glanced back, Miss Whittaker inclined her head in regally gracious thanks.

She was distinctly stiff, a managing female with a strong line in condescension, yet Alaric was grateful she wasn't the swooning, weeping, helpless sort. Monty would be in his element soothing the weeping chaperon, but Alaric had never had that skill; distraught ladies made him want to run—far away.

After a second's thought, he crouched by the body and, once again, gently lifted the same arm he'd earlier moved.

Constance studied him, then she walked to the body and crouched on the opposite side. "What are you doing?"

He glanced at her. His hazel eyes were sharp, their expression shrewd as he studied her face. On the evidence thus far, he seemed decidedly more intelligent—more direct and straightforward—than any of the others she'd met at Mandeville Hall.

Eventually, he said, "If her limbs are stiffening, and they are, then she was killed at least four hours ago. Given it was cool overnight—and that delays the stiffening—it seems likely she was killed more like eight hours ago."

She frowned. "It's just after nine o'clock now, so possibly an hour or so after midnight."

He nodded and gently set Glynis's arm down.

She hesitated, then reached for Glynis's other arm, the one closer to her. As soon as she raised it, she felt what he had; it was as if the muscles were locking in place. Carefully, she set the arm down. She debated, then looked at him. "You said you were attending the house party. As you knew what Glynis was wearing last evening, I assume you attended the same event. Did you happen to notice if she went outside with any man?"

Carradale met her eyes—and she knew he was deciding whether to tell her something. Then his lips—lean and mobile and curiously visually magnetic, at least for her—twisted, and he said, "Glynis strolled the terrace with me—that was at her suggestion, which others overheard. But that wasn't that late, and I returned her to the drawing room. I left her with a group of others—including Mandeville and Monty—then I quit the house and rode home."

Constance tried to imagine how and why Glynis was where they'd found her. "She must have gone outside later, with some other man."

"Possibly." Carradale rose, hesitated for a heartbeat, then offered her his hand. She gripped it—feeling the strength in both hand and arm as he closed his fingers around hers and drew her to her feet.

She almost felt flustered and inwardly scoffed; no man had ever rattled her senses. What she felt had to be a lingering effect of shock. Then his reply registered, and she frowned and looked at him. "Why 'possibly'?"

He met her gaze, held it for an instant, then replied, "Did she leave the house before or after the gathering broke up? If after, then it's possible she ventured out on her own, either to meet someone else—man or woman—or simply to get some air."

She looked down at the necklace of bruises marring the white column of Glynis's throat. "No woman did that."

"No—it was a man. But depending on when and why she left the house, it's possible that the only person who knew she was outside was"—he followed her gaze and rather grimly concluded—"whoever did that to her."

Constance continued to look down at Glynis's body, and the responsibility that habitually weighed on her shoulders seemed to grow heavier. She'd come there to rescue Glynis…only to find her already dead. Anger and more rose within her. "I swear I will not rest until your murderer is caught. And hanged."

She felt Carradale's sharp gaze touch her face and linger, then he said, quite simply, "Indeed."

The single word carried a full measure of lethal promise. In pursuing justice for Glynis, evidently Constance wasn't—and wouldn't be—alone.

CHAPTER 2

*A*long with the stony-faced Miss Whittaker, Alaric paced toward the house in the wake of the footmen carrying the door on which they'd placed Glynis Johnson's body.

The Amazon had waited with him until the footmen had arrived, then had overseen the lifting and transferring of her cousin's lifeless form with a stoic calm Alaric had had to admire.

Now, however, as they paced side by side across the forecourt and up the porch steps, he sensed grim determination overtake her—visible in the adamantine set of her features and the steely light that infused her eyes.

He recognized the sentiment because he shared it. Glynis Johnson had been a blameless soul who had not deserved to have her life cut short. The murder might not have occurred on Radleigh land, yet it was close enough—in some strange way, it seemed to fall within his purlieu—and as such, a degree of responsibility to see justice done and Glynis avenged fell on his shoulders.

Carnaby, looking more rattled than Alaric had ever seen him, met them in the front hall. "Ah…" The normally unflappable butler looked helpless. He stared at the body, decently shrouded in an old curtain.

Miss Whittaker drew herself up. "Do you have an ice house?" Her delivery was even and commendably assured.

Carnaby blinked and faced her. "No, ma'am. But we have a cool store beyond the wash house, if you think that would do?"

She seemed to consider, then nodded. "That will probably be an acceptable alternative. If there's a table...?"

"Yes, ma'am." Carnaby had regained some of his composure. "We'll place the poor young lady there." He gave brisk directions to the footmen. As they moved off, going deeper into the house, Carnaby faced Alaric and Miss Whittaker. "If you would, my lord, the master and all the other guests have gathered in the drawing room. They're waiting for you and Miss Whittaker to discuss what next to do."

Alaric hid a frown; what needed to be done next should have been obvious.

A sidelong glance at Miss Whittaker—at the frown in her eyes—suggested she thought the same.

Alaric gestured to the drawing room. "If you're ready...?"

She drew in another fortifying breath, then nodded and, with a determined stride, led the way.

A footman hurried to open the door, and Alaric followed her—into a scene of mild panic and general chaos. A cacophony of chatter and shrill exclamations engulfed them, and they halted.

No one noticed their entrance, all too busy hypothesizing and frightening themselves with wild speculation. For several moments, Alaric and Miss Whittaker stood silently just inside the door.

Eventually, Alaric glanced at Miss Whittaker and confirmed that she was surveying the company just as he had, but in her case, through cold and, he suspected, very clear eyes.

No doubt she, like he, had leapt to the conclusion that Glynis's murderer was, most likely, in the room.

Gradually, the babel of voices grew more distinct, allowing various comments and observations to be distinguished. Several ladies were claiming to have been friends of the deceased, while the gentlemen were unanimous in praising Glynis's character. Nothing said was untrue, yet...

Half a minute later, Miss Whittaker put her finger firmly on the anomaly. Her voice low, for Alaric's ears alone, she murmured, "I wasn't aware Glynis was such close friends with all these people."

Cynically, he replied, "She wasn't—at best, they were recent acquaintances. I got the impression she hadn't met the majority of those here prior to arriving two days ago."

"Then why...?"

"Because they're not sure how to behave, and most are overdoing things." When she sniffed disparagingly, he added in a mild tone, "You have to allow for the fact that most if not all of those here have not previously been confronted by the violent death of an acquaintance—a member of a house party they are attending."

After a second, she cut a sharp glance his way; sensing it, he met her eyes, then arched a brow. "Have you?" she asked. "Been confronted by the violent death of an acquaintance?"

He returned his gaze to the assembled company. "Not as such, but I have had to comfort a friend whose mother met a ghastly end, so I have that experience to guide me."

Just then, Edward, standing to one side of the fireplace, beside the chair in which Percy had slumped, noticed Alaric and Miss Whittaker. Edward dropped a hand on Percy's shoulder, gripped, and lightly shook his cousin. When Percy blinked and looked up, Edward tipped his head, directing Percy's gaze to Alaric and Miss Whittaker, and said something—presumably pointing out to Percy that it was time to address the immediate issue.

Alaric had noted that Percy had been staring blankly—blindly—across the room. He hadn't been contributing to the dramatic exchanges; indeed, he'd seemed deaf to the clamor around him.

Now, instead of rising and taking charge, Percy spoke to Edward and waved—clearly inviting his cousin to do what needed to be done.

Edward straightened, then patently ready to assume command, moved to stand squarely in front of the fireplace. Facing the room, he raised his voice. "If I could have everyone's attention?"

Gradually, the conversations quieted until, finally, absolute silence held sway. Everyone had turned to look at Edward.

He cleared his throat, glanced at Alaric and Miss Whittaker, then said, "I believe the correct procedure is that we should summon the local magistrate."

A wave of comments ensued. Edward listened and waited, but ultimately, no one disagreed.

As the voices faded, Alaric spoke. "I'm sure Sir Godfrey Stonewall will do his best, but I believe that under the new system, any suspicious death is supposed to be reported to Scotland Yard."

Horror filled the faces turned his way, then the protests began.

"What a horrible suggestion, Carradale." Prue Collard shuddered.

"You can't possibly be serious!" William Coke sounded close to choking.

"I say, no call for such extremes," Fletcher said.

"I've heard the inspectors are overzealous individuals who treat everyone—absolutely everyone—as if they're the basest criminal," Henry Wynne reported.

"Stuff and nonsense!" punctuated by a cane hitting the floor came from Mrs. Fitzherbert. "I'm surprised at you, Carradale."

As the refusals to countenance calling in Scotland Yard continued, Alaric inwardly sighed. One would have been forgiven for imagining he'd suggested bringing in the newshounds; indeed, judging by the tenor of some of the protests, the newshounds would have been preferable to the clodhopping, flat-footed, bumbling denizens of the fabled Scotland Yard—the descendants of Peel's Bow Street runners.

Miss Whittaker frowned at him. "You're not arguing."

He arched a brow. "I'm resigned. I never thought they'd agree, but I felt the point needed to be made." After a second, he remarked, "At least this way, no one will balk at sending for Stonewall."

Sure enough, as the protests faded into grumblings, with some opining that Alaric had only made the suggestion to throw the proverbial cat among the pigeons, Edward conferred with Percy, then once more raised his voice. "I'll send for Stonewall—he's the local man here."

When many looked his way, Alaric inclined his head in acceptance; it wasn't, after all, his house.

Miss Whittaker was still studying him as if he was some strange specimen. As Edward strode from the room, presumably to consult with Carnaby, and the other guests returned to their speculation, she inquired, "Why not Stonewall?"

Alaric shifted his gaze to meet hers. "You'll see. Then again, who knows?" He shrugged. "He might have changed." He doubted it, but anything, he supposed, was possible.

Miss Whittaker bent her frown—the one he'd already realized meant she was trying to puzzle something out—on him. "Stonewall is—presumably—closer. And perhaps he'll take one look and summon Scotland Yard himself. He can do that, can't he? That might be more effective."

Alaric's reply was a dry "We can but hope."

The door opened, and Edward came in. He walked to his previous position before the hearth, turned, and informed everyone that the magistrate, Sir Godfrey Stonewall, had been summoned.

Everyone waited, patently expecting some direction. Edward looked at Percy—many others did as well, Alaric and Miss Whittaker among them—but as before, Percy seemed disinclined to take the lead. He still looked ashen, as if the shock of the murder had knocked him for six and he hadn't yet got his mental legs under him.

Or more likely, in Alaric's estimation, a realization of the consequences of it becoming known, as it inevitably would, that such an unsavory murder had occurred at his house, during a house party he was hosting, had started to impinge on Percy's awareness and had—perhaps unsurprisingly—scuppered all confidence.

Alaric could attest that Percy was definitely not the strong and decisive sort, that he'd always lacked confidence in unexpected situations. His patent inability to step up and lead the company now was entirely consistent with his known character.

Edward cleared his throat and, when everyone looked his way, said, "I gather Stonewall is unlikely to arrive before the afternoon. Perhaps, in the circumstances, it might be best to go over what information we have of Miss Johnson's movements during the evening just past. Who knows? By sharing what we observed and assembling all the facts, we might unearth a clue, which we can then lay before Stonewall and perhaps get through his visit with less fuss."

Constance bit her tongue against the urge to inform the company that she didn't care how much fuss it took to identify the man who'd killed Glynis—and that they shouldn't care, either. But she was a realist, and people of this ilk always seemed to measure the cost of things in terms of how much they, personally, would be put out. But even more pertinently, learning all the company knew of Glynis's movements the previous night ranked high on Constance's list of immediate objectives.

She felt Carradale's gaze touch her face, as if he could read her thoughts—feel her impulses. A second later, he murmured, "Just wait. They'll perk up at the thought of sharing what they know—it's an occupation very close to gossiping."

Despite the weight that had settled about her heart, she almost smiled.

He touched her arm, then gestured to an unoccupied armchair. "This," he murmured, "is likely to take some time."

She walked to the chair and sank down; the position—nearer to the door than the other settings—gave her a decent view of all the company as they gathered their thoughts. Carradale fetched a straight-backed chair from against the wall and placed it alongside the armchair. He sat as the gentleman who had summoned the magistrate stated, "Perhaps we should start from a moment when we can all agree Glynis was present in the drawing room."

Constance glanced at Carradale and quietly asked, "Who is that gentleman—the one who just spoke?"

"Edward Mandeville. He's Percy's older cousin."

She nodded as a lady with brassy-blond ringlets raised a hand.

"Glynis and I were together, chatting with Monty and Robert for a time. Then we four joined Carradale, and after some time, Glynis asked him to escort her out onto the terrace."

Constance wasn't surprised at the salacious glances cast at the gentleman beside her.

For his part, he didn't seem to notice. Instead, his expression entirely serious, he nodded. "Miss Johnson declared she needed some air. She and I walked the terrace for about ten minutes. She didn't say anything to suggest she was in any way frightened, much less that she feared for her life or even held reservations over any man present."

The realization that Glynis apparently had had reason to fear one of the men present registered in most minds and eradicated all inclination to levity. Every face grew somber.

"Subsequent to our stroll in the moonlight," Carradale continued, "I returned with Miss Johnson to the drawing room, and we joined the group that included Percy, Monty, Cyril and Caroline Hammond, and Colonel Humphries."

An older gentleman with a military mustache humphed. "Remember that quite clearly. You left soon after."

Carradale inclined his head. "Indeed. The last I saw of Miss Johnson, she was chatting with Cyril and Caroline."

The Hammond pair, apparently brother and sister-in-law, took up the tale. Consequently, others chimed in, various members of the company growing animated as they either related their interaction with Glynis or confirmed seeing her talking with someone else.

Minute by minute, interaction by interaction, the assembled guests traced Glynis's movements as she'd circulated among the groups in the drawing room. As she listened, Constance realized that although Glynis had to have been somewhat out of her depth in this company, she'd managed to hold her own among them quite creditably; no one spoke of her with anything less than respect and, at minimum, mild liking. From no quarter—not even the other unmarried young lady—did Constance sense any animosity.

Why, then, had Glynis been killed?

The question triggered some other avenue of thought, but before she could follow it, the brassy-haired lady—Carradale had murmured that the lady's name was Mrs. Prudence Collard—looked around the circle of faces and stated, "I believe that brings us to the end of the evening. We retired then, didn't we?"

The other ladies agreed. "We ladies went up the stairs first," a Mrs. Humphries said. "I assume Miss Johnson was with us."

Mrs. Collard was frowning. "I'm sure she was." She looked around at the other ladies, inviting their confirmation. "Surely, she must have been?"

After an instant's pause during which the other ladies plainly consulted their memories, Mrs. Hammond stated, "I, too, had thought Miss Johnson was with us, but I cannot say for certain that I saw her retire."

The ladies looked at each other, waiting for someone to say they had seen Glynis, but no one spoke.

Then the oldest lady in the room, a Mrs. Fitzherbert, who Carradale had explained was a relative of Mandeville's there to lend countenance, rapped the floor with the tip of her cane. "It's simple enough to check." She turned beady eyes on one of the ladies, a youthful widow by the name of Mrs. Cleary. "You, Rosamund Cleary, were sharing a room with Miss Johnson, were you not?"

"Yes..." Mrs. Cleary didn't sound all that sure.

"Well, gel—did the chit reach the room last night or not?"

Mrs. Cleary, who, like many of the ladies, had been rather pale, blushed. She hesitated, then under the weight of the gazes of everyone there, admitted, "I...can't say. I wasn't in the room at that time...indeed, for some hours. All I know is that she wasn't there when I got back, and her bed hadn't been slept in."

A ripple of murmurs and sly looks suggested all too clearly where Mrs. Cleary had been—dallying with one of the gentlemen.

Mrs. Fitzherbert snorted. "Well, that's no help."

The old lady's snide tone sparked a flash of resistance in Mrs. Cleary. She straightened and, in a firmer voice, declared, "Be that as it may, I was on the terrace, at the rear corner, a little while later—just taking the air after everyone had retired upstairs." She glanced swiftly around at all the faces, then looked down at her hands. "And I saw a gentleman come out of the shrubbery."

Eyes grew round, then everyone glanced at their fellows.

An uncomfortable pause ensued.

Carradale broke it. "Which gentleman?"

Mrs. Cleary looked at him. "I don't know. The moon had set, and there wasn't enough light to see clearly—just enough to be sure that it was a gentleman I saw." She glanced around again, this time openly assessing all the men, then looked back at Carradale. "I can't even say that it was one of the gentlemen in this room. I didn't see his face or anything else to identify him."

"In which direction did he go?" Constance asked.

Mrs. Cleary blinked at her, then her gaze grew distant. After a second, she replied, "Toward the house." She refocused on Constance. "He walked toward the front of the house, but I didn't see if he went inside or not."

By the expressions of studied blankness that flowed over most faces, it was plain what everyone believed the sighting meant. Constance wished she could look every way at once—to take in the reaction of each and every gentleman. She raked as many faces as she could. Did any look guilty? Or furtive or even conscious?

She noted that beside her, Carradale was also surveying the other men. He was, she realized—assuming the staff at the Hall and at his home could be counted on—the sole male present who could not have been the man Mrs. Cleary saw. Not unless he'd gone home and come back, but that would be easy to prove, and she doubted Carradale was the sort of man who would expect staff—both at the Hall and at his home—to lie for him in a matter of murder.

Regardless, given all she'd sensed and seen in the shrubbery as they'd stood over Glynis's body, she truly did not believe him in any way involved. There'd been too much anger at the waste of Glynis's life seething just beneath his surface.

After a too-prolonged silence, Monty Radleigh blinked owlishly. "I... say. That's something of a turn-up."

As if the simple words had somehow penetrated when the prior discussion had not, Percy Mandeville, host of the house party and owner of the house, slowly straightened in the chair in which, until then, he'd been slumped. His expression suggested sudden resolution.

Constance watched him, wondering...

Percy opened his mouth...then shut it. Three seconds later, after staring blindly straight ahead, he slumped back in the chair and covered his eyes with one hand.

His reaction sent a ripple of unease through the gathering. Hard on the heels of that, a palpable sense of panic started to swell, with every gentleman looking increasingly agitated, increasingly defensive.

Then Edward Mandeville offered, "Perhaps the gentleman was out taking the air, too."

The panic deflated like a pricked balloon. Relieved murmurs of "No doubt" and "That's it" abounded, and the fraught moment dissolved as everyone looked at their fellows, waiting for a gentleman to admit he'd been outside and must have been the man Mrs. Cleary had seen...

No one spoke.

Unease returned, creeping like an oppressive fog over the company. Once again, neighbor glanced sidelong at neighbor, at this man, then that, wondering...

Eventually, Edward Mandeville, still on his feet before the hearth, shifted and said, "I believe we've done all we can. Now, we must wait for Sir Godfrey to arrive, consider all the facts we can place before him, and decide on his verdict." Edward glanced at Percy, who hadn't stirred; his hand still concealed his face. "Perhaps," Edward went on, "in the circumstances, we should spend the intervening hours in quiet pursuits."

Edward looked around the gathering, but no one argued. He straightened and nodded. "I'll have Carnaby inform everyone when Sir Godfrey arrives."

Several seconds passed, then the ladies exchanged glances and rose. The rustling of their skirts filled the otherwise silent room as they filed out of the door, followed by the gentlemen—no doubt to find some quiet nook and gossip about Glynis and speculate...

Constance hauled her mind from that tack. She couldn't do anything about Glynis's reputation, not until they found the murderer and learned why he'd killed her.

After a moment's thought, Constance glanced at Carradale, who hadn't yet risen.

He'd apparently been waiting to catch her eye. With a tip of his head, he indicated the door. "Shall we?"

She rose, and he came to his feet. It wasn't often that she met a man tall enough—with a personality robust enough—to make her feel...not the largest person in the room. Carradale accomplished the feat without trying.

As they fell in at the rear of the stream of guests, she murmured, "Can we believe Mrs. Cleary? Or is it possible she invented the tale of the man leaving the shrubbery to pay back the old lady—or perhaps to divert attention from her own activities?"

Looking down as they walked, Carradale didn't immediately reply, but as they neared the door, he met her eyes. "I think we must believe her. Aside from all else, she's never been the sort to invent tales, much less purely to make herself important. I've never heard of her courting that sort of attention."

She arched her brows. After a moment's thought, she said, "In that case, she was brave to speak out."

"Indeed." Carradale followed her into the front hall. "Especially as it seems she might well have glimpsed Glynis's murderer."

In the front hall, the guests were sorting themselves into groups—some for the library, others for a walk in the rose garden, still others to sit quietly in the morning room or to convene about the billiard table.

Constance saw no benefit in joining any of the groups. She paused just outside the drawing room door, debating what to do next.

Alaric studied the surprising Miss Whittaker's expression, then gently touched her arm. When she looked at him, he gestured to the front door. "After all that, I need some fresh air. Would you care to join me?"

She regarded him for a second, then nodded. "Fresh air sounds like an excellent idea."

Alaric wasn't sure why her ready acquiescence so pleased him, but there were several questions he wanted to put to her. He nodded to the footman stationed by the door. He opened it; as Alaric followed Miss Whittaker through, he informed the footman, "We'll be on the front terrace if anyone has need of us."

"Yes, my lord."

"You can close the door."

"Indeed, my lord."

Miss Whittaker heard and glanced back, but she made no demur. She looked around, then walked to the right, to where a semicircular outcrop at the front corner of the terrace offered a stone bench, also semicircular, running beneath the balustrade. It was the perfect spot to sit and share information; no one could overhear, and they would see anyone approaching.

She sat with a sibilant rustle of petticoats. Alaric claimed a seat opposite so they could easily see each other's faces.

He held her gaze for a second, then said, "If we are to catch your cousin's killer, it might be helpful for us to share what we know."

She arched her brows. Her unspoken question *What did he have to offer?* hung in the air between them.

Despite all, he almost smiled; she was prickly, ready to be defensive, yet he sensed she would do whatever she had to to avenge her cousin. "I know a great deal about Percy and Mandeville Hall and also quite a lot about each of the guests. You, in turn, know about your cousin. If we pool our knowledge, we're liable to get further faster."

After a second of regarding him assessingly, she inclined her head. "If you're willing, then yes. I agree."

He inclined his head in return and leapt in. "First, was this event the sort of party your cousin normally attended?"

"No. Obviously. That's why, as soon as she heard of Glynis's plans to attend, her mother came and begged me to come south and fetch Glynis home."

"Home being where?"

"Kilburn. North of Derby." She pinned him with her green gaze. "Glynis was normally a biddable girl, but she could be stubborn. Her mother, my grandfather's cousin Pamela, isn't strong, yet she was set on giving Glynis her Season. They spent the earlier months of the year in London, in a rented house. Toward the end of the Season, as the weather warmed, Pamela fell ill and had to return to the country—the air of the capital didn't agree with her. Glynis begged to remain for a little while longer—until the lease on the house expired—and as Mrs. Macomber was willing to continue in her role of paid chaperon, Pamela agreed. However, Pamela expected Glynis to return home last week. Instead, Glynis sent a letter saying she'd been invited to Mr. Mandeville's house party and had accepted, and that she would return home after the house party ended." She paused, then added, "From what little I gleaned from Mrs. Macomber before we found Glynis's body, she hadn't been convinced it was appropriate for Glynis to attend, but Glynis overrode her objections."

She sighed. "Sadly, I can imagine that all too readily. As I said, Glynis could be stubborn. The family can't hold Mrs. Macomber to blame for Glynis being here. She was hired to be Glynis's chaperon at social events, not her keeper."

Alaric nodded. A leased house in town and a paid chaperon who knew suitable hostesses wasn't an unusual arrangement for county gentry wanting to puff off their daughters in London society. But... "That begs the question of why Glynis was here—more specifically, what prompted her to accept Percy's invitation." He paused, then in the interests of the sharing he'd been the one to suggest they indulge in, went on, "I know Percy quite well, and I was surprised to discover not only your cousin but also Miss Weldon, another unmarried young lady, and her chaperon present at this event. In the past…suffice it to say that this wasn't the sort of house party unmarried young ladies would be expected to attend."

Miss Whittaker's expression hardened. "So Glynis—and this Miss Weldon—weren't Mandeville's usual sort of guests?"

"No." He couldn't fathom why Percy had invited either young lady. Alaric met Miss Whittaker's fine green eyes. "If you like, I'll undertake to ask Percy why he invited your cousin."

"Please do. I would like to know his reasons myself—and so would her poor mother and Grandpapa."

Alaric frowned. "Glynis's father?"

"Died two years ago, or I assure you he would have been here himself."

Her tone suggested that the Whittaker clan took care of their own—and judging by her presence and what Alaric had seen so far of her character, in no uncertain terms. He allowed faint puzzlement to creep into his expression. "If you don't mind me asking, why was it you—a relatively young lady and unmarried yourself—who Glynis's mother approached?"

"Because I'm not that young, and since the death of my parents nine years past, I've been acting as, in effect, my grandfather's agent. He's the head of the wider family, but is now chair-bound. When Pamela learned her daughter wasn't coming home as expected and, instead, had come to this house party, I was, naturally, the one she appealed to—and therefore, the one who came."

She paused, then added, "I arrived in the village last night and put up at the inn. This morning, I reached here as the company were rising from the breakfast table. I spoke with Mr. Mandeville and several others—your cousin Monty among them—in the front hall. Mr. Mandeville sent a footman to fetch Glynis, but she couldn't be found. Once we all realized she wasn't anywhere inside the house, Mr. Mandeville organized a search of the grounds. Monty kindly volunteered to be my guide, and as you saw when we found you, Mrs. Macomber, who, unsurprisingly, had been thrown into a panic, trailed behind us."

Alaric had fixed on her earlier revelations and what they suggested of both her character and the way her family saw her. "You didn't travel from Kilburn alone?"

The look she threw him was the equivalent of telling him not to be silly. "Of course not. My maid and my groom are with me."

Mildly, he said, "You might want to send for them, along with your luggage. I know Percy—or rather his housekeeper, Mrs. Carnaby—will find you a room."

Her haughtiness dissolved as she thought. "I'll wait to hear what the magistrate says." She cast him a sharp glance. "I gather he doesn't meet with your approval."

He lightly shrugged. "Sir Godfrey Stonewall is a pompous ass who thinks far too much of himself and his appointment. However, I haven't crossed paths with him for several years—it's possible he's acquired wisdom in the intervening time."

She studied him—his face, his eyes—for several seconds, then humphed. "Obviously, we'll see."

He realized he'd somehow got trapped in the shifting hues within her green eyes. Inwardly frowning, he hauled his mind back to business and refocused his wayward senses. "As to Glynis being here, she must have had a reason. What was it, and did that reason, or the simple fact of her being here, precipitate her murder?"

Constance couldn't fault Carradale's reasoning but... "I have no answer as to her reason for accepting Mr. Mandeville's invitation." She paused, thinking of Glynis, of the girl Constance had known. Staring unseeing at the balustrade, she mused, "I wouldn't have said Glynis was flighty, but rather that she was intent on enjoying life. In a wholly innocent way." She refocused on Carradale—and told herself she didn't need to pay so much attention to the dark beauty of his face. "You said you'd attended the earlier days of the house party. How did Glynis appear to you? Did you observe anything strange? Did you glean any hint as to why she was here or, at any time, sense that she was afraid of anyone?"

His gaze turned inward, and he remained still as—she assumed—he thought back over the past days. Eventually, he said, "If I had to give my opinion of her mood, I would have said she was happy. Sunnily so and pleased with her world." His hazel eyes refocused on Constance, his gaze direct and rather piercing—eagle-like in its predatory quality, although in that regard, rake though he assuredly was, she sensed no threat from him. He went on, "She was bright and breezy, yet I saw no evidence that she was aiming her smiles at any particular man, if that's crossed your mind."

Constance softly snorted. "Of course it's crossed my mind. I know Glynis well enough to guess that her primary interest in attending this house party would almost certainly have had something to do with a gentleman and the prospect of a potential betrothal. It's difficult to imagine her pushing to accept Mr. Mandeville's invitation if not at the behest of—or in pursuit of—some gentleman."

"Perhaps not, but I saw no indication of any particular man being her target—and over the years, I've developed a reasonable facility for gauging such things, especially at events like this."

She hadn't needed the reminder of the sort of man she was dealing with, yet he'd made the comment in a matter-of-fact manner. Given his confidence in his expertise... "When you walked with her on the terrace last night, what did you talk of?"

His brows rose in thought, then he replied, "It was largely the usual small talk. Nothing that stands out or that was in any way revealing." His eyes held hers for a moment, then he went on, "There was one thing— which might owe less to reality than to me reading too much into her behavior. However, for what it's worth, from the way she engaged with me on the terrace, I assumed she was intent on *appearing* to flirt with me."

While she could readily imagine Glynis doing so, Constance picked up his emphasis. "Appearing?"

He nodded. "She...went through the motions, as it were. No one else was on the terrace to see her performance at close range—only me." He shrugged. "And I admit I found it entertaining. Amusing and a touch intriguing, because I had to wonder if she was intent on using me as a façade to screen the true reason she was here—meaning which gentleman she actually had her eye on."

She hesitated, then said, "Can you be sure she wasn't trying to make another gentleman jealous?"

"Had that been her purpose, she would have done better to have clung to my arm in the drawing room, where the entire company would have seen. As it was, they could glimpse us through the windows, but the bulk of her performance—if eliciting jealousy was her aim—would have been wasted. Instead, it was her idea to claim my arm for a stroll in the evening air, and she didn't seem intent on us being on display."

She frowned. "But surely—with the pair of you going outside alone— the others might imagine..." She looked at him and arched her brows.

He gave a dismissive huff. "You're clutching at straws. Take it from one with more than a decade of experience, Glynis was not trying to make any other gentleman jealous."

She was intrigued enough to ask, "How can you be so sure?"

"Because she wasn't constantly glancing over her shoulder—or anywhere else—to see if he, her putative lover, was watching."

The reason for their discussion wasn't anything to smile about, so she compressed her lips against the urge, but his bone-dry delivery left her in little doubt that, more than once, he had indeed been used as a means to prod another gentleman to action.

Swiftly, she cast her mind over the points they'd touched on—and felt somber sadness engulf her once more. Just for a few seconds, the grief she was holding at bay had eased...

She glanced sharply at Carradale and found him watching her. And realized that, while he'd been answering her questions and furthering their understanding of the circumstances surrounding Glynis's death, he'd also been...distracting her from the shock and sadness that, no matter how hard she endeavored to suppress it, lay waiting, hovering at the edge of her mind.

"I didn't know Glynis all that well—not like a sister." She had no idea why she felt she needed to tell him that; perhaps because he was being understanding, and she wasn't sure she deserved his sympathy. "There were too many years between us, and we lived in different towns."

His gaze remained steady. "Nevertheless, it had to have been a nasty shock. She's one of your kin, after all."

If she acknowledged the shock, the emotional turmoil that had erupted when she'd looked down at Glynis's body, Glynis's pretty face grotesquely distorted...a potent combination of grief and rage would swamp her, and she would rail and lose direction. With grim determination, she forced the emotions back into the box in which she'd trapped them and slammed down the lid. She met Carradale's gaze head-on. "To my mind, the best way I can mourn Glynis is by ensuring justice is done and that her murderer is caught and hanged."

His gaze steady on her face, he inclined his head in agreement. "She was an innocent in all the ways that count—such as she deserve to be avenged."

"Exactly." She thought of their questions and what they might do to find answers. "Mrs. Macomber might have been ineffective in reining Glynis in, but she's not without eyes and ears and a degree of common sense. Presumably, she'll know why Glynis wanted to come to Mandeville Hall—she must at least know something of that." She paused, then sighed. "Of course, I'll have to wait until she recovers enough to attain coherency." She met Carradale's eyes. "Seeing Glynis like that…overset her."

She caught the fractional upward twitch of his lips and felt she'd at least partly paid him back for his attempt to lighten her mood.

A throat being cleared had them both looking toward the front door.

The butler, Carnaby, a surprisingly thin, aesthete-looking individual, regarded them impassively. "Ma'am, your lordship, if you would care to partake, we've arranged a cold collation in the dining room."

"Thank you, Carnaby," Carradale said.

The butler bowed and withdrew.

Alaric looked at his Amazon; she didn't appear to be the sort of female who would consider starving herself to be a good idea, even in the present circumstances. When she glanced his way, he arched a brow at her. "I suspect this afternoon is going to be a long one. We should keep up our strength."

She studied his face for a second, then observed, "You said that with a certain authority. I believe I'll take heed."

He rose as she did and fell in beside her as she made for the door.

As he reached for the doorlatch, she added, "It does seem wise to fortify ourselves before spending hours dealing with a magistrate who goes by the name of Stonewall."

Alaric grinned entirely spontaneously and briefly met her eyes, then he opened the door and followed her over the threshold—into the deadening hush of a house hosting a company all of whom suspected that their number included a gentleman with, metaphorically at least, blood on his hands.

CHAPTER 3

To Constance's dismay, she discovered that Carradale's assessment of Sir Godfrey Stonewall was all too accurate. Stonewall proved to be a pompous ignoramus and arrogant with it.

The magistrate was in his later middle years and clearly liked his food. His coat strained over his paunch, and judging by the way he stumped around, supporting his bulk with a cane and grumbling when he needed to take the steps up to the front door, he suffered from gout.

In addition to being of irascible temper and unprepossessing mien, Sir Godfrey lost no time in getting on her bad side; on entering the house, after shaking Percy Mandeville's hand, Stonewall ignored her, Carradale, Monty Radleigh, and Edward Mandeville, along with all the other guests hovering farther back in the hall, and suggested that he—Sir Godfrey—and Percy should repair to the library and "settle this business," for all the world as if Glynis's murder was nothing more than a bothersome occurrence.

To her relief, Edward frowned and insisted that he, as an older member of the family, should be present as well, then Carradale calmly pointed out that what knowledge Percy had was second-hand at best, while he, Carradale, had been the one to discover the body, while Constance—he included her with a glance and a half bow—was the deceased young lady's relative, and Monty had been present when the body was found as well.

Sir Godfrey huffed and puffed, but when neither Percy nor any of the other guests supported his view, Sir Godfrey grumpily consented to meet with Carradale, Constance, Edward, and Monty, along with Percy. With what was doubtless supposed to be an ingratiating glance at the other guests, Sir Godfrey declared that he saw no reason to inconvenience them further.

Constance noted that none of the guests appeared particularly grateful.

Edward glanced at Percy, then suggested the drawing room as a more appropriate venue. Once inside with the door shut, after Constance sank onto the sofa, with Monty alongside, Carradale and Edward found straight-backed chairs and positioned them facing the fireplace, while Percy took one of the armchairs beside the hearth. Sir Godfrey settled in its mate and disgruntledly barked, "Well—tell me what happened."

Unperturbed by the edict—as if such boorish, offhand behavior was no more than what he'd expected of the man—Carradale recited the bald facts of arriving at the stable that morning and walking to the house via the path through the shrubbery and discovering Glynis's body. He concluded with "Miss Johnson had obviously been strangled." He glanced at Constance and Monty. "At that point, I was joined by Mr. Radleigh and Miss Whittaker—Miss Johnson's cousin."

"Mrs. Macomber, Miss Johnson's chaperon, was with us as well," Monty supplied.

"Indeed." Constance fixed Sir Godfrey with a severe look. "As Lord Carradale says, it was instantly apparent that my cousin had met her death at some man's hands. As both his lordship and Mr. Radleigh confirmed that she was wearing the same gown as she had worn the previous evening and her body and gown were damp with dew, it seems clear that she was killed during the early hours—sometime after the other guests retired."

Edward glanced at Percy, who finally seemed to be pulling himself together, but Percy waved at Edward to speak.

"We," Edward said, "by which I mean all those here, attending the house party, pooled all we know of Miss Johnson's movements last night." Briskly, he outlined what the company collectively believed to have been Glynis's actions through the evening's gathering. "Sadly, no one has any recollection of Miss Johnson's whereabouts after the gathering broke up and the company retired upstairs."

When Edward fell silent, Carradale said, "The one additional potentially relevant fact is that one of the other ladies, out taking the air on the terrace a little later, saw a gentleman come out of the shrubbery through the entrance beyond which Miss Johnson's body was later found. The other lady did not see the man well enough to identify him."

"I see." Sir Godfrey had assumed what he no doubt imagined was a judicial expression. Frowning, he stroked his chin. From under his bushy eyebrows, his beady eyes shifted from Percy to Monty to Carradale, where his gaze lingered, then he glanced at Edward before returning his attention to Percy. "How long's this party been running, heh? And what about your guests—any rum customers among them?"

The suggestion succeeded in rousing Percy. "Good Lord, no!" He stared at the magistrate for a second, then dragged in a breath, straightened in the chair, and made an effort to explain that the house party had commenced on Sunday afternoon, so the previous evening had been only the second of a projected six nights. "Everyone is…was planning to stay until Saturday. As usual."

"I've heard that you host this house party every year," Sir Godfrey said. "I can't recall any bother at any of the previous years' events."

Percy looked taken aback. After a second, he responded, "If by bother you mean murder, then certainly not. Indeed, we haven't had anything untoward occur before. Not at any event I've hosted."

"Quite right, quite right." Sir Godfrey seemed to realize he'd come perilously close to insulting a well-born landowner. "If you can tell me about your guests—I take it they are frequent visitors here?"

"Some certainly, but I've known most—including all the gentlemen—for years." Percy's attitude toward the magistrate was hardening, his accent growing more clipped. "All come from good families and are well established in society."

"Naturally, naturally." Sir Godfrey nodded gravely. He frowned, appearing to sink deep into consideration of the facts, then he drew in a portentous breath, looked around at them all, and stated, "From all you've told me, it seems obvious the poor young lady went out to take the air and fell victim to a passing itinerant. A gypsy, perhaps."

When everyone stared at him in patent disbelief, Sir Godfrey airily waved. "Only to be expected if a pretty young thing goes walking alone in the country at night."

Constance felt as if she'd been struck. For the first time in her life, she was, quite literally, speechless.

Carradale and Percy shifted, then Carradale coldly inquired, "Forgive me, Sir Godfrey, but do you have any evidence of a homicidal itinerant in the neighborhood?"

Sir Godfrey's color rose, and he puffed up like a challenged rooster. "No need for evidence beyond what we have—it's perfectly obvious it must be some wanderer." His tone turned contemptuous. "Who else, pray tell, could it have been?"

With unimpaired and decidedly chilly calm, Carradale replied, "My people have reported no sightings of anyone unusual in the vicinity. They usually send word if any stranger is lurking in the woods."

"None of my farmers have said anything, either." Despite his continuing pallor, Percy seemed determined to hold his own. "And it's the wrong season for gypsies around here."

"I have to wonder," Carradale said, his gaze steady on Sir Godfrey's face, "if this matter shouldn't be reported to Scotland Yard. I was under the impression that it's currently the case that all murders are to be brought to the Yard's attention to ensure a proper investigation."

Sir Godfrey recoiled. "Nonsense! What use would they be, heh? Londoners, the lot of them, with no understanding of how matters are dealt with in the counties."

Constance, along with Carradale and Monty, looked at Percy. He was frowning, clearly debating which side of the argument he should support.

Edward, too, was frowning. When Percy didn't immediately speak, Edward said, "I'm not at all sure that inconveniencing everyone by bringing in the Metropolitan Police would be a good idea."

Constance drew in a long breath and stated, "My cousin was not merely inconvenienced. She was *murdered*!"

Her forceful, whip-like tone jerked Edward and Sir Godfrey to attention; both looked at her, almost in surprise.

Edward recovered first. "My apologies, Miss Whittaker. I merely meant that bringing in outsiders might be counterproductive. I can't see how they will get to the bottom of this any more expeditiously than the local authorities."

"Exactly so," Sir Godfrey stated.

As Constance, too, didn't know that the investigators of Scotland Yard would be any improvement over the local constable, and from all she'd heard, they might well be worse, she compressed her lips, narrowed her eyes on both men, and glared—primarily at Sir Godfrey—and let her expression state her position; she would be damned if she allowed

Stonewall—or Edward Mandeville—to sweep Glynis's death under any carpet.

A tentative tap on the door distracted them all.

Alaric turned, along with everyone else, and saw the door open and Rosa Cleary look in. Seeing them, she hesitated, then clearly girded her loins and came in.

As she walked forward, Alaric got to his feet, as did the other gentlemen.

Rosa's gaze fixed on Sir Godfrey. She halted at the end of the sofa beside Alaric. "I thought…that is, I wanted to be sure that what I saw last evening was made clear."

From under beetling brows, Sir Godfrey frowned at her. "And you are?"

At his aggressive tone, Rosa paled and looked to be on the point of bolting.

Alaric crisply stated, "This is Mrs. Rosamund Cleary—the lady who glimpsed the gentleman leaving the shrubbery last night."

Rosa tipped up her chin. "Yes. That's right."

"Indeed." With a welcoming gesture, Miss Whittaker—Constance—invited Rosa to sit beside her on the sofa; Monty readily moved along to give her space. "We're grateful for your assistance, Mrs. Cleary."

Alaric noted the look Constance shot Sir Godfrey.

In response, the magistrate grumbled, but as Rosa sank onto the sofa and Constance joined her and the other men resumed their seats, Sir Godfrey had no option but to do the same and allow Rosa—encouraged by Constance—to recount what she had seen.

Sir Godfrey's first reaction was to challenge Rosa over the man's station. "Surely, given you couldn't see well enough to recognize the man, he might have been some itinerant. Or one of the gardeners or grooms?"

"No." Rosa's chin firmed, and her gaze remained steady. "On that point, I'm quite certain. He was a gentleman—by dress, by confidence and stride, by his hair and cravat—I saw clearly enough to see all that. I didn't see his face or even his profile, or anything singular by which to identify him, but he was most certainly a gentleman…although whether he was one of the gentlemen presently in this house, I can't rightly say. He might have come from elsewhere."

"But when last you saw him, he was walking toward the house,"

Alaric put in. "You said he was heading toward the front door, which would, at that time, have been on the latch."

Rosa nodded. "Yes. That's correct."

Sir Godfrey had been frowning direfully, transparently displeased to have such information so forcefully placed before him, but now his expression cleared. "Aha!" He looked at Rosa, then at Percy. "Clearly, Mrs. Cleary here saw one of your gentlemen out taking the air—just as she was. The gentleman had no doubt gone for an innocent walk in the shrubbery—nothing suspicious about that, heh? He must have passed out of the shrubbery before the incident with Miss Johnson occurred. Yes, yes." Sir Godfrey warmed to his theme. "Nothing to it. All perfectly innocent, what?"

Clinging to patience—knowing that was the only way to deal with Sir Godfrey—Alaric evenly said, "Unfortunately, none of the gentlemen will admit to being the man conveniently out taking the air. As you say, if any had been that man, engaged on a perfectly innocent walk, there should be no reason not to own to it. However, none will. And as one might expect, that has inevitably given rise to a cloud of suspicion that now hangs over the head of every gentleman here."

That was, perhaps, overstating things—at least at present. But it needed no stretch of the imagination to foresee that if the murderer of Glynis Johnson wasn't identified, the possibility of being guilty could well deepen to the level of a social stigma that attached to all the gentlemen there, despite only one having done the deed.

Imperturbably, Alaric went on, "As the senior peer present"—with such as Sir Godfrey, it never hurt to remind him of title and station—"my opinion is that, in such unfortunate circumstances, in addition to the justice owed to Miss Johnson and her family, the interests of all the guests will also be best served by a thorough investigation—one leading to Miss Johnson's murderer being caught."

Invoking social opprobrium—the blame for which some might later lay at the magistrate's door—was, in Alaric's view, the fastest way to get Sir Godfrey to give the murder the attention it was due. Holding Sir Godfrey's gaze, Alaric continued, "Many of the gentlemen guests present have yet to marry, and these days, fond mamas and papas are wont to look askance at any suitor with unresolved questions hanging over his name."

Sir Godfrey harrumphed. He looked down, clearly canvassing his options, then he cast Alaric a malevolent glance. "And how will you feel, my lord, when it's you being questioned, heh?"

Alaric arched his brows. "I'm only too happy to be questioned by you or anyone else. I'm not staying at the Hall but at Carradale Manor, and I had left for home an hour or more before last night's entertainment ended. My movements can be verified by Mandeville's and my own staff. I wasn't here when Miss Johnson was murdered." He allowed his voice to grow colder. "But other gentlemen were, and in light of Mrs. Cleary's sighting and the lack of any gentleman admitting to being out taking the air, I suggest you will need to satisfy yourself and all those here that one of the company is not the murderer before washing your hands of this case."

Sir Godfrey was known to be an irrationally stubborn man; his scowl only deepened and his resistance, palpable, hardened.

Constance's clear tones cut through the simmering silence. "The Whittakers might not be local, however, I can assure you that my grandfather has many highly placed friends, and he will not be pleased to learn that the murder of his cousin's daughter was not accorded a thorough and exhaustive investigation and that the man responsible wasn't brought to justice."

The calculation in Sir Godfrey's eyes suggested he didn't know whether to risk Constance's grandfather's ire or not.

"It seems to me," Alaric said, "that given the circumstances, the least you can do is to properly investigate."

"Humph!" Sir Godfrey's exclamation was less trenchantly resistant than before. "Don't try to tell me how to do my job—of course I'll properly investigate..." Blinking, Sir Godfrey broke off. "If that's what's called for."

Alaric endeavored to make his next statement as much of a suggestion as he could. "That will mean instructing everyone to remain at the Hall until you can be sure who the murderer is—one of the company or otherwise. Of course, that way, if anyone seeks to leave prematurely—or actually runs—that could surely be taken as an admission of guilt, don't you think?"

From experience, Alaric knew Sir Godfrey was suggestible. The magistrate appeared to be imagining how such an investigation might go...

Eventually, Sir Godfrey turned to Percy. "Is that what you want, then?

A thorough investigation? Surely you don't wish to have this matter further inconvenience your guests to that extent."

Percy stared at Sir Godfrey as if seeing him clearly for the first time. The magistrate's last question appeared to have stripped away any lingering shock and seized and focused Percy's wits. "No." The word was cold, sharp, and decisive. "However, Miss Johnson was killed— *murdered*—in my house. Under my roof, so to speak, where she should have been safe. Where she was, in effect, under my protection. Nothing can erase that or the duty I therefore must assume to ensure all is done— every last stone turned—to identify the murderer and bring the miscreant to justice."

Alaric felt like applauding; Percy had finally found his backbone.

Percy cast a glance at Edward—reminding Alaric of Edward's purpose in being at Mandeville Hall. Regardless, Percy, his voice gaining strength, declared, "And as Carradale pointed out, my guests—the gentlemen at least—will not be best served by having an unsolved murder in their past, one they might be suspected of having committed." Percy met Alaric's eyes and, seeming to draw strength from the contact, concluded, "I agree with Carradale. For everyone's sakes, a thorough investigation must be mounted and Miss Johnson's murderer apprehended."

"I entirely agree," Constance stated, sparking murmurs of agreement from Monty and Rosa, too.

Alaric looked at Edward, but he was looking down at his clasped hands. Given his self-appointed role of defender of the family's name, Edward's resistance to the notion of a full-scale investigation was under-standable. It wasn't, however, tenable in the circumstances, and Edward appeared to have accepted that.

Sir Godfrey remained recalcitrant to the last. He cast a long look at Alaric, who coolly arched his brows in response, hoping very much that Sir Godfrey would take as read the threat Alaric hadn't voiced—that if Sir Godfrey failed to mount an adequate investigation, Alaric would inform Scotland Yard himself.

Something of his thoughts must have reached Sir Godfrey, because with a final harrumph, he surrendered. "Very well." Briefly, he flung up his hands, then pushed to his feet. "If that's what you all want, then that's what you shall have, although mark my words, it'll prove a dead end. The man responsible is long gone. But we'll question and be thorough—just don't later say I didn't warn you." He fastened his gaze on Constance,

Rosa, and Monty and pompously advised them, "Investigations are never pleasant."

Constance returned his look coldly. "I'm quite certain that being murdered was not a pleasant experience for my cousin."

Sir Godfrey blinked, then swung to face Percy, who had also risen. "As Carradale suggested, I'm ordering everyone residing under this roof to remain here, on the estate, until my investigation's complete." He glanced sidelong at Alaric. "You, my lord, may continue to sleep in your own bed, but you must not leave the area of the combined estates."

Alaric inclined his head in ready acceptance.

Sir Godfrey turned back to Percy. "Will you inform your guests, or shall I?"

"I'll do it." Looking as if he wanted to be rid of Sir Godfrey, Percy gestured somewhat curtly to the door.

Sir Godfrey acknowledged the others with nods, then stumped toward the front hall. "I've appointments this afternoon," he declared, his customary arrogance resurfacing. "I'll return tomorrow morning with the constable to begin my investigation."

Alaric refused to rise to the bait. What could be more important than murder, especially the slaying of an apparently blameless young lady? He caught Constance Whittaker's eye and saw that she, too, was biting her tongue. As she and Rosa Cleary and Monty joined him and they followed in Percy and Sir Godfrey's wake, Alaric murmured, "I believe we should be appropriately grateful for small mercies."

"Evidently," Constance replied.

Edward trailed them as they entered the front hall. Percy was seeing Sir Godfrey off. Monty gallantly offered Rosa his arm; she accepted, and the pair went off, presumably in search of the other guests. Edward looked in that direction, then turned and made for the stairs.

Sir Godfrey left, and Percy turned from the door. He saw Alaric and Constance and nodded to them, then strode off in Monty and Rosa's wake.

Constance drifted in the same direction; Alaric kept pace beside her. She glanced around, confirming no one else was within earshot, then murmured, "Mrs. Macomber dosed herself with laudanum and is still too sedated to question."

Alaric halted, and she paused beside him. He trapped her gaze. "I asked Percy why he'd invited your cousin. He said it was merely because he'd thought she would enjoy the stay, and he'd been asked to invite Miss Weldon as well, and so had thought the invitation not inappropriate."

"Hmm." After a moment, the Amazon—despite knowing her name, he still thought of her as that—grudgingly admitted, "I suppose that's understandable."

Alaric didn't add that when he'd asked his question, Percy had looked at him blankly—strangely—for several seconds before bleakly offering his reason: that he'd thought she would enjoy it. There'd been emotion behind the words—guilt of a sort, not so much in a personal sense but more in the vein of failing as a host, along with something else. Failing someone he'd been attracted to? Alaric had to wonder. From what he'd seen, Miss Johnson had caught the eyes of several gentlemen present, but not in any over-lustful fashion. Innocents were not the favored prey of the unmarried gentlemen there, and Glynis Johnson had given no sign what-ever of angling for an illicit liaison. No—she'd been gay and carefree and utterly blameless…at most, possibly seeking to attract one particular gentleman there.

Constance glanced around the now-empty front hall, then looked at Alaric. "Perhaps by the time Sir Godfrey returns, we might have more definite evidence of murder—and of the murderer."

Alaric feared that was unlikely, yet they'd succeeded in wringing from Sir Godfrey as much as—indeed, more than—he'd hoped. Electing to focus on that positive, he inclined his head, then waved her toward the side corridor down which the sounds of other guests could be heard, predictably exclaiming over the news of Sir Godfrey's edict.

Constance allowed Carradale to lead her to the morning room. There, they found the other guests giving vent to their thoughts, speculations, and what seemed largely pro forma grumblings about being confined to the Hall estate for the duration of Sir Godfrey's investigation. As Constance had gathered that they'd all expected to remain until at least Saturday morning, she judged the grumblings as being merely for show—what people felt they should say in such circumstances.

Carradale excused himself and went to speak with his cousin and Percy Mandeville. Constance found her eyes tracking him as he crossed the room, appreciating his easy, loose-limbed stride… She blinked and looked away. Telling herself she was grateful for a chance to again survey the company, she hugged the wall and studied the groupings scattered about the room. Studied the gentlemen.

Despite accepting—as she suspected many there now secretly did—that one of the gentlemen present might be a murderer, she found it impossible to pick out one as more likely to be the villain…indeed, to be the sort of man who would strangle a lady at all. Although presently understandably subdued, all the gentlemen appeared personable, even likeable; they were an easygoing, socially confident lot, not overtly villainous in any way.

Yet it was almost certain that one of them had put his hands about Glynis's throat and choked the life out of her.

The sobering thought reminded Constance of another duty awaiting her. After one last glance around the company, she slipped out of the door and went to find the housekeeper.

Mrs. Carnaby was all sympathy rolled up in refreshing practicality. She conducted Constance to the cool room off the laundry, along the way briskly advising that they'd summoned the local undertaker from Salisbury. "Given the time, he's not likely to be here until tomorrow, but John Wilson's a good man—he'll handle the body with all due respect, and you can rely on him to carry out whatever arrangements you decide on." Mrs. Carnaby opened the cool room door and stood back.

"Thank you." Constance paused on the threshold, scanned the room, then said, "My grandfather's house lies north of Derby. Your husband was kind enough to dispatch a letter for me a few hours ago. Miss Johnson's mother lives close to my grandfather's house, and I expect she'll have sought refuge with the rest of the family there."

"Indeed, miss. John Wilson will be able to arrange to have the body taken north for you—just let him know the direction." Mrs. Carnaby nodded toward the shroud-draped figure resting on a trestle table. "Our old cook is used to laying out. She's done what she can to set your young lady properly at peace. Anything else you need, you just let us know." She paused, then added, "We're right sorry to have had such a thing happen here. Please accept the staff's sympathies on the young lady's sad passing."

Constance ducked her head. "Thank you."

Mrs. Carnaby bobbed, then turned and walked away. Constance looked at the shrouded body. There was no one else in the room. She closed the door, then advanced on the table. After a second of steeling herself, she reached for the top of the sheet and drew it down.

She remembered that the still faintly protuberant, staring eyes had been closed when she'd come upon Carradale and the body. Presumably Carradale had drawn down Glynis's lids; it seemed the sort of thing he would do. Now, with her features further smoothed, Glynis looked to be sleeping. The only sight that marred the illusion was the necklace of ugly bruises that circled her white throat. Someone—given that Mrs. Macomber was still unresponsive, presumably the old cook or Mrs. Carnaby—had found a white cotton nightgown with a high, lace-edged collar that partially concealed the dark marks.

Constance looked down on the distant cousin she'd been sent to fetch safely home and, again, the sense of failure—of failing in that task—swamped her.

Focusing on Glynis's face, taking in the sweetness still apparent, Constance murmured, "Our poor Glynis—who did this to you?"

Two seconds later, a light tap on the door drew her from her unhappy thoughts. The door opened to reveal one of the upstairs maids.

Halting just inside the room, the maid bobbed a curtsy. "Beggin' your pardon, ma'am, I'm to report that your maid and groom have arrived with your things, and as you requested, we've set you up to share the poor young lady's chaperon's room."

"Thank you." Earlier, on hearing that Constance had put up at the village inn, Percy had invited her to stay at the Hall; while Constance valued the privacy and anonymity of staying at an inn, if she was to find Glynis's killer, being on site was surely preferable, and she'd accepted Percy's offer.

The maid went on, "And Mrs. Carnaby wanted me to ask if you'd like one of us to spell your girl while she's watching over Mrs. Macomber, ma'am."

Constance thought, then replied, "My thanks to Mrs. Carnaby and the staff. Until Mrs. Macomber wakes, if one of you could spell Pearl whenever she requires it, that would be helpful." She should remember to tell Pearl she was referred to as a girl; that would make the middle-aged lady's maid laugh.

The maid—a girl in truth—bobbed again. "I'll let Mrs. Carnaby know, ma'am."

The girl turned, then stepped back and held the door—allowing Carradale to enter.

He directed a vague smile and a nod at the girl. "Milly."

Milly bobbed again. "Your lordship."

For an instant, Constance wondered if there was anything between the pair, if Carradale and the maid had...

Constance blinked. Carradale was a local; of course, he would know the maid's name. And while it was impossible to miss his rakish side, all she'd seen suggested he wasn't the type to be constantly on the prowl, sniffing after anything in skirts. He was a reserved and aloof wolf, if there was such a thing—picky and needing a challenge to stir him. Where she got such an assurance from, she had no idea, but whatever prey he settled on, she felt certain it would be no relatively helpless maid.

Indeed, despite the exchange, he seemed to have barely registered Milly's presence; his gaze had swung to Constance all but immediately, and there it remained as he crossed the small room to stand on the opposite side of the table.

Only then did he lower his gaze to Glynis's face.

Alaric was battling surprise and had to own to being curious as to why, despite the dead body between them, the primary focus of his senses was the Amazon facing him. He'd been informed by Mrs. Carnaby—who had known him since he'd been in short-coats—that in the staff's estimation, Miss Whittaker was "a proper lady" and sane and sensible to boot. The latter assessment was high praise, indeed; Mrs. Carnaby did not bear fools gladly and usually sniffed and tipped up her nose at the foibles of the tonnish ladies Percy invited to stay.

Aware that he wasn't the only one subject to the prods of curiosity, he glanced briefly at the Amazon's strikingly attractive face. "I remembered something from last night, and I wanted to check."

That, of course, guaranteed him her full attention; the mystery was that he craved it.

"Oh?" She stepped closer to the table and looked down at her dead cousin. "What did you remember?"

He reached for the high ruffle that largely concealed Glynis Johnson's slender throat. "I need to see the base of her neck. Do you mind if I undo the collar?"

She frowned, but waved at him to proceed. "Not if it gets us any closer to identifying who did this."

He slipped the top two buttons of the nightgown free, then spread the halves of the collar, exposing Glynis's throat to the collarbones. He bent closer, examining the purple blotches left on the fine white skin. He pushed the cotton ruffle farther back, with his eyes following a line toward Glynis's nape, and found, all but hidden beneath the heavy bruising, what he'd thought might be there.

Feeling a spark of elation, he pointed to the side of the throat, just above the point where neck met shoulder. "There. Can you see it?" He eased back a little to allow her to lean closer and examine the area. "The mark left by a chain."

He looked and confirmed, "It's repeated here, on the other side." He straightened and looked at the Amazon; head bent, she was minutely examining the tiny marks left on the side of Glynis's throat. "When I saw your cousin yesterday evening, when we strolled on the terrace and then when I left her with Percy and the others, she was wearing a gold chain with some pendant—some weight—on it."

Slowly, frowning more definitely, the Amazon straightened. "So presumably she was still wearing the chain when she met the murderer."

"So one would think."

"The chain's been ripped off—that's what left those marks." She met his gaze. "What was the pendant—the thing she had on the chain?"

"I don't know. She wore it beneath her bodice."

For a second, they stared at each other, then she said, "I suspect this is —or at least might be—new evidence to lay before Sir Godfrey tomorrow."

"Possibly." He glanced at the body, then looked at the Amazon. "If you've finished here, perhaps we might take a stroll."

"In the shrubbery?"

Dead body or no, his lips lifted. "That was my intention."

With care and due reverence, she did up the buttons he'd undone, resettled the nightgown's collar, then drew the sheet once more over her cousin's face.

Then with a last, lingering glance at her cousin's shrouded body, she rounded the table.

When she looked at him, he waved her to the door. "We have at least half an hour before it'll be time to dress for dinner."

Keen not to waste any of those minutes and therefore wishing to avoid the other guests, he directed her to the nearest exterior door—the one at the base of the west wing stairs. They quit the house and strode swiftly toward the forecourt to circle around to the shrubbery.

The instant they were out of the house, Constance glanced sidelong at Carradale; with his long legs, he was easily keeping pace with her, not something all men could do. It was her habit to plot and plan ahead, to thoroughly assess all options in advance for any scenario where she might be called on to make a quick decision. They crunched across the fore-court, and she fixed her gaze forward, looking across the lawn to the shrubbery entrance, still some way off. "Earlier, when Stonewall was here, you suggested that Scotland Yard should be called in. Based on all the protests voiced by the others and all I've heard elsewhere, I wouldn't have thought bringing in Peel's men would be something you would support."

He cast her a quick, rather cynical glance. "I understand the protests, and I can imagine what you've heard. But the days of heavy-footed Runners creating havoc for no good reason are very much in the past. The Metropolitan Police Force of today is a very different beast to its origins. It's evolved into an authority to be reckoned with, a weapon of law and order that isn't to be sneezed at—not at all."

She studied him as he looked down at the grass before his feet.

"I've seen them in action," he went on, "albeit from a distance, and there's a particular inspector who specializes in cases such as this—cases of murder within the ton." He looked up and caught her eye. "If this case is reported to Scotland Yard, then unless there's something more socially pressing on his plate—like the murder of a nobleman—the case will be assigned to an Inspector Stokes. And whenever he works on cases within the ton, Stokes calls on two…colleagues, I suppose one would call them. The Honorable Barnaby Adair—the Earl of Cothelstone's son—and Adair's wife, Penelope, who is connected to more of the haut ton than I can enumerate."

She frowned. "So this Inspector Stokes works hand in glove with two members of the haut ton?"

He nodded. "I don't know how the association started, but it's been in existence for a good many years and is accepted by the powers that be in the police force." They neared the entrance to the shrubbery. "For what it's worth, my experience of Stokes and Adair, brief though it was, suggests that they will be relentless and thorough, but also sensitive to the nuances those not accustomed to the ways of the ton might not comprehend."

"I see." They passed under the cool shade of the archway cut into the high hedge that bordered the shrubbery. As they turned and approached the spot where Glynis had lain, she added, "You speak highly of them—I'll put my trust in that." A very strange decision for her; she rarely trusted anything men said. "If nothing comes of Sir Godfrey's investigation, I—or rather, my grandfather through me—will press for Scotland Yard to be called in."

His gaze already quartering the ground around the spot where he'd found Glynis's body, Carradale inclined his head. "Do. I'll press with you, and I suspect Percy will, too. He's not as spineless as his recent behavior has painted him, and as he is the owner of the house in which the crime took place, his voice will carry additional weight."

She accepted that with a nod and settled to search alongside him. "The chain was gold?"

"Yes. Rose-gold and not that thick. The usual weight of chain on which young ladies wear small pendants."

They searched through the thick grass, then poked and peered into the hedges on either side of the short passageway that led from one of the shrubbery gardens to the entrance.

After several silent minutes of parting leaves and pushing aside branches, he observed, "We won all the concessions from Sir Godfrey that, to this point, we needed to secure. Yet you seem…dissatisfied. Not satisfied, at any rate."

She glanced sharply at him, but he was busy searching and wasn't looking at her. After several seconds—feeling almost as if she couldn't help it—she opened her lips and said, "I mentioned that I was sent to fetch Glynis—to fetch her safely home. I arrived in the village on Monday evening. I could have come straight here and demanded that Glynis leave with me immediately. If I had, she wouldn't be dead. Instead, I allowed social niceties to guide me—I thought it would create too much of a scene for both her and me if I barged in during dinner. So I did what I thought was the right thing and waited until the next morning…and by then, she was dead." She paused, then went on, "I will always regret my decision to wait. I know her murder is not my fault, yet regardless…I feel that I've failed. Failed the trust the family put in me to rescue her from whatever she'd got herself into and bring her safely home."

His "Ah yes. The weight of familial responsibility," uttered in a matter-of-fact tone that suggested he truly understood, was the last reply she'd expected.

Instead of making her feel silly for her thoughts—her persistent and irrational emotion—his words suggested that her reaction, at least for her and possibly for him were he in the same straits, was natural and understandable.

Feeling insensibly better, she said, "As things stand, the only appropriate response I can think of is to ensure that Glynis gets justice."

"Indeed. And as I mentioned earlier, you're not alone in pursuing that goal."

They continued to search—high, low, and everywhere between.

Alaric was far too wise to say anything more regarding the emotions he could sense behind her dramatically arresting features. Her eyes were particularly fine—a clear green, like a fern-shadowed woodland pool— but she wouldn't like knowing just how easy he was finding it to read the vicissitudes of her thoughts in their depths.

Eventually, Constance straightened and looked around one last time. "Not even a piece of the chain. If it was ripped away by main force, a chain of that thickness might well have broken into more than one section."

"True." He straightened. "But we haven't found anything." He glanced around, then pointed to the spot where Glynis had lain; the grass was still crushed enough to show. "She was there." He took two steps back toward the entrance, then mimed having his hands around a throat and flinging the body away… He shook his head. "Even if he flung her rather than just opening his hands and letting her fall, he couldn't have been standing farther away than this."

"And we've searched that far and beyond." She scanned the area and grimaced. "It isn't here."

She turned back to see him resettling his coat. Sober, he met her eyes. "It's not here—which suggests the murderer took it. Judging by the marks on your cousin's neck, it seems whoever he is tore it from her."

"Which," she concluded, "leaves us to wonder what it was that Glynis wore so secretively on the chain."

She turned toward the shrubbery entrance, and he fell in alongside her.

"Have you had a chance to speak with Mrs. Macomber?" he asked. "She might well know what Glynis's pendant was."

"I tried, but sadly, she's still too sedated to even rouse. I suspect she took sufficient laudanum to ensure she slept until morning."

They stepped out of the shrubbery and headed for the front door.

After a moment, he shot her a glance. "It's tempting to think that Glynis was murdered for whatever was on that chain."

She met his eyes. "But what sort of pendant could possibly be worth murdering a young lady for?"

He tipped his head to her. "That's a very good question."

~

Unsurprisingly, dinner that evening was a subdued affair, but with Constance to make up the numbers of ladies, at least there wasn't a glaring gap about the board.

She was now glad that Pearl had insisted on packing her bronze-silk evening gown, the matching slippers, and her pearls; the accoutrements allowed her to move among the other guests without standing out sartorially. Not that she cared about such things, but she was aware others did, and she wanted the ladies to feel at ease in her company, the better to elicit comments about Glynis that might lead them further in pursuit of the murderer.

With that aim in mind, when the ladies rose from the table and trailed back into the drawing room, Constance said, "I noticed there's a conservatory. Does anyone else feel like a stroll to study the plants?"

Five other ladies leapt at the chance to be elsewhere; no doubt the drawing room held memories—echoes of the previous evening when Glynis had moved among them.

Mrs. Collard led the way, explaining that she'd already ventured into the heated atmosphere of the conservatory; she quickly added that she had something of a green thumb and had been drawn to see what Mandeville had growing, then named several species of plant that she declared Mandeville—or more correctly, his gardener—had succeeded in cultivating.

Constance knew next to nothing of what might be grown in a conservatory; on crops and orchards, herbs and vegetables, she was close to being an expert, but her knowledge of exotic species was essentially nonexistent.

Luckily, Mrs. Collard was matched in knowledge by Mrs. Finlayson, and while their small company wended this way and that along the tiled paths between the groupings of pots and planters, the pair entertained the rest—Miss Weldon and her chaperon, Mrs. Cripps, Mrs. Cleary, and Constance—with a running commentary on matters horticultural.

Constance strolled slowly at the rear of the group beside Mrs. Cleary. Rosamund Cleary seemed unsettled and skittish—ready to jump—which was hardly to be wondered at. Despite wanting to interrogate Mrs. Cleary in case she'd seen more than she'd said, Constance felt that, at least at that moment, it would be unkind to press the woman. She was already nervous, as if the realization that the murderer was very likely in the house, under the same roof, had sunk into her awareness in a more definite way than it had with the other ladies.

Constance suspected that the rest of the guests believed themselves mere bystanders, not in any way connected with Glynis or her death and so immune from any threat.

The more she dwelled on the situation, the more Constance's respect for Mrs. Cleary's courage in speaking up and reporting what she'd seen grew. In response, Constance adopted a quietly encouraging mien and hoped Mrs. Cleary might share a comment—something that would allow Constance to ease into a conversation about the figure Mrs. Cleary had seen leaving the shrubbery the previous night.

Sadly, she hoped in vain.

When the time came to return to the drawing room and they filed out of the conservatory, Mrs. Cleary had managed to utter not a single useful word, although she had made the effort to share her opinion on the best species of palms for decorating a ballroom.

Even with that, her tone, at least to Constance's ears, had sounded brittle.

In the end, she wasn't sure if Rosa Cleary was skittish because she was truly frightened or because she was a nervous sort and utterly distracted.

The route between the conservatory and the drawing room lay via a long corridor that ran past the billiard room. The billiard room door was still yards ahead of them when it opened and a horde of gentlemen streamed out. To Constance, tall enough to see over the other ladies' curls, it seemed as if every male guest had taken refuge in the billiard room and all were now intent on hurrying to join the ladies for tea. Talking, settling coats, and briskly striding toward the drawing room, the men had come through the door already turning in that direction; not one noticed the six ladies coming along the corridor.

Mrs. Collard gave an audible sniff, which caused Constance and Mrs. Cripps, who was walking beside her, with Miss Weldon on her other side, to cynically smile.

Then Rosa Cleary gasped and halted.

They'd been walking three abreast, with Rosa in the middle in front, ahead of Mrs. Cripps.

Behind Mrs. Collard, Constance saw Rosa's left hand dart out and grip Mrs. Collard's wrist.

Instantly, all the ladies gathered around.

"Are you all right, Rosa?" Mrs. Finlayson inquired.

"You've gone dreadfully pale," Miss Weldon observed.

Mrs. Collard closed her hand over Mrs. Cleary's, shifting her arm to be ready to support her in case she fainted. "Do you need to sit down, dear?"

With the change in positions, Constance found herself standing beside Mrs. Collard. Able to see only Mrs. Cleary's profile, Constance saw her lower her eyes, until then apparently wide, then Rosa Cleary sucked in a breath, closed her eyes, and briefly shook her head. "No, no—it's nothing. Just a turn."

"A turn, dear?" Mrs. Cripps solicitously inquired. "Are you sure?"

Rosa drew in another long, bracing breath and opened her eyes. "Yes. I...sometimes get them. It's of no moment, I assure you."

"Oh!" said Miss Weldon. "That must be so trying."

Along with the other more experienced ladies, Constance wasn't convinced.

Rosa managed a smile, but it was patently strained. "Indeed, it is." She dipped her head to Mrs. Collard and included the others with a glance as she said, "Thank you all. I'm quite recovered now."

As if to demonstrate that, she drew back her hand, stiffened her spine, and waved down the corridor. "We should get on—all the men are before us."

Constance looked ahead and glimpsed the last of the men turning briskly in to the front hall. They—at least the last stragglers—must have heard the ladies' exclamations, but in typical male fashion, they hadn't dallied. No doubt, they were terrified of being drawn into a discussion of some female malady.

Then again, they probably had looked—Constance vaguely thought they had—but the instant Rosa had declared it was nothing, they'd hurried to make themselves scarce.

Considering such behavior nothing more than to be expected of men —gentlemen or otherwise—Constance continued with the other ladies as they made for the drawing room. The tea trolley should have arrived by now.

They reached the front hall, but instead of continuing on, Rosa stepped toward the stairs. She still looked distinctly peaky. "If you would be so good as to make my excuses, I believe I'll go straight to bed."

"Of course, dear," Mrs. Cripps said.

"We'll tell Mrs. Fitzherbert if she asks, but truthfully, I doubt she'll notice," Mrs. Collard said.

"You're still a trifle pale, my dear," Mrs. Finlayson said. "We'll hope it's nothing a good night's sleep won't cure."

Rosa assured them all that was so. With wishes for a good night's rest following her, she went upstairs.

Constance noted that Rosa went up rather quickly; she dallied long enough to make sure Rosa didn't trip or fall, then turning her mind to wondering how to engineer a moment—several moments—alone with Mrs. Cleary on the morrow, Constance followed the other ladies into the drawing room.

She'd been right. The tea trolley had already arrived. With an inward sigh, she lined up to accept her cup of overbrewed tea from Mrs. Fitzherbert's gnarled hand.

CHAPTER 4

a piercing scream jerked Constance awake. Eyes wide, she sat up, clutching the covers; her heart thumped, then started to race.

"Oh no. What now?" She scrambled out of the bed, grabbed her night robe, shoved her arms into the sleeves and her feet into her slippers, spared a glance for Mrs. Macomber—still in a drugged sleep—and rushed out of the door. Hurriedly belting the robe, she ran toward where she'd thought the scream had come from—farther along the wing containing the rooms assigned to the ladies of the party.

Toward the end of the corridor, Constance saw a maid, her hands over her mouth, her eyes staring, backing out of a room. The maid's gaze remained locked on what lay beyond the open door...

Constance's lungs seized; a sense of looming horror gripped her.

Other doors opened. As Constance sped past, several guests looked out; some—the gentlemen who had spent the night in one or other of the ladies' rooms—came out and strode after her.

Constance reached the maid, who had halted, frozen, just outside the room. The girl was breathing in ragged gasps.

Constance took the maid by the shoulders and steered her around so her back was to the corridor wall and she was no longer seeing whatever was inside.

Then Constance whirled and, with Guy Walker and Robert Fletcher on her heels, rushed into the room.

They pulled up just beyond the threshold, their feet coming to faltering halts at the sight that met their eyes.

On the bed, Rosa Cleary lay on her back, wide eyes staring upward. Her head was tipped back on the pillow, her mouth partly open as if she'd cried out, and her hands had clenched into claws, gripping the sheets to either side.

Her legs had thrashed violently, churning the covers.

She was very definitely dead.

Constance was dimly aware of others pushing into the room behind her. Unable to drag her eyes from the sight of a woman who only hours before had been very much alive, giving in to the pressure of bodies behind her, she slowly stepped forward and around the side of the bed.

She looked into Rosa's face and saw terror etched in her features— in those staring, now-blind eyes with their expression of horrified disbelief.

Several of the ladies had peered in; gasps and wails—quickly cut off —came from beyond the door.

Most of the gentlemen—stony-faced and grim—had pushed into the room, but they remained closely bunched, blocking the door.

Then Percy arrived. "What's happened?"

Constance tore her gaze from Rosa Cleary's face and looked up as the gentlemen shuffled and let Percy through, into the clear space at the foot of the bed.

She studied Percy as his gaze fell on Rosa's body. Already hollow-eyed and pasty, he lost every vestige of color, and his eyes widened until it seemed they would fall from his head. As Constance had done, he stared. "Oh God. No—not Rosa as well."

His shock and the stunned grief in his voice struck Constance as entirely genuine. No man could be such a good actor.

The gentlemen before the door shifted again, and Edward Mandeville appeared. He walked forward, halting to stand shoulder to shoulder with Percy.

After a second of looking down on Rosa's body, Edward humphed. "This is very distressing. I heard that she was unwell last night and retired early. Perhaps she had a weak heart."

Constance frowned. "I don't think she died of any malady."

His expression registering faint distaste, Edward lightly shrugged. "I admit I know little of such things." His gaze went past Constance; she followed it to the small table beside the bed—to a vial of laudanum standing beside a glass of water. "Perhaps it was an accident. I understand many women are addicted to that stuff."

Still frowning, Constance looked at the body. "Laudanum kills while the victim sleeps—they simply never wake." At the edge of her vision, she noticed the ivory-white of a pillow tucked down beside the head of the bed, half hidden by the drapes that hung there.

She looked up as Percy waved at the body and, in a choked voice, said, "It's obvious Rosa was awake when she died."

Edward's frown deepened until it approached an aggravated scowl. "Perhaps she was. But surely there must be some mundane explanation for her death."

Everyone—including the men still crowded before the door—looked at Edward in disbelief.

Constance remembered the comments various members of the company had made regarding Edward's presence at the house party—that he'd been sent by Percy's family to ensure nothing scandalous occurred. Given Edward's role, in the circumstances, it was perhaps unsurprising that he did not want Rosa's death to be another murder.

Dismissing Edward and his wishes, Constance looked at Percy. "I believe the proper course of action is to summon a doctor to confirm the cause of death."

Percy blinked at her, then nodded. "Yes. That's what we should do."

"And perhaps," Constance went on, "we should send for Lord Carradale. He knows the situation here and will also know the doctor and can assist with deciding what action should be taken once we have the doctor's verdict."

"Yes." Percy nodded more decisively.

Several of the men behind him nodded, too; Constance had noted that most of the guests had confidence in Carradale as one who knew how to navigate the pitfalls of their world.

Percy turned and tried to see over the wall of men. "Carnaby—are you there, man?"

"Yes, sir," the butler replied from the corridor.

"Send for Dr. Swale," Percy ordered. "Tell him we've a lady found dead in her bed and need his services urgently. And also send to Carradale and ask him to come as soon as he can."

"Indeed—at once, sir."

The gentlemen before the door started to file out of the room.

Constance hesitated; she wanted to look at the pillow hidden beside the bed, but didn't want anyone to know she'd spotted it. She also didn't want anyone straightening Rosa's legs and fingers and closing her eyes before the doctor and Carradale had viewed the body. To her mind, how the body lay was the most critical evidence that Rosa's death had been anything but natural.

She didn't glance again at the hidden pillow but instead advanced with her arms spread to gather and herd Percy and Edward, along with the other men, out of the room ahead of her.

She followed them into the corridor and closed the door behind her. Up and down the passageway, guests were gathered in small groups, discussing the latest horror in shocked and somber tones. The ladies looked as shaken and rattled as, inside, Constance felt. Glynis's death had been a shock, but Rosa's death—under the same roof beneath which they'd all been sleeping—went well beyond dreadful into outright frightening.

To Constance's mind—and she was sure in many others—they had a murderer in their midst.

She cleared her throat and, when everyone looked her way, said, "This may sound insensitive, but as we are all wide awake, early though it is, it might be best to dress and go down to breakfast and"—she glanced at the door behind her—"vacate this area."

Carnaby had dispatched footmen to do his master's bidding; as pale and as distressed as anyone, he remained in the corridor, obviously waiting to carry out any further requests the guests might make. He added his encouragement to Constance's. "Breakfast will be ready momentarily, should anyone feel so inclined."

"I'm not sure I could eat anything." Prue Collard looked at the door behind which Rosa lay. "But I do think you're right about us all going downstairs. We don't need to hover within sight of...our latest tragedy."

Constance inclined her head; she couldn't have put it better.

Unsettled, wary, and uncertain, the guests dispersed, retreating to their rooms to dress before heading downstairs.

Once they were alone in the corridor, Constance turned to Carnaby. "There's a lock on this door, but no key. Do you have it?"

"Yes, miss. The key will be in the housekeeper's room—we don't leave keys in the locks, as the guests are prone to forgetting and locking the doors, and then the maids can't get in."

"Of course. But I believe we should lock this chamber until the authorities have made their decision about what caused Mrs. Cleary's death."

"Indeed, miss." Carnaby glanced around and spotted a maid waiting nervously by the servants' stairs. He beckoned her nearer and sent her for the key.

Constance had been thinking; no one but she and the staff would know the door was locked. "As well as locking the door, I believe it would be best to station two men from your staff on guard, here in the corridor. Then if anyone attempts to gain entry, perhaps one of the men could come and fetch me?"

"Of course, miss. If I might say, that's a wise precaution. There are always those who have a ghoulish fascination with the dead."

Especially murderers who want to hide their tracks. Constance merely nodded. She waited until the maid returned with the key and Carnaby locked the door. He regarded the key, then presented it to her. "Perhaps you should hold this, miss."

She looked at the heavy key resting in the butler's palm, then reached out and took it.

Two footmen arrived, and Carnaby directed them to stand guard before the door to Rosa's room and to report to Constance if anyone approached, wanting to get inside.

With all as secure as she could make it, with a grateful nod, Constance left Carnaby and his guards and hurried back to the room she shared with Mrs. Macomber.

Constance scrambled into her day gown. Her maid, Pearl, arrived as she was settling the bodice; while Pearl did up the tiny buttons closing the back, Constance related what had happened.

Grimly, Pearl offered, "I can sit with the body, if you want."

"I don't think that's necessary—the door's locked, and we've got guards outside." Constance glanced at Mrs. Macomber. "I would rather you kept an eye on Mrs. Macomber. I—Carradale and I—really need to know if she can shed light on any of this, or at least on why Glynis was murdered."

"Has to be the same man, surely. But why'd he do Mrs. Cleary in? Might she have known who he was—or known enough to guess?"

Constance stilled. "Those are excellent observations and questions." She twitched the sleeves of her gown into place. "But now that Mrs. Cleary's gone, it's going to be much harder to learn the answers."

After allowing Pearl to brush out her hair and tame the long tresses into a plaited coronet, Constance left Pearl to her vigil beside Mrs. Macomber's bed and hurried back to where the two footmen stood guard outside Rosa's door.

She glanced up and down the corridor, but saw no one lingering in the shadows.

"Most of the guests have gone downstairs to breakfast, miss," one of the footmen reported. "Some of the ladies looked a mite green—they seemed ready enough to get away from here."

"I see. Do you have any idea how long Lord Carradale will be?"

"Shouldn't be long, miss," the other, older footman said. "His lord-ship's not one to dally when asked for help."

Realizing she meant to wait for Carradale to arrive, the older footman fetched a straight-backed chair for her and placed it against the wall. Constance sat and waited, trying to suppress her impatience.

Five minutes later, she heard footsteps—boot steps—pounding up the back stairs. She leapt to her feet as Carradale appeared at the end of the corridor; the relief that flowed through her was powerful enough to make her blink.

He strode forward; sharp and startlingly intense, his hazel gaze locked on her face. "I received a garbled message that one of the guests had died." His gaze lingered on Constance for a moment more, then he drew breath and glanced at the door before which the footmen had come to attention.

Constance remembered how to breathe, found her tongue, and gestured to the door. "It's Rosa Cleary. The maid who brought up her washing water found her quite obviously dead in her bed."

Alaric frowned. "Last evening, I heard she'd retired early—that she'd suffered a turn. Had she sickened or been taken ill?"

Constance drew in a fortifying breath. "I don't believe it was anything like that." She reached into her pocket and drew out the key. "But come and look and see what you think."

She unlocked and opened the door, then stood aside and waved him in. She followed and watched as his steps slowed, then halted. From the foot of the bed, he studied the body.

Constance closed the door, then went to the side of the bed. "After the maid screamed, I reached the room first. I made sure nothing was touched or altered."

"Good." The word was even, yet weighted with emotion; when he raised his gaze and met her eyes, she identified the emotion as impotent fury. "She was murdered, too."

Not a question. Constance nodded. "I believe she was smothered." She drew back the heavy curtain that framed the head of the bed and pointed to the pillow thus revealed. "With that."

Alaric looked at the pillow. "Did you move it?"

"No—I haven't touched it yet." Constance glanced questioningly at him, and when he nodded, she gripped the pillowcase by one corner and carefully tugged it free.

He moved to her shoulder and watched as she turned the pillow over.

She held it up, angling it so the light from the window slanted across the pillowcase's surface. They both studied the ivory cotton; several smudges of pale color were discernible, along with a more definite hint of an impression of parted lips, marked by the soft plum-colored lip paint Rosa had favored.

Constance glanced at the body. "She wasn't that young—she wore powder on her face and rouge on her cheeks and painted her lips."

He nodded. "And she was, beyond question, murdered." After a second's thought, he added, "Quite aside from by whom, what we don't know is why. Why kill Rosa?"

She set the pillow down beside the bed. "As my maid suggested, the most likely reason, surely, is that Rosa somehow knew enough to at least guess who murdered Glynis."

She paused, her expression suggesting she was thinking back, reviewing something. Then she offered, "That turn Rosa had last night—she insisted it was nothing, just a slight faint—but what if it wasn't?" She met Alaric's eyes. "We were in the corridor when the gentlemen came out of the billiard room. Could Rosa have seen something—something about one of the gentlemen—that shocked her and caused her to come over faint?"

He studied her green eyes, lit with compassion and determination. They were eyes he could get lost in, but...not yet. Not now. "You mean she recognized something about one of the gentlemen that made her suspect he was Glynis's murderer—the man she'd glimpsed coming out of the shrubbery that night."

"Yes. The first time she'd seen him—leaving the scene of Glynis's murder—the light was poor. Last night, while the corridor wasn't ablaze with light, it was better lit. She might have recognized him then, when she hadn't before."

"Striding out of the shrubbery entrance and striding out of the billiard room." He tipped his head. "I grant it's possible."

Constance frowned and looked down at the body. "But if she recognized him, why didn't she say? Rather than retire early—calling attention to her 'turn'—and giving him a chance to creep in while she slept and smother her."

Alaric looked down at the remains of what had once been a vibrant lady. Rosa Cleary hadn't been a saint, but she'd by no means deserved to have her life cut short. He stirred. "Perhaps our speculation is misplaced, and it truly was just a turn. However, the murderer might have reasoned as we just did and decided he needed to ensure Rosa didn't tell anyone of anything she recognized—now or later."

He thought, then added, "I believe we can be certain of one thing— Rosa's reaction last night was enough to sign her death warrant."

Constance pointed to a small vial on the nightstand. "She very likely took a dose of laudanum to help her sleep. That would have made her even easier prey. No surprise she didn't wake in time to scream."

He nodded. "Given she saw the gentlemen exiting the billiard room last evening and had an obvious reaction of some kind, whether she recognized Glynis's murderer or not didn't matter. Our gentleman murderer thought that she had, or at some point would, and so he killed her."

Constance met his eyes, and he read in hers her unqualified agreement.

He held her gaze for an instant more, then looked at Rosa's body and grimly stated, "It's time to get Sir Godfrey back."

Together with Percy and Edward, Alaric and Constance were waiting in the library when Sir Godfrey arrived.

The portly magistrate stumped through the door, then leaned on his cane to bend a disgruntled eye on Percy. "What's this, then, Mandeville? Another murder, you say?"

The dark rings beneath his eyes emphasizing his pallor, Percy flatly replied, "So we believe." He gestured to the door. "You'd best come and take a look."

Sir Godfrey shuffled around. "Who is it, then? One of your stable hands? Perhaps it was he who did away with the chit in the shrubbery."

The suggestion was so inapt, it left them all momentarily dumb-founded.

Alaric recovered first. "No—another of the female guests was discovered smothered in her bed this morning."

"Mrs. Rosamund Cleary." Constance's tone was quietly condemnatory. "The lady who reported seeing a gentleman leaving the shrubbery around the time Glynis met her end."

The news set Sir Godfrey back on his heels. He stared at Alaric, then looked at Percy. "Oh."

Thereafter, Sir Godfrey made no further comment as he trailed Percy and Edward up the stairs. Alaric and Constance followed. When they reached Rosa's room, Constance drew out the key; while she unlocked the door, she explained her part in the discovery and that she'd ensured nothing in the room had been altered since the body was found.

Sir Godfrey gave her an odd look, but when she stepped back and waved him inside, he ventured in—and stopped short just over the threshold. After several moments, he swallowed and said, "Ah. I see."

All hint of his customary bluster had fled.

Alaric followed Constance into the room. She went to the side of the bed and lifted the heavy curtain aside to reveal the pillow. "This pillow was tucked down here, out of sight." She reached down and lifted the pillow, then turned it and displayed the face of the pillowcase to Sir Godfrey, Percy, and Edward. "If you look closely, you can see the marks left by Mrs. Cleary's powder and rouge and also her lip paint."

His hands crossed on the head of his cane, on which he was leaning heavily, Sir Godfrey craned forward and peered, then, his face losing what little color he'd retained to that point, he nodded. "Yes." His voice sounded strangled. "I see."

"If any evidence beyond what you can see in the bed was required to determine that Mrs. Cleary was murdered," Alaric grimly stated, "I contend that pillow and case puts the matter beyond doubt. Rosa Cleary was smothered."

Constance added, "Almost certainly by the same man who murdered my cousin, Miss Johnson."

In a voice devoid of emotion, Percy said, "Carradale and I checked with Carnaby, and he swears the house's doors and windows were all locked last night. Given Miss Johnson's death, the company retired early, and Carnaby and the footmen made doubly sure there was no way that any itinerant"—Percy gave the word contemptuous emphasis—"could gain entry."

"Further to that, Carnaby checked again this morning, and no door or window shows signs of being forced," Alaric stated. "So unless you wish to postulate that two ladies being murdered at one house on two consecutive nights is the work of two different murderers, one an itinerant and the other someone who is residing under this roof, then we have a double murderer who is almost certainly one of the gentlemen currently staying at Mandeville Hall."

Alaric caught Sir Godfrey's gaze. "In my opinion, you should summon Scotland Yard immediately."

He wasn't all that surprised when, after a fractional hesitation, Sir Godfrey nodded. Realization, followed by swift calculation, had gleamed in the magistrate's eyes; investigating a double murder committed by a gentleman at a ton house party held the potential for all manner of social mantraps that—pride be damned—Sir Godfrey would prefer to avoid.

"Harrumph! Yes." Having made his decision, Sir Godfrey was eager to extricate himself with all speed. He turned from the bed and addressed Percy. "I'll send a message by courier as soon as I get home. Regardless, anyone the Yard sends won't reach here before tomorrow afternoon at the earliest." Sir Godfrey started for the door. "I will, of course, return to consult with the inspector sent to take charge and offer him my insights. Until then, my earlier edict regarding everyone remaining at the Hall must stand."

Constance returned the pillow to where it had been. Seeing Sir Godfrey almost at the door, she frowned. "Sir Godfrey—what about the bodies?"

"Heh?" Sir Godfrey, Percy, and Edward had all started for the door. All three looked back, the magistrate with his bushy eyebrows rising.

Hiding her exasperation— *men!*—Constance waved at the body in the bed. "We can't leave Mrs. Cleary like this. And what of my cousin's remains?"

Sir Godfrey regarded Rosa's body anew. "I'm sure whoever is sent will want us to keep things the way they are as far as possible. But as for the bodies, they should, I believe, be placed on ice, or at least somewhere cool, until the inspector from Scotland Yard releases them."

Unsure, Constance glanced at Carradale. He dipped his head. "The cool room here holds temperature reasonably well. If the inspector arrives tomorrow afternoon, which he should, that should suffice."

Percy looked at Rosa Cleary's body, then met Constance's gaze. "I'll get Carnaby to arrange moving...Rosa."

Satisfied, Constance nodded. Nevertheless, as she and Carradale followed the other three out of the room, she locked the door once more.

She strolled beside Carradale in the wake of the others as they went down the main stairs, through the front hall, and out onto the front porch.

Together with Carradale, she halted beside Edward and Percy and watched as Sir Godfrey's footman helped hoist his master into his coach. Calling out a last promise to send a courier to London with all speed, Sir Godfrey rattled away down the drive.

Edward, whose expression had remained a mask of rectitude for the duration of Sir Godfrey's visit, snorted softly. "An investigation run by Scotland Yard. Viscount Mandeville will be furious. And I can't imagine how your mother and her cronies will react to the gossip. As for the rest of the family, I believe I can state with absolute assurance that they will be horrified."

His expression close to blank, Percy regarded his cousin for a silent moment, then said, "At least Scotland Yard will get to the bottom of it."

"Perhaps," Edward scoffed. "But at what cost?" With an abrupt shake of his head, he stalked back into the house.

Percy sighed. He raised a hand and rubbed the bridge of his nose. "He means well, but he's so damned focused on the family's reputation, he simply doesn't consider..." Belatedly realizing a lady was present, Percy looked up and grimaced. "Forgive me, Miss Whittaker."

She smiled briefly. "No need. I understand your frustration."

"Yes, well." Percy looked into the front hall. "I suppose I had better go and explain to the others what's happening." He pulled a face. "At least having to remain shouldn't prove a problem." To Constance, he explained, "The house party was to run until Saturday."

"So I understood." Today was Wednesday. If the inspector from Scotland Yard arrived tomorrow afternoon, he would have less than two days before the guests started agitating to be allowed to leave.

Percy sighed again, then nodded to Constance and Carradale and walked into the house.

Constance watched him go, then turned to Carradale. "Will you remain at the Hall, or do you need to return to your home?"

He met her eyes, then said, "No. I'd intended to spend most of my days this week here, and now...I rather think I want to be on hand, in case anything else happens."

"In case the murderer gives himself away in some fashion?"

His features hardened. "Indeed."

She looked in the direction Percy had gone. She compressed her lips, then eased them and admitted, "I'm still not sure what I feel about Scotland Yard being involved." Briefly, she glanced at Carradale. "My instincts run more along the line of Edward's—that nothing but greater scandal will ensue."

Carradale shook his head. "I'm almost certain the commissioner will send Stokes—if he's available. And all I've seen and heard suggests he's a sensible and reasonable man, one with insight into the world of the ton and how it operates."

She studied his face. "You're speaking from experience."

He dipped his head in acknowledgment. "I wasn't directly involved, and my interaction with Stokes himself was brief, but I know Adair—the gentleman who often acts as Stokes's partner with, I gather, the commissioner's consent—and Adair is an earl's son and is more than aware of all the ins and outs of our world. He's also inherently trustworthy."

He'd said as much before—or at least had alluded to it—but that he spoke from personal knowledge went a considerable way toward reassuring her that she wasn't going to see her cousin's name dragged through any mud.

Side by side, they started walking back into the house.

"At least with Scotland Yard on the case," Carradale continued, "you can be assured of a properly conducted investigation." He met her eyes. "In terms of securing justice for your cousin and Rosa Cleary, getting Scotland Yard involved is the most critical thing we needed to do."

She found herself faintly smiling, not just at his words but at the determination and intent investing them. It was comforting to have confidence that however grimly she was set on catching Glynis's and now Rosa's killer, Carradale's commitment matched hers.

CHAPTER 5

*A*t a little after four o'clock on Thursday afternoon, Senior Inspector Basil Stokes of Scotland Yard looked out of the window of the carriage that was bowling up a gravel drive and beheld his destination, Mandeville Hall.

A Gothic-style building in pale brown stone, the central house had been added to over centuries; like some crouching beast, it appeared to have spawned two sprawling wings and—like horns—two rather pretentious turrets. The central building was three stories high, while the wings were two stories with attics above. A long, stone-balustraded terrace stretched along the front of the house and appeared to continue down the left side. Mature woodland crowded close on the right and, it seemed, the rear, but on the left was held back by an extensive array of established hedges.

The sweeping drive ended in an oval forecourt before the stone steps leading up to the porch and the front door.

Seated next to Stokes and leaning forward to peer at the house, the police surgeon, Pemberton, grumbled, "About time. If the nobs have to kill each other, why can't they do it in London?"

Stokes grunted; he wasn't best pleased to have been sent into deepest Hampshire either. "At least it isn't Yorkshire." With the new arrangements in place, Scotland Yard—in the person of its inspectors, sergeants, and constables—could be called on to take charge of investigations into serious crimes anywhere in the country.

He glanced across the carriage at his constables, Morgan and Philpott. He would miss Sergeant O'Donnell, but the older, more experienced man had had to be left at the Yard to tie up the loose ends pertaining to a string of jewel robberies in Hatton Gardens.

As their carriage—not the usual lumbering Yard conveyance but a faster, lighter hired coach—swept around the last bend in the drive and the front porch, until then largely obscured by the canopies of the trees bordering the drive, came into clear view, Stokes caught sight of a tall, dark-haired, elegantly yet somehow negligently attired figure lounging against one of the porch pillars.

Stokes blinked and leaned forward, eyes squinting against the westering light.

Pemberton shot him a glance. "Who is he?"

"I've met him before…once." Stokes flicked through his capacious memory. It hadn't been that long ago… "Carradale. Lord." Intrigued, he added, "A denizen of Jermyn Street. I didn't expect to see him here."

"Hmm. Will he be useful? Can we trust him?"

"He's acquainted with Adair. If I read their interaction correctly, they've known each other for years." Stokes replayed what he could remember of his and Barnaby Adair's short interview with Carradale while pursuing a case previous year. "Carradale seemed a decent sort. So yes, potentially useful."

Possibly very useful. Stokes was distinctly pleased to discover he had a contact already in the household.

The carriage slowed, then halted. Stokes opened the door and climbed down. He looked up at Carradale, nodded to signify recognition, and started up the steps.

Carradale pushed away from the pillar and came to meet Stokes. Somewhat to Stokes's surprise, Carradale held out his hand and said, "I hoped they'd send you."

Grasping the proffered hand, Stokes arched his brows. "In that case, I'm glad not to disappoint."

Carradale's mobile lips twitched, but then he sobered. His gaze moved past Stokes to Pemberton as the surgeon stumped up the steps, his telltale black bag in hand.

Stokes gestured to Pemberton. "Our police surgeon. He needs to examine the bodies."

Pemberton touched the brim of his black hat and nodded to Carradale.

"My lord. If you could direct me to the deceaseds, plural, I'd like to get started immediately. I'm expected to return to London tonight."

"Of course." Carradale turned to the open door. "Carnaby."

The butler came forward and inclined his head to Stokes and Pemberton, then looked at Carradale. "My lord?"

"Mr. Pemberton needs to examine the bodies. Please show him to the cool room."

"Indeed, my lord. At once." To Pemberton, Carnaby said, "If you'll come this way, sir."

With an "I'll come and make my report before leaving" to Stokes, Pemberton went, pacing alongside Carnaby, his focus already on his work.

Carradale stared at the surgeon's retreating back. When Carradale glanced at Stokes and realized he'd noticed, Carradale said, "I'll be interested in hearing his findings."

Stokes allowed his brows to rise. After a second, he said, "I take it you're staying here."

"Yes and no. I'm attending the house party, along with about twenty others. However, my own house is just through the woods, so I haven't been spending my nights here. I've attended through the days and evenings, and as I'm an old friend of the owner—Mr. Percival Mandeville—and was acquainted, however briefly, with you, Percy asked, and I agreed to meet you and act as your liaison with the other guests, as well as with Percy and the staff."

Inwardly, Stokes rejoiced; his task had just got immeasurably easier. "You know everyone?"

"Some better than others, but yes—we run in the same circles."

Excellent. Stokes felt much more confident of catching his man sooner rather than later. In acknowledgment of Carradale's willingness to act as go-between, he said, "If you were glad to see me, then I expect you'll be even happier to hear that Adair's on his way. Along with his wife, who is shockingly adept at ferreting out social secrets."

Fleetingly, Carradale grinned. "Mrs. Penelope Adair—indeed, her reputation is legion, even among this set." He paused, then admitted, "Given the season, I didn't dare hope Adair might be available."

"Well, if one can talk of luck in the face of murder, in this instance, it was on your side—the Adairs deposited their son with his doting grandparents at Cothelstone Castle and came down to attend a house party near

Andover. I sent a courier before I left London. I'll be surprised if they aren't here soon."

Carradale looked relieved. "That's…excellent news."

Stokes nodded. "Meanwhile, I haven't received any detailed information. The magistrate simply wrote that two women—ladies attending this house party—have died in suspicious circumstances, one on Monday night and the other on Tuesday, again sometime during the night."

Carradale grimaced. "As far as it goes, that's accurate."

"But not terribly informative." Stokes glanced at the house. "I would appreciate having a better notion of what happened before I go in and meet possible suspects." He held up a finger. "One moment."

At the bottom of the steps, Philpott and Morgan were waiting for orders. "Usual procedures," Stokes said. "Philpott—you're with me. Morgan—go and charm the cook and the maids and see what they can tell us."

"Aye, sir." Morgan grinned and snapped off a salute, then he turned and made his way around the house.

Carradale watched him go, then looked back at Stokes. "Your constable appears to know his way about a country house, at least when it comes to ingratiating himself with the staff."

"That he does—an invaluable trait." Stokes arched a brow at Philpott, who quietly extracted his notebook and pencil, then Stokes looked back at Carradale. "The beginning is always a good place to start."

Carradale gathered his thoughts, then offered, "The house party officially commenced on Sunday afternoon. All the guests were here by then, and I'd ridden over from Carradale Manor—there's a bridle path between the stables of the two houses."

"Did you notice anything unusual on Sunday—or on Monday, during the day?"

Carradale thought before shaking his head. "No. Nothing at all. As far as I saw, everyone behaved entirely normally." He met Stokes's gaze. "It was a good group—a felicitous choice of guests. Everyone seemed to be getting on, and there was no hint of any tensions. Mandeville—Percy, that is—and I commented on the ease of the company on Monday evening, during what was effectively a soirée, held in the drawing room."

"So when did Monday's death occur, and who died?"

Carradale's expression turned grim. "The first to die was a Miss Glynis Johnson. Sometime after the company retired—so more correctly in the early hours of Tuesday—she was strangled just inside the shrubbery. At about that time, another guest, a Mrs. Rosamund Cleary, was taking the air on the terrace. She saw a gentleman leave the shrubbery and make for the house. The light was poor, and she couldn't see who it was, but she was certain the man was a gentleman and that he headed for the front door, which at that hour was still unlocked."

Stokes closed his eyes and stifled a groan. "Don't tell me—this Mrs. Cleary is the other lady now dead."

He opened his eyes to see Carradale nod.

"A maid found Mrs. Cleary dead in her bed on Wednesday morning. There was a pillow tucked down beside the bed. Those of us who've seen Mrs. Cleary and examined the pillowcase believe the pillow was used to smother her while she slept. She might well have taken laudanum to help her sleep, but it was clear she'd thrashed in the bed before she…died."

The last word was said with both sorrow and distaste. And not a little underlying anger.

Stokes eyed Carradale. "Did you know Mrs. Cleary well?"

Carradale's gaze snapped to his, then his lips twisted. "Not in the way you're thinking. But I had been acquainted with her for…it must be nine years. Ever since her husband died and she started moving in the same circles I did."

Stokes registered Carradale's use of the past tense and wondered, but the point was unlikely to be relevant to the investigation. He glanced at the hedges beyond the end of the long front terrace. "Is that the shrubbery over there?"

Carradale looked over his shoulder. "Yes. It's extensive."

"You said Miss Johnson's body was found just inside—who found it?"

"I did." Carradale turned back and met Stokes's gaze. "I'd ridden over after breakfast to join the company for the day. I left my horse with the stableman, Hughes, and was walking up to the house—I always take the path through the shrubbery, as it avoids having to go through the kitchen and disturbing the staff."

Stokes nodded his understanding. He debated, then said, "You're going to have to go through everything for Adair and Penelope—I can't imagine they won't turn up in the next half hour or so. Given that, instead of you telling and me hearing all twice, while the light's still good, I'll take a look at where you found Miss Johnson's body."

Carradale waved down the steps. "The fastest route is via the fore-court, along the front of the terrace, then across the lawn."

On reaching the gravel of the forecourt, Stokes glanced at the front door, then fell in beside Carradale, matching his long strides. "Am I correct in thinking we're retracing the route that the gentleman who was glimpsed leaving the shrubbery would have taken?"

"Going by what Rosa said, had he been a member of the house party, then yes. He would have come this way." As they rounded the corner of the house, Carradale pointed along the terrace that continued down that side. "From the shrubbery entrance, I normally make for the steps and the side door there"—he was pointing to steps leading up to a door set between windows midway down the terrace—"but that door gives onto the library and, late at night, would likely have been locked."

"That suggests the gentleman knew the ways of the house well enough to make for the front door."

Carradale waggled his head. "In case guests want to walk at night, Percy makes a point of mentioning that the front door is the last to be locked and that very late. Any of the guests would have known."

Stokes humphed.

Carradale led him to an archway cut in the thick, high hedges that, it seemed, enclosed quite a large section of the garden. "There are five discrete gardens within the shrubbery. The hedged paths link them—like corridors between rooms."

Halting just inside the archway, Stokes saw what Carradale meant. The grass there was lush underfoot, rendering the "corridor" one with green walls and floor and blue sky for a ceiling. Noting an area three yards on where the grass was still partially flattened, Stokes pointed. "She was there?"

"Yes." Carradale's tone held the taut undercurrent of anger again. He walked to the spot and looked down. "Just there." Then he looked further and waved beyond the end of the walk. "I passed through three of the five gardens to reach here. The other two gardens are on the other side of the entrance."

Stokes crouched and examined where the body had lain—it was just possible to make out—then he raised his head and scanned the area. "This seems an odd place to meet—so close to the entrance. Perhaps Miss Johnson and the gentleman had been walking together in one of the gardens and had started back toward the house when some argument blew up."

Carradale shrugged. "Either that or she came out expecting to meet someone, but ran into the murderer instead."

"Then whoever she was supposed to meet should have found her, or at least mentioned the aborted meeting the next day." Stokes looked up at Carradale and arched his brows. "What if she merely went for a walk in the night air and the murderer ran into her as she was heading back—possibly having followed and lain in wait?"

Carradale wrinkled his nose. "That's theoretically possible, but as Miss Johnson was an unmarried young lady of unblemished reputation hoping to attract a reasonable offer, and she didn't strike me as a silly twit, I would class her walking alone late at night in an unfamiliar garden filled with high hedges and dark shadows as highly improbable."

Stokes grunted and rose. "So, tell me—you found her body on Tuesday morning. Why wasn't the Yard informed then?"

"Ah—you have the local magistrate, Sir Godfrey Stonewall, to thank for that." Carradale paused, then added, "And, of course, Scotland Yard's still-lingering unsavory reputation."

"That's been more imagined than real for the past decade."

"Even so. Adverse reputations can take decades to redeem, especially within the ton."

Stokes merely humphed, then caught the rustle of skirts briskly nearing. He turned as a tall lady—only an inch or so shorter than Stokes himself—appeared framed in the archway through the hedge. Her eyes landed on Stokes, and she walked forward, inclining her head politely if with reserve, then she looked at Carradale.

Carradale had straightened. "Inspector Stokes—this is Miss Whittaker. She's a distant cousin of Miss Johnson and arrived on the morning we found Glynis dead."

"Indeed." Miss Whittaker's gaze was measuring as it lingered on Stokes's face. "Circumstances being what they are, I cannot say that I'm delighted to make your acquaintance, Inspector, but Lord Carradale has assured me I should be glad that you're here. I was sent by my family to fetch Glynis home from this event, but to my sorrow, I arrived too late."

"Miss Whittaker came upon the scene just after I had discovered Miss Johnson's body."

"I had arrived in the village the evening before and decided to wait until morning to speak with Glynis. I now regret I didn't come straight on to Mandeville Hall—had I done so, Glynis would not be dead."

"I see." Stokes had been doing some assessing of his own. Over the years, he'd learned to read the subtle cues carried in the way members of the ton and higher gentry interacted with each other; he wondered if

Carradale had made a conscious decision to move closer to Miss Whittaker, or if she knew how revealing it was that she'd accepted Carradale's nearness without so much as a batted lash. *Hmm.* However, all he said was, "If you were among the first to find Miss Johnson's body, I'll need to speak with you at length."

"I was also among the first to view Mrs. Cleary's body," the formidable Miss Whittaker stated. "After Glynis's death, Mr. Mandeville —Percy—kindly offered me houseroom. Given Glynis's chaperon is presently still sedated and cannot be moved, I accepted his offer and have been residing at the Hall since." She glanced at Carradale, then looked back at Stokes. "Lord Carradale and I have essentially joined forces to ensure my cousin's death—and now that of Mrs. Cleary as well—are properly investigated and the murderer brought to justice. If the matter had been left to the magistrate, all would have been swept under the proverbial rug as a mere inconvenience."

Stokes blinked. "I see." He had to wonder how any magistrate had thought to get away with such a response with a lady of Miss Whittaker's caliber involved.

The sound of a carriage coming quickly up the drive reached them.

Stokes felt a modicum of relief. It occurred to him that Miss Whittaker and Penelope Adair would get on famously; they seemed cut from a similar cloth. "With luck, that will be the Adairs." He glanced at Carradale.

"His lordship explained that Mr. Adair and his wife often assist you in cases such as this." Miss Whittaker turned and led the way out of the shrubbery.

When Stokes looked at Carradale, the man merely shrugged and waved for Stokes to precede him.

Stokes did; once beyond the archway, with the silent but industrious Philpott bringing up the rear, he and Carradale fell in on either side of Miss Whittaker as she determinedly strode for the forecourt.

The light traveling carriage had barely halted and was still rocking on its springs when the door opened and Barnaby Adair stepped down. He saw Stokes approaching, noted his companions, and raised a hand in greeting. With his other hand, Adair gripped his wife's gloved hand and assisted her to the gravel.

Penelope retrieved her fingers from her husband's clasp, shook out her skirts, and looked around with interest—not to say blatant curiosity. And not a little relief. Delivered at close to noon, Stokes's note advising them of a case with which he would be glad of their assistance if they could spare the time had arrived at a fortuitous moment. The house party she and Barnaby had felt pressured to attend had turned out to be even more political than they'd feared; a legitimate excuse to cut short their attendance had come as a godsend, one they'd fallen on with alacrity. That the house party had also been in Hampshire, just north of Andover and not at all far away, had been the cream on their cake.

On top of that, as she was expecting their second child but was thankfully not yet showing, Penelope was keen to have something with which to occupy her mind—to keep said mind away from dwelling on her occasionally queasy stomach.

She had great hopes that this investigation would prove an effective distraction.

After a quick survey of the house—an older place with Gothic pretensions—she followed Barnaby's lead and focused on the people accompanying Stokes and Constable Philpott across the lawn. She narrowed her gaze on the gentleman. "Isn't that Carradale? The friend of Hartley Galbraith—his erstwhile landlord? And you know him as well, and of course, I've seen him in passing in town."

Barnaby nodded. "That is, indeed, Carradale. I think his estate is nearby—somewhere in Hampshire, at least—but I have no idea who the lady is."

Penelope put on her best smile. "She appears to be leading the men. How intriguing."

Barnaby humphed as the trio reached the forecourt; gravel crunched as they approached.

The lady halted at a polite distance; Stokes and Carradale flanked her. A full head taller than Penelope, the lady possessed a statuesque figure, while her severely cut and otherwise unremarkable morning gown—in a shade of plum that Penelope herself was fond of—suggested that the lady hailed from the upper gentry rather than the aristocracy. However, the excellent fabric and styling plus the simple yet finely wrought gold chain about the lady's throat declared that, regardless of her social status, her family was relatively well heeled.

Stokes nodded to Barnaby and Penelope, and Carradale inclined his head to them both. Stokes waited for the noise of the carriage rolling off around the house to fade, then made the introductions. He concluded with "As Carradale found the first body and was joined within minutes by Miss Whittaker—who had been sent by the victim's family to fetch her home from this event—and Miss Whittaker was also among the first to view the second body, I suggested that we wait for you to join us before Carradale and Miss Whittaker give us a rundown of events as they know them."

"An excellent idea." Penelope turned bright eyes on Carradale and the interesting Miss Whittaker. "You might begin, Miss Whittaker, by telling us why your family wished your cousin to come home."

Miss Whittaker blinked, but after a moment's hesitation obliged, explaining that her family, with her grandfather as its head, had deemed the event unsuitable for her distant cousin, Miss Glynis Johnson. "It was felt that this was not an event an unmarried lady, chaperoned or not, should attend." Without further prompting, Miss Whittaker outlined the timing of her arrival in the nearby village and her subsequent call at Mandeville Hall the following morning. "I expected to be able to collect Glynis and her chaperon, Mrs. Macomber, and depart—Glynis wouldn't have argued with me—but instead..." She paused, then glanced at Carradale.

He shifted, then said, "I think it better if I start on the Monday evening." Succinctly, he described what he knew of events during the gathering in the drawing room, including his thought that Glynis Johnson might have claimed his escort for a stroll on the terrace in order to make a point with some other gentleman present, although he had no idea in which gentleman her interest lay or exactly what her point might have been. He also mentioned the gold chain about her throat and that a pendant of some sort had weighed it down, yet Miss Johnson had kept whatever she wore on the chain concealed.

The details of the following morning, when he'd found the body, were quickly told, and then, between them, he and Miss Whittaker related the salient points of that day, including the discovery that the chain and what-ever had been on it appeared to have been ripped away, almost certainly by the murderer. Also, that a Mrs. Rosamund Cleary had reported seeing a gentleman leaving the shrubbery at about the time Miss Johnson had been killed, but that Mrs. Cleary hadn't seen the man well enough to iden-tify him. Consequently, despite the magistrate's attempts to blame some fictitious passing gypsy, there was every reason to believe that the murderer was one of the gentleman presently residing at the house—specifically, the gentleman Mrs. Cleary saw.

"How many gentlemen are there on our suspect list?" Penelope asked.

Carradale mentally counted, then replied, "If you include all the gentlemen who were sleeping under the Hall's roof, there are ten."

Stokes nodded. "No doubt we'll shorten that list soon enough." He glanced at Philpott, who had been scribbling throughout. "Let's get the names of all the guests from Mr. Mandeville later." Stokes frowned, then glanced at Carradale and Miss Whittaker. "When you mentioned your host, both of you specified a Percy Mandeville. Are there more Mr. Mandevilles present?"

"Just one other—Edward Mandeville, Percy's cousin." Carradale lightly grimaced. "He's older and, as you'll discover, pompous and arrogant. He apparently took it upon himself to attend to ensure nothing of a scandalous nature occurred to blot the family escutcheon."

"Ah." Barnaby nodded in understanding. "I take it that, in the past, Percy Mandeville's house parties have been...racy if not outright licentious." He glanced at Miss Whittaker. "That explains your family's aversion to having Miss Johnson attend."

Miss Whittaker nodded. "That was what we had heard and feared."

"To give Percy his due, while in the past these yearly parties of his were on the licentious side, this year, while I'm sure several affairs are being conducted under the Hall's roof, the tone of the event has been much more sedate." Carradale shrugged. "I put it down to the guests having attained a degree of wisdom, but perhaps Percy inviting two unmarried young ladies and their chaperons also contributed to the more acceptable tone. None of those here are of the ilk to seduce or act in a way that would shock innocent young ladies."

"How...interesting." Penelope had to wonder what had caused Percy Mandeville to change his spots, so to speak. And possibly Carradale, too, although in his case, while any experienced lady with eyes would instantly place him in the too-dangerous-to-know class, she understood that when it came to his liaisons, he had always been rigidly discreet. A rake he might be, but an aloof and distant one, a gentleman who kept his private life private.

"Very well. So that's the first murder in brief." Barnaby arched his brows at Carradale and Miss Whittaker. "Now tell us about the second."

Miss Whittaker drew in a deeper breath and embarked on a clear and concise recitation of events, covering Mrs. Cleary's strange turn in the corridor in the evening, followed by her retiring early, then Miss Whittaker waking to a maid's scream and discovering Mrs. Cleary smothered in her bed. Between them, she and Carradale described the evidence that supported that conclusion, then Carradale swiftly sketched the details of their subsequent encounter with the magistrate and Sir Godfrey's agreement to call in Scotland Yard.

Carradale concluded by outlining the present state of play, namely that both bodies had been preserved as well as possible pending the Yard's advice—Stokes broke in to inform them that Pemberton had traveled down with him and was conducting his examination as they spoke—that they'd locked up the second murder scene for what that might be worth, and that Sir Godfrey had at least had sense enough to decree that all the guests had to remain at the Hall until Stokes gave them leave to depart.

Barnaby frowned. "When is the house party due to end?"

"Saturday morning," Carradale replied.

Barnaby grimaced. "It's already Thursday afternoon." He met Carradale's eyes. "I suspect we'd better learn who's on the guest list now rather than later."

Penelope saw understanding dawn in Carradale's eyes. He thought, then grimaced as well. "Leaving aside the ladies, in addition to the two Mandevilles, we have Mr. Henry Wynne, the Earl of Dorset's nephew, the Honorable Mr. Guy Walker, Mr. Robert Fletcher, heir to Viscount Margate, Viscount Hammond, Mr. William Coke, Colonel Walter Humphries, and Captain Freddy Collins."

Barnaby sighed and looked at Stokes. "Finding our killer just turned urgent. You might be able to persuade some of the guests that they need to remain here until we've identified the murderer, but your chances of holding the likes of Wynne, Walker, and Fletcher, much less Coke and even Humphries, are slim to none."

Stokes pulled a face. After a moment, he looked at the house. "Let's cross that Rubicon when we come to it. But if we are going to be pressed for time, I suggest that now we have some inkling of what happened, we'd better make a start."

Penelope settled her spectacles on the bridge of her nose. "Before we march in and start asking questions, are we all agreed that, based on what we currently know, our working hypothesis is that Miss Johnson was strangled by one of the gentlemen staying at the Hall, that he ripped the chain and whatever pendant she was concealing from about her neck, left her lying on the grass in the shrubbery, and returned to the house via the front door—along the way being glimpsed by Mrs. Cleary, but as a gentleman she couldn't identify. The next evening, Mrs. Cleary's turn in the corridor led the murderer to assume that she had recognized or would recognize him, and subsequently, he silenced her by smothering her in her bed." Penelope looked around the faces of their small group. "Is that it?"

The others took a moment to think through her words, then nodded or murmured agreement.

"Excellent!" Penelope turned to the porch and the open front door. "Now we know where we stand, I suggest we forge on."

She led the way up the steps, unsurprised that Miss Whittaker quickly caught up with her and kept pace. They walked together over the threshold and into the cool dimness of the front hall and found the butler waiting.

"What is it, Carnaby?" Carradale asked as, with Barnaby and Stokes, he joined Penelope and Miss Whittaker.

The butler—Carnaby—swiftly studied their faces, then settled on Stokes. "Inspector?"

Stokes nodded. "I'm Inspector Stokes of Scotland Yard, here to investigate the deaths of Miss Glynis Johnson and Mrs. Rosamund Cleary."

"Indeed, sir. And I wish to assure you that the staff hold themselves ready to render whatever assistance we may." Carnaby drew himself up. "However, if we might beg a small indulgence, time is getting on, and we have a houseful of guests to feed—is it at all possible to put off any questioning of the staff until later?"

Stokes thought, then replied, "Given the hour, I can't see us getting around to interviewing the staff until tomorrow. If any member of the staff has information pertaining to the murders that they feel should be brought to our attention immediately, they can give that information to Constable Morgan, who I believe is currently in the servants' hall."

Obviously relieved, Carnaby nodded. "Indeed, sir, he is. I'll instruct the staff to inform him of any urgent matter." Carnaby stepped back and gestured to a closed set of double doors. "The company are waiting in the drawing room, along with the magistrate, Sir Godfrey Stonewall. If you're ready—"

"Stokes! Before you get caught up..." Pemberton, the police surgeon, came lumbering up from the rear of the front hall. He dipped his head to Barnaby and Penelope. "Adair. Mrs. Adair."

"What can you tell us?" Stokes asked. "Anything to make my life easier?"

"Well, I can confirm that you're dealing with two murders—one by strangulation, the other by smothering. No doubt about either, and both likely committed by a man..." Pemberton's gaze had passed to Miss Whittaker. After a moment, he faintly grimaced and amended, "Or a very strong woman. Height is also necessary—whoever strangled Miss Johnson was at least several inches taller than she."

Penelope glanced at Miss Whittaker. "How tall was Miss Johnson?"

Miss Whittaker dryly replied, "She was of average height."

Pemberton nodded. "Just so." He immediately returned his gaze to Stokes's face. "Neither lady was interfered with in any way. Whoever killed them simply wanted them dead."

"Could the two murders have been committed by the same man?" Barnaby asked.

"Yes, and I would hope that was the case, or else you have two murderers under one roof." Pemberton focused on Stokes. "Anything else you want to know?"

"Yes. According to Carradale, earlier in the evening, Miss Johnson had been wearing a chain and pendant that someone—possibly the murderer—subsequently ripped off. Any idea when the chain was taken?"

Pemberton nodded at Carradale. "Indeed—well spotted. And yes"— the surgeon returned his gaze to Stokes—"comparing the marks left by the chain to the bruises about her throat, I would say the chain was wrenched off at or very soon after the time of death."

Stokes and Barnaby both nodded.

Miss Whittaker spoke. "Doctor, I'm a relative of Miss Johnson. Might I ask whether I can now make arrangements to have her body returned to our family?"

Penelope listened with half an ear as Pemberton, Stokes, and Miss Whittaker discussed and agreed on the release of Miss Johnson's body. As Stokes bluntly said, "Given the time that's elapsed since death and Pemberton's undoubted expertise, I'm confident we've got all we're likely to get from the dead."

Looking smug at Stokes's praise, Pemberton accepted his hat from a footman and bade them all goodbye.

Stokes watched him go, then turned to the others, still gathered in a circle in the middle of the front hall. Lowering his voice, he said, "It appears that whatever Miss Johnson was wearing on that chain was important to our murderer."

Penelope nodded. "Could it—whatever it was—have precipitated her death? Did the sight of it enrage the murderer? Or was it something he knew she had, and he wanted it? Perhaps wanted it back?"

"All good questions," Barnaby said. "But what I want to know is what the pendant or whatever was on the chain actually was." He looked at Miss Whittaker. "Surely Miss Johnson's maid would know."

"Glynis didn't have a maid with her," Miss Whittaker said. "We could ask if any of the household's maids was seeing to her—I haven't yet had a chance to follow that up."

"We can ask tomorrow." Stokes glanced at Philpott, confirming he was making a note.

Miss Whittaker continued, "Glynis's chaperon, Mrs. Macomber, might know what was on the chain, but after seeing Glynis dead—she was with me when I reached the shrubbery—she grew hysterical and had to be sedated. Sadly, when she woke the next day, before I could speak with her, a maid told her of Mrs. Cleary's murder. After that, Mrs. Macomber grew so excessively distressed that the doctor recommended she be kept sedated for at least two more days, and he left a strong sedative. Unfortunately, Mrs. Macomber seems to have been powerfully affected by the draft, and she's still sleeping too deeply to rouse—at least not to any purpose."

Stokes grimaced. "So we'll have to leave that until the morning, too."

Penelope frowned. "If the murderer thinks Mrs. Macomber might know something that might help identify him..." She glanced at Miss Whittaker.

"Just so," Miss Whittaker returned grimly. "But I've arranged to share Mrs. Macomber's room, and when I'm not there, my maid is on duty and knows not to leave Mrs. Macomber alone."

"Good." Barnaby nodded approvingly. "So we can rest easy that we're not going to wake tomorrow to find another dead body."

"Indeed," Miss Whittaker replied; Penelope thought she suppressed a small shudder, which was hardly to be wondered at. Coming upon one dead body, and that of a relative, was bad enough; coming upon two in quick succession would try any lady's courage—even, Penelope suspected, her own.

"Right, then." Stokes looked around their small circle. He nodded to Penelope and Barnaby. "We're as ready as we can be." To Carradale and Miss Whittaker, he said, "It would be helpful if the pair of you went in first and preserved the appearance of not being any more connected with the three of us than the other guests. Indeed, you are both on our suspect list until you're formally cleared of involvement by the testimony of others, principally members of staff. Meanwhile, however, if you would, you could act as two extra pairs of eyes and ears—it's more likely the guests will lower their guard around you two than us, and you might gain some valuable insight."

More mildly, Barnaby said, "Please don't imagine you'll be committing any social solecism in observing and reporting on your fellow guests' reactions. In cases of murder, nothing is sacred beyond our duty to the dead."

"Specifically," Penelope said, "our duty to identify and capture the murderer."

Carradale and Miss Whittaker exchanged a glance, then both looked at Stokes, Penelope, and Barnaby and nodded. "We'll do as you ask," Carradale said.

"Indeed." Miss Whittaker's chin set, determination writ large in her face. "Nothing can possibly be more important than seeing the blackguard who murdered two innocent ladies brought to justice."

With that declaration, she and Carradale turned, crossed the hall, and went into the drawing room.

Stokes, Barnaby, and Penelope waited for a full minute in silence, then Stokes turned and led the way—into what, for him, was the equivalent of a lion's den.

Immediately becoming the cynosure of all eyes, Stokes calmly walked into the room and halted facing the fireplace about which the majority of the company were gathered. Rather than flank him, Barnaby and Penelope halted a few paces inside the door—in support, but not in any way detracting from Stokes's authority.

"Good afternoon," Stokes gravely said. "I am Senior Inspector Stokes from Scotland Yard. My men and I are here to investigate the recent deaths of Miss Glynis Johnson and Mrs. Rosamund Cleary."

A heavyset gentleman peered around Stokes, nodded to Barnaby, then looked at Stokes. "And Adair and his wife?"

"Are, as is often the case in investigations such as this," Stokes responded, "officially assisting Scotland Yard."

Another gentleman standing by the fireplace frowned in puzzlement, but before anyone could ask anything more, Stokes focused on a portly gentleman with pinched features who was seated in one of the armchairs closest to the hearth. "Sir Godfrey Stonewall?"

Leaning heavily on his cane, the magistrate pushed to his feet. "Indeed, Inspector. And while I'm sure you understand that none of us here are pleased to see you, in the circumstances, it seemed best to ask Scotland Yard for assistance."

Unperturbed, Stokes replied, "All murder investigations are, these days, reported to the Yard. As the representative of the commissioner, I have assumed all responsibility for this case and, henceforth, will report to London." Before Sir Godfrey could decide whether to be huffy about being virtually dismissed, Stokes continued, "I understand you've made no advance in identifying the gentleman responsible for the murders."

Sir Godfrey blinked. "Er...no. That is, I did wonder if it might be some itinerant in the case of Miss Johnson, but with Mrs. Cleary..." Sir Godfrey's face fell into lines of grave concern. "Of course, there might be two murderers."

"One hopes not." Stokes formally inclined his head to Sir Godfrey. "If you have nothing more to tell me, sir, I believe we need delay you no longer. Thank you for making time to hold the fort here. The Yard appreciates your support. Perhaps as a last gesture, you might direct me to the owner of Mandeville Hall."

Penelope compressed her lips to stifle a grin. Stokes had clearly been working on tact and charm.

"What? Oh—yes." Sir Godfrey waved at the wan-looking gentleman in the chair opposite the one Sir Godfrey had vacated. "Mr. Percival Mandeville."

Percy Mandeville rose to his feet and—wearily and warily—inclined his head to Stokes. "Inspector."

Stokes nodded back, then looked at Sir Godfrey. "The Yard will inform you of the outcome of the investigation in due course."

"Er...right. Yes, of course." With no alternative offering, Sir Godfrey muttered a farewell to Percy and directed a general bow to the assembled company, then Sir Godfrey stumped to the door, which a footman opened for him.

Stokes watched Sir Godfrey leave; he waited until the door was shut before turning to address the Hall's owner. "Mr. Mandeville. I'm sure I don't need to stress how serious the crimes committed here are." His gray gaze wintry, Stokes surveyed the guests seated on the sofas and chairs. "I understand Sir Godfrey has already informed you that no one is to quit the property until such time as the investigation allows it. That edict will remain in place. However, my men and I will endeavor to complete all the necessary interviews, searches, and other investigations as soon as possible. Depending on the outcome, I may be able to lift the injunction against leaving sooner rather than later."

All the guests were hanging on Stokes's every word.

Satisfied, he returned his gaze to Mandeville. "Regarding the crimes, the police surgeon has examined the bodies and confirmed that both ladies were, in fact, murdered. We are, therefore, seeking to identify a man—apparently a gentleman residing under this roof—who has already killed twice." The bald statement of a fact the guests must already have deduced nevertheless sent a ripple of unease through the company.

"More," Stokes relentlessly continued, "we believe Mrs. Cleary was murdered because Miss Johnson's killer believed she might have recognized him—perhaps not then and there, but the prospect had arisen. Consequently, I urge any of you who have any inkling of who the murderer might be to speak with or send word of your suspicions to me, to the Adairs, or to my constables as soon as possible. Sharing any information you have is the best way to protect yourself from coming under attack from the murderer."

Now the guests were looking sidelong at each other, which, Penelope knew, had been Stokes's intention—to put them on guard and get them watching each other.

He made a production of looking at the clock on the mantelpiece. "As it's already late and dinnertime is nigh, we will hold off commencing our formal interviews until tomorrow morning. Until then, you're free to do as you wish, as long as you remain in the house or on the grounds. However, I will ask that you give your names and home addresses to my constable"—Stokes gestured to Philpott, standing just inside the door —"before leaving the room."

Formally, Stokes inclined his head to the company, sweeping them with his steely gaze. "Thank you for your attention. I look forward to your cooperation in bringing this distressing episode to a speedy resolution."

With a last nod to Percy Mandeville, Stokes turned and walked to join not Penelope and Barnaby but Carradale and Miss Whittaker. "If you would both remain for a moment," Stokes said, his voice loud enough to be heard by those nearby, "I would like to question you further as to the finding of Miss Johnson's body."

Carradale met his eyes, then somewhat stiffly inclined his head. "As you wish, Inspector."

Clearly, Carradale knew how to play a part.

Miss Whittaker noted Carradale's distance and mimicked it; her expression aloof, she dipped her head the merest fraction in acquiescence.

Stokes turned and watched the other guests file out, all pausing at the door to give Philpott names and addresses as requested. None made any fuss. From all Stokes could see, no one appeared to be jibbing under his rein. Yet. He sighed and murmured, "I always live in hope that during such exchanges, the murderer will stand up and bluster and try to have me thrown out. I don't suppose either of you noticed any unexpected reaction?"

Carradale softly humphed. "No. This lot have learned to be circumspect. I doubt you've much chance of surprising the murderer into giving himself away."

"As for the ladies," Miss Whittaker said, "they were all listening avidly, but at your suggestion of reporting anything they know, they all looked around at each other. None appeared to think the danger you alluded to applied to her."

Stokes grunted.

The owner, Percy Mandeville, was the second last to leave. Stokes nodded at the gentleman who followed Percy out. "Is that the other Mandeville? Edward, the cousin?"

"Yes." Carradale faintly frowned. "He seems to have elected himself Percy's guardian."

Morgan slipped into the room and closed the door. After consulting with Philpott, both constables crossed to join Stokes. Barnaby and Penelope also came up.

Stokes arched a hopeful brow at Morgan, but the baby-faced constable shook his head. "Nothing to report, sir. The staff are all properly rattled, but also properly tight-lipped."

Stokes humphed. "We'll see how they feel tomorrow, once the reality of an investigation takes hold."

Penelope widened her eyes at him. "Given the time, I agree that postponing all interviews until tomorrow was unavoidable. So what now?"

He compressed his lips, then let them twist in a grimace. "Normally, we'd have already studied the scenes of both crimes, but in this case, both scenes are long cold, and if anything incriminating had been left behind, the murderer has had ample opportunity to remove it."

"Except that Mrs. Cleary's room has been kept locked from shortly after the body was found." Miss Whittaker produced a key and handed it to Stokes. "It's an old, heavy lock, not that easy to pick or force."

Stokes took the key and weighed it in his palm, then glanced at Barnaby, Penelope, and his men. "If the room is secure, we'll do better searching it tomorrow, in better light." He sighed and met Barnaby's eyes. "It's been a while since I had a case in the country—the different rhythms of life and of the case itself take some adjusting to."

"Indeed," Penelope said. "And in this instance, the most difficult aspect is the time constraint—the short period we have before keeping the guests here becomes a battle in itself."

Barnaby grimaced. "Essentially, we have one day—tomorrow." He met Stokes's eyes. "We have to make some significant advance by day's end or face mounting pressure from the guests to be allowed to leave on Saturday."

Turning grim at the reminder, Stokes nodded curtly. "We'd best find a place to lay our heads for the night."

"Try the Tabard Inn at Wildhern," Carradale said. "It's the closest and decently comfortable. Use my name. The innkeeper is Peters. He's trustworthy."

"I stayed there on Monday night," Miss Whittaker volunteered, "and can vouch for the beds."

Barnaby nodded. "We'll go there."

"Meanwhile"—Stokes regarded Carradale and Miss Whittaker—"you two could assist by keeping your eyes and ears open through the rest of the evening. I'm hoping all the others in the company will view the time you've spent with us as merely due to our questions rather than you actively assisting us. The longer they believe that, the longer they'll remain unguarded in your presence."

Carradale and Miss Whittaker nodded.

"We'll do our best," Miss Whittaker confirmed.

"What we're looking for," Penelope said, "is anything that seems the least bit odd—out of place or out of character."

"Anything," Barnaby said, "that doesn't ring true."

Carradale inclined his head. "We'll observe as we can, but I feel compelled to point out that, thus far, our murderer has maintained a cool head and shown no inclination whatsoever toward giving himself away."

CHAPTER 6

*A*lthough it wasn't quite time to change for dinner, most of the other guests appeared to have retreated to their rooms, no doubt to consider what being at a house party with a murderer might mean for them, socially speaking.

For some, Alaric suspected, the answer wouldn't be all bad; being the bearer of juicy gossip opened doors in the ton.

He needed to return to Carradale Manor and change for dinner and the evening's entertainment, whatever that might now prove to be, but first...

After seeing Adair, Stokes, and company off to the village, on returning to the front hall, instead of leaving Miss Whittaker at the base of the stairs, he touched her arm and glanced upward. "There's an alcove off the gallery that will allow us to speak privately without actually being in private. I'd like to know your thoughts on events thus far."

She looked at him in the very direct way he was coming to expect from her, then nodded. "Indeed. I wouldn't mind hearing your opinions as well."

He walked with her up the stairs and ushered her into the gallery that ran down one of the odd wings of the house. The alcove at the nearer end was open to the gallery itself; it wasn't visible from the entrance to the gallery, yet anyone drawing near on the polished oak floors would instantly be heard. Built into one of the turrets of the house, the circular alcove offered deep window seats that ran around the perimeter beneath windows that looked out over the gardens.

Miss Whittaker observed and approved. As she drew in her skirts and sat, she looked up at him and remarked, "A useful spot."

"Percy and I have often found it so."

"You've known our host for a long time, haven't you?"

He sat opposite her and waved toward the woods. "We're neighbors with no other families of similar station close. Although Percy's several years my junior, throughout our childhoods, during the months we both spent in Hampshire, we were together for much of the time."

"Do you also know Edward Mandeville well?"

He shook his head. "I know Edward more by repute—via Percy and Percy's older brother—than by direct exposure. Prior to this house party, I'd only met Edward a handful of times at family events." He caught her green eyes. "But turning to the investigation of your cousin's and Rosa Cleary's murders, are you comfortable with Scotland Yard's intervention?"

She arched her brows. "I wouldn't say comfortable. Resigned, yes, and perhaps, now that I've met Inspector Stokes and his…I suppose the Adairs are consultants of sorts, then I'm rather more accepting of the notion that placing the investigation into their collective hands is our best hope for catching the murderer."

She held his gaze, then her lips twitched, and she added, "I was watching the other ladies and some of the gentlemen, too, and I got the distinct impression that Stokes was a great deal more civilized than they'd expected."

He felt his lips lift fractionally in response. "One can only hope the realization will make the others more amenable to assisting in whatever way they can." He paused, then, his gaze steady on her eyes, went on, "I appreciate the reasoning behind Stokes's request for us to continue to observe the others, but again, I deem it unlikely that the murderer, who thus far has remained entirely unruffled, will suddenly grow nervous or guilty and give himself away. And despite the edict that keeps all the others here, you are not a guest as such and therefore not subject to it, any more than I am."

He wished he could foresee how she would react to his next suggestion; regardless, he felt compelled to make it. "I hope you won't consider this impertinent, but there is a murderer in this house, under this roof, and there's no real call for you to remain here and expose yourself to potential danger. You could retreat to the inn with Stokes and the others. There can be little question that you would be safer there."

As she frequently had, she held his gaze in a direct and forthright manner. No blushes, much less any lowering of her gaze, and to his relief, he saw calculation behind the limpid green. After a moment, she tipped her head to one side, still studying him. "I understand your argument, and no—in these circumstances, with a murderer lurking, I don't consider your suggestion impertinent. However, quite aside from being the investigative team's eyes and ears among the guests, just in case the murderer does stumble and give himself away, as Rosa Cleary's death and its aftermath demonstrated, at least one of us needs to be here—with the house party—all the time. If I hadn't reached Rosa's room so quickly, I'm perfectly sure she would have been moved, and the signs of violent death might well have been erased."

He couldn't help a cynical snort. "The others would have straightened her limbs and all but laid her out before they thought of informing anyone."

"Precisely." She paused, then added, "While I sincerely hope we have no more deaths, there's always the chance something might crop up that points to the murderer—something others won't see for what it is and will helpfully assist in destroying or concealing it."

He couldn't argue, but his anxiety—an emotion he'd rarely felt over anything yet couldn't deny he felt now—didn't abate. The notion of Miss Constance Whittaker being in any sort of danger...exercised something inside him he hadn't known he possessed. "Very well." The soundness of her reasoning left him with only one option—only one way to blunt the prick of an exceedingly pointed concern. "I'll have a word with Percy and Carnaby—they'll find me a room here." He refocused on Miss Whittaker's fine eyes. "Until we have the murderer by the heels, I'll remain under this roof, too."

With you.

Her eyes, locked with his, widened a fraction, then proving that she was more intelligent than the average, she inclined her head. "That might well prove a sensible move."

Where the words came from, he didn't know; he was too well versed in sophistication to make such a blatant move, yet.... "Would you think me presumptuous if I used your first name—Constance?"

Unblinking, she studied him for a second, then evenly replied, "Only if you refuse to extend the same courtesy to me—and I don't know your first name."

"It's Alaric."

Her brows rose. "That's very old."

"My family's very old."

Her lips twitched. "It suits you—and not because it's old."

Still holding her gaze, he arched one brow. "Just as, I suspect, your name suits you."

She stilled for a second, then inclined her head. She rose. "I had better go and change."

"As had I." Now was not the time to push his luck. He got to his feet and followed her from the alcove.

Later that evening, Barnaby pushed back from the table in the private parlor of the Tabard Inn. Comfortably replete, he surveyed their small company. "It's like old times." He looked at Stokes. "Just you, me, and Penelope, with your constables to hand."

Stokes nodded and leaned back in his chair.

The door opened. Penelope looked, then smiled and waved the two maids in to clear the remnants of what had proved a very acceptable repast.

After the door had shut behind the maids and their trays piled with dishes, the three friends sat and stared unseeing at the uninformative table; after a day of traveling, then having so many details of not one but two murders thrust upon them, none of them were feeling loquacious.

Glancing at the other two, Stokes felt certain that, like him, they were missing the children and Stokes's wife, Griselda. Normally, with an investigation afoot, they would all have come together before dinner to share the known facts, then after dinner, it was their habit to go over the salient points of the case...

Stokes shook himself; he surveyed Barnaby, then Penelope, seated beside him. "We need to assess and plan our campaign. Let's have Philpott and Morgan in and see where we are."

Penelope duly roused herself. By the time the two constables arrived and drew up chairs to the table, she'd wrestled her mind from thoughts of her son, Oliver, who was no doubt thoroughly enjoying himself with his paternal grandparents, and refocused her wits on the murders. As the others settled, she said, "Why don't we recount what we think we know and then see what loose ends present themselves—what facts we might tug on to unravel the case."

Stokes grunted an assent and commenced a recitation of the bare facts as they knew them.

Despite there being two successive murders to describe, the bare facts didn't take long to state.

"I think we have to conclude that Mrs. Cleary's murder was secondary to Miss Johnson's murder, not just in time but in intent," Barnaby said. "It seems unlikely Rosa Cleary was killed for any reason other than that the murderer believed she'd realized who he was."

"Or if she hadn't already guessed his identity, that she soon would, and the threat of that wasn't something the murderer would accept." Penelope met her husband's gaze. "Whether Rosa Cleary knew who he was or whether she ever would have known is neither here nor there. All that mattered was that the murderer wasn't willing to let her live and risk her exposing him."

Barnaby tipped his head in agreement.

"Nevertheless"—Stokes glanced at Philpott and Morgan—"it would be preferable to establish an unequivocal link between Mrs. Cleary's murder and her putative knowledge of Miss Johnson's murderer."

Morgan was jotting in his notebook. "It's possible the staff noticed something. Most of the nobs don't even see the footmen and maids and reveal more than they realize."

Stokes grunted; Morgan often turned up evidence via some obscure staff member who'd seen something they hadn't thought was relevant. "See what you can ferret out. Meanwhile..." He looked at Barnaby.

"Meanwhile," Barnaby responded, "given the time constraint, I suspect we need to focus on why Glynis Johnson was murdered. In the general way of things, it's not a murder one might have expected. Jealousy, money, revenge, or rage—on the face of it, none of those motives seem to fit. She was twenty years old, and according to Miss Whittaker, this year's Season was Glynis's first—it seems unlikely she would have gained enemies in such a short time."

"And what enemies she might have garnered would most likely be female, not anyone capable of strangling her to death," Penelope dryly remarked. After a second, she went on, "But I agree that learning why Glynis was murdered should be at the top of our list. Given that Miss Whittaker was sent to fetch her away, how was it that Glynis even came to be at such a house party?"

"And," Stokes said, "there's the mystery of what she was wearing on that chain around her neck."

Penelope nodded. "She kept it hidden—why?"

"More," Barnaby said, "as the murderer took whatever the bauble was, was it the reason he killed her?"

He, Stokes, and Penelope looked at each other, then all three nodded.

"Right, then." Stokes straightened and stretched his back. "That's enough questions to be going on with. Let's get some sleep, and we'll start pressing as hard as we can for our answers immediately after breakfast."

Percy had instructed Carnaby to give Alaric the room in the family wing he'd used on past occasions when he'd stayed overnight at the Hall.

The evening had proved remarkably short. After a quiet dinner at which all conversation was, understandably, subdued, the company had thought to entertain themselves with music, but after Miss Weldon had played three gloomy airs, the consensus had been that muted conversation was more appropriate.

As soon as the tea trolley had been wheeled in and cups of tea consumed, the guests had made excuses and drifted off to their beds.

Or to whichever bed they were currently sharing.

Alaric had kept Percy company; his childhood friend had still seemed stricken and not recovering from the shock as fast as Alaric had expected. Sufficiently so for Alaric to flirt with the notion that Percy might have been smitten with Miss Johnson, although of that Alaric had seen no sign —not while Glynis Johnson had been alive and still smiling.

Finally closing the door of his room, still pondering Glynis's bright smiles, Alaric cast his mind back over the days before she'd been killed; was there any clue there as to any specific gentleman being the particular recipient of those smiles?

His memories were reasonably clear, yet still he couldn't see it— couldn't pinpoint any man as Glynis Johnson's particular interest.

He halted by the bed, shrugged out of his coat, tossed it on a chair, and muttered, "And I could be reading far too much into what I sensed in her."

While he undressed, he dispassionately reappraised all the gentlemen present. Logically, each and every one had to be considered a suspect, yet...

Alaric couldn't see either Percy or Monty as the murderer. Not because he thought them incapable of killing—very likely all men were capable of murder given sufficient motive—but because he was confident neither Percy nor Monty would be able to behave with any degree of savoir faire afterward. Neither had the stomach nor the strength of personality to be able to conceal their inner turmoil—and they would, most definitely, be in turmoil had they committed murder.

And that was just one murder. Two… For such as they, that would be impossible.

"If they'd killed just once, they would be panicking—all but incapable of functioning." They would be falling apart; of that, he was absolutely certain. And despite Percy's…whatever it was, he wasn't falling apart.

"So—not them." Who else could he strike from the suspect list?

By the time he slid between the cool sheets, he'd realized he couldn't discount any of the other men. More, he knew several potentially pertinent facts about Wynne, Fletcher, Walker, and Colonel Humphries—facts that could have given rise to a motive for murdering Glynis Johnson.

Alaric settled on his back, his head cushioned in the pillows, and stared at the ceiling as he debated keeping what he knew to himself.

In the end, he concluded that—as Adair had stated—in matters of murder, the usual unstated ton prohibitions did not apply. He would have to tell Adair, at least, and let those more experienced than he decide how relevant those gentlemen's proclivities were.

With that settled, he closed his eyes and willed his mind from all thoughts of men and murder.

A minute later, he realized he'd succeeded admirably, because images of Constance Whittaker now filled his mind.

His eyes firmly closed, he allowed himself to dwell on those far more fascinating visions.

At some point, he smiled, and his thoughts segued into dreams.

At nine-thirty the following morning, Stokes arrived at Mandeville Hall with Barnaby, Penelope, Philpott, and Morgan. His first act was to request that Percy Mandeville and his guests gather in the drawing room. Once the company was assembled, Stokes, alone, addressed them, stating only that interviews would commence shortly, that each guest would be seen individually, and that all were requested to remain in that room until all interviews were complete.

The last request caused some consternation, but after Stokes assured them the interviews would be conducted as quickly as possible, the grumbles faded.

He scanned the room, then nodded to Carradale. "My lord, if you would join us." Constance Whittaker was seated beside Carradale. "And Miss Whittaker, too. We would like to go over your statements."

The other guests seemed relieved not to have been called first.

Stokes ushered Carradale and Miss Whittaker into the front hall, where Barnaby and Penelope were waiting, along with Philpott; Morgan had already retreated to his usual station in the servants' hall. Stokes nodded toward the front door. "Let's go."

He'd wanted Barnaby and Penelope to see the spot in the shrubbery where Miss Johnson had died. More importantly, however, being out in the shrubbery would give him a chance to ask Carradale and Miss Whittaker if they'd learned anything more during the previous evening.

"Nothing," Miss Whittaker stated. "As might be expected, everyone was subdued and, overall, not saying much." She paused, then added, "Interesting, now I think of it—one would imagine the other ladies would have comments to make to me regarding Glynis and her interactions with the gentlemen present, but no."

Penelope turned from surveying the hedges. "It might well be that Rosa Cleary's death is acting as a deterrent to any who might have pertinent information."

Stokes looked grim. "Sadly, that's all too likely."

Carradale had been pointing out to Barnaby the route from the stables; he turned and added, "There was nothing of note I observed among the gentlemen. However, I did remember a few snippets of information about four of the company that might be relevant regarding a motive for murder."

Stokes's brows rose. "Indeed?" He glanced at Barnaby and Penelope. "If you two have seen all you want here, I suggest we repair to our interview room."

The butler, Carnaby, had informed Stokes that, as per his request, a small parlor toward the rear of the house had been set aside for Scotland Yard's use.

The parlor proved to be well chosen, out of the way of any guests but of a suitable size and with a desk and sufficient chairs for their purpose.

Stokes, Barnaby, and Penelope drew up chairs behind the wide desk, while Carradale set two chairs before it. After seating Miss Whittaker with his customary elegant grace, he sat beside her.

Stokes leaned his forearms on the desk and focused on Carradale. "So what have you remembered?"

Carradale looked at Barnaby. "Have you heard the tales about Wynne?"

Barnaby's expression blanked for a second, then his blue eyes hardened. "That he's...shall we say aggressive over getting what he wants, including with the ladies?"

Carradale nodded. "That said, I believe he'd taken up with Rosa Cleary. I can't imagine Miss Johnson as being at all to his taste."

Penelope wrinkled her nose. "We don't need another motive for Rosa's death. Let's leave Wynne and his aggressiveness to one side—at least for the moment."

"My thoughts exactly." After a second, Carradale continued, "Fletcher and Walker share a particular trait—they don't take rejection well. While I can't imagine either pursuing any revenge to the point of murder, I can imagine them bailing up Miss Johnson over a suspected liaison with some other man, and given her inexperience, she might have said or done something that caused them to lose control."

"Like scream?" Penelope suggested.

Carradale's eyes widened. "I hadn't thought of that, but that would almost certainly push either of them to silence her—not intending anything permanent, but..."

Grimly, Barnaby nodded. "Sadly, I can see it. From what I know of both men, they are quick to take offense, and both have mercurial tempers."

"Both are also tall enough to have been the murderer," Miss Whittaker observed.

Stokes nodded to Philpott, who was sitting unobtrusively by the door. "Move Fletcher and Walker higher on our list." He looked at Carradale. "Who was the fourth man?"

"Colonel Humphries." Carradale glanced sidelong at Miss Whittaker. "Without wishing to impugn Miss Johnson's character in any way, the colonel is known to have a wandering eye. If he'd taken up with Miss Johnson in London and continued to pursue her here..." Carradale blinked. "I suppose, really, that the motive applies more to Mrs.

Humphries than the colonel, and my mind boggles at the thought of meek and slight Mrs. Humphries strangling anyone."

"Unless Glynis was foolish enough to threaten to make a public brouhaha." Penelope looked at Miss Whittaker. "Is that likely, do you think?"

Miss Whittaker frowned. After a moment, she said, "Sadly, I didn't know Glynis well enough to be able to give you a definitive answer. She and I weren't close. However, once Mrs. Macomber wakes, we can ask her if Glynis had met the colonel in London."

"Is Mrs. Macomber likely to wake soon?" Stokes asked. "We have several key questions to put to her."

"We expect her to wake properly sometime today," Miss Whittaker replied. "My maid is sitting with her and will send word the instant Mrs. Macomber is compos mentis."

"Good." Stokes jotted a note in his notebook. He flipped back through the pages, then looked at Carradale and Miss Whittaker. "I think we've extracted all we can from the pair of you to this point. However, I'd like to ask if you're willing to sit in the next room"—he tipped his head to where a door to the adjoining room stood ajar—"out of sight, and listen to our interviews with the rest of the guests. Normally, I wouldn't ask such a thing, but we're up against it time-wise, and if someone lies, we won't have time to backtrack and check with others to catch them out."

Stokes closed his lips on further persuasion and waited, his gaze on Carradale and Miss Whittaker.

The pair exchanged a long glance, then Carradale looked at Stokes. "If that's the fastest way to identifying the murderer…then yes. I'll do it."

Miss Whittaker nodded, but added nothing more.

Together with Stokes, the pair rose. He saw them settled in the next room, then returned to the desk. Reclaiming his chair, he glanced at Barnaby and Penelope, seated to either side. "As we're all agreed that Miss Johnson's murder is the precipitating event, and Mrs. Cleary was murdered as an outcome of that, I propose we focus on the first murder. If we can identify Glynis Johnson's murderer, we'll have our man."

Barnaby and Penelope both nodded in agreement.

Stokes looked at Philpott. "Let's start with the host. Ask the footman outside to fetch Mr. Percy Mandeville."

Percy Mandeville came in looking nervous and unsure, but not in a guilty way.

Penelope's first question was why he'd invited Miss Johnson, an unmarried young lady, to an event more normally the province of the married-and-racy, not to say licentious set.

Percy's expression blanked. He blinked slowly, then, his tone flat, offered, "I'd met her in town. Freddy Collins and I...we started talking that perhaps it was time to change things somewhat, perhaps make the house party a bit *less* racy, and why not invite two good-looking young ladies..." Percy swallowed. "Freddy suggested Miss Weldon, and Miss Johnson was an acquaintance, so..." He looked down at his hands, clasped tightly between his knees. "I invited them both." He quickly looked up. "And their chaperons, of course. There was never any intention of them being...harmed in any way..." His voice faltered and he breathed, "Oh God."

The shock that still held him was obvious.

After a moment, Stokes took up the questioning; he led Percy through the events of Monday evening, confirming the movements of Glynis Johnson as far as Percy knew them. He denied noting anything out of the ordinary, any altercation or disagreement with any of the men—not even any specific interaction with one.

"Well, other than strolling on the terrace with Alaric—Carradale, that is." Percy stared at Stokes. "But I think that was just that she wanted some air and saw Carradale as...safe. He's more mature, and he's not the sort to pursue young ladies."

Penelope arched her brows, but then nodded. "That was insightful of her and essentially correct."

Stokes confirmed that Carradale had left for home before the guests retired.

"Yes." Percy added, "We talked and chatted for about an hour more, then the ladies went up, and the gentlemen followed." He paused, then said, "Miss Johnson should have been with the other ladies."

"You didn't see her elsewhere?" Stokes asked.

"Edward and I brought up the rear, and I went to my room. I didn't see Miss Johnson anywhere about."

"As to your movements during the night, can anyone confirm where you were? And come to that, can you confirm the whereabouts of anyone else?"

Faint color touched Percy's pallid cheeks. "Er...no. I spent the night alone, in my bed."

After Percy, they called in Edward Mandeville. Carradale had described him as arrogant and pompous, and for Stokes's money, stiff-rumped could be added to the list. Edward was thrown off balance by having to face both Stokes—who he patently regarded as a social inferior—and Barnaby and Penelope, who were unquestionably of higher social rank than he. In the interests of getting on as fast as possible, Stokes left the interrogation to Barnaby. As Edward hadn't been acquainted with the guests prior to meeting them at this party and his attention seemed to have been primarily on Percy and his interactions, in the matter of Miss Johnson, they had little joy of Edward.

When asked as to his movements during Monday night, he looked faintly shocked, then stated unequivocally that he'd retired to his room and had remained there throughout.

Next came Mr. Montague Radleigh, Carradale's cousin. He hadn't met Glynis before the party, and although he seemed quite observant, about Glynis, he could tell them no more than Percy.

"Although," Stokes said as the door closed behind Radleigh, "he did confirm everything Percy Mandeville said."

Radleigh had also spent the night in his allocated bed; given the reluctance with which he admitted that, they were inclined to believe him.

Thereafter, they proceeded as rapidly as they could through the guests, alternating between ladies and gentlemen. Most could corroborate at least a part of Glynis Johnson's movements during Monday evening, and more tellingly, no one contradicted the information offered by anyone else.

Neither Fletcher nor Walker showed any hint of consciousness over Miss Johnson; if either was the murderer, he was an excellent actor, which—as Penelope later pointed out—was entirely possible. Both men remained high on the suspect list.

Penelope made a point of asking every guest—male and female—if they had any idea what bauble Miss Johnson had worn on the chain about her neck. Many hadn't noticed the chain, and those who admitted doing so had no idea of what had been hanging on it.

When it came to where people were over the critical hours of Monday night, a surprising number claimed to have spent the night alone in their beds. The only gentlemen to be provided with alibis were Colonel Humphries, whose wife, Maude, swore he'd been snoring beside her the whole night, Mr. William Coke, whose wife, Margaret, gave much the same response as Maude Humphries, and Viscount Hammond, who—refreshingly—admitted to spending the night with Mrs. Gibson in her room, a claim Mrs. Gibson subsequently rather haughtily verified.

Of interest, Mr. Henry Wynne's alibi proved to be unverifiable; he claimed to have been in his room with Mrs. Cleary. "We met at the rear corner of the side terrace and agreed to adjourn to my room—she was sharing a room, but I had a room to myself." Almost glowering at having to explain, he grudgingly continued, "I went upstairs first, and she joined me about ten minutes later. She didn't mention seeing the gentleman come out of the shrubbery, but we weren't there to chat."

Beyond that, Wynne could tell them nothing; as he pointed out, he hadn't been interested in Miss Johnson, so he hadn't been watching her.

In surprisingly good time, they reached the end of the interviews of those above stairs.

Stokes pushed back from the table and raised his voice. "Carradale. Miss Whittaker. Would you join us?"

The pair appeared and resumed the seats the interviewees had recently vacated. "No one lied that I could tell," Carradale said.

"From what little I've gathered over the past days, no one said anything out of character. I detected nothing false," Miss Whittaker offered.

Penelope frowned. "Do you mind, Miss Whittaker, if we switch to first names? It seems the time for formality between us is long past. My name is Penelope."

Constance Whittaker inclined her head. "Please call me Constance."

"Barnaby," Barnaby said.

"Alaric," Carradale responded. "But I've been Carradale to most for a very long time."

Stokes grunted. "No one—not even my wife—calls me anything other than Stokes."

Penelope grinned and caught Constance's eye. "That's true. He remains forever Stokes."

Stokes stirred. "Now we've got the niceties out of the way, to the case." He glanced at Alaric and Constance. "You two are formally suspects until we can speak with those staff members here, at Carradale Manor, and at the Tabard Inn who can verify your movements. Obviously, that's purely a formality. However." Stokes rapidly counted down a list in his notebook. "Now we've interviewed all the guests and eliminated a few, we still have eight gentlemen without alibis."

"And," Barnaby said, slouching in his chair and sliding his hands into his trouser pockets, "we still have no sighting of Glynis between the time the ladies retired upstairs and her being found dead the next morning. It seems remarkable that no one saw her."

"That's something we'll need to push with the staff." Stokes made another note in his book. "Someone had to have seen her."

Barnaby shrugged. "Staff are often more observant than their masters."

"So we can hope," Stokes returned.

"We also have no information as to what Glynis was wearing on her chain—the object that might have caused her to be murdered," Penelope said. "It's possible a maid assisting Glynis might have glimpsed it, but we really need to speak with Mrs. Macomber."

Constance nodded. "We'll be told when she wakes."

Silence fell, then Stokes tapped his notebook with the end of his pencil. "The thing that worries me most is that we've got no real hint of any strong motive. We can hypothesize and imagine what might have been, but as yet, with not one guest mentioning any altercation or even tension between Miss Johnson and anyone else, there's precious few facts to follow."

Barnaby drew his hands from his pockets and straightened. "I believe that's our cue to get on with investigating." He caught Stokes's eye. "But before we adjourn to the servants' hall, might I suggest that a report to those still corralled in the drawing room might be in order?"

Stokes arched a brow. "How so?"

"There's no need to tell them we have a list of eight suspects. Given they already entertain erroneous views of how Scotland Yard and its investigations operate, why not simply say that the interviews are proceeding, but that there's nothing of any moment to report at this point and, without actually stating it, reassure the murderer that we're not closing in on him." Barnaby's expression hardened. "We want no more murders."

Stokes grunted. "We aren't closing in on him. But I take your point." He shut his notebook and straightened. "I would rather he—whoever he is —believes he's safe and need do nothing more."

"Hmm. And making such a statement will give us an opportunity to observe how it's received," Penelope said. "Will anyone show, however fleetingly, relief—or even guilt?" She swung her gaze to Alaric and Constance. "Apropos of watching everyone at once, might I suggest that you two leave and make your way to the drawing room by a circuitous route? Perhaps via the gardens. It will be to our advantage to preserve for as long as possible the appearance of you not being allied with the investigators."

Stokes glanced at the clock on a sideboard. "We can give you ten minutes."

Alaric rose and held Constance's chair as she came to her feet. He nodded to the three on the other side of the desk. "Until later." With that, he escorted Constance out of the parlor, down a corridor, and out onto the side terrace.

Strolling easily, they made their way to the corner and around onto the front terrace and so to the drawing room, entering through the open French doors. Others asked where they'd been and if they'd heard anything; smoothly Alaric explained that they'd been the first to be questioned and, subsequently, had strolled the gardens, waiting for the others to be released.

Other than a few humphs, no one made any further comment. A love seat near the windows was the only vacant seating; Alaric touched Constance's arm and nodded in that direction. They'd just made themselves comfortable, seated side by side with, courtesy of their heights, a reasonable view of the room's other occupants, when the door opened and Stokes, Barnaby, and Penelope walked in.

While Barnaby and Penelope hung back by the door, Stokes walked forward to claim center stage.

Alaric found his respect for the man growing; this wasn't Stokes's milieu, yet he commanded attention with a calm professionalism that was impressive.

Glancing at his fellow guests, Alaric sensed he wasn't alone in thinking that.

"I've come to inform you of progress thus far and to thank you all for your patience." Stokes's deep voice riveted his audience. "As of yet, we have garnered no facts that point to Miss Johnson's and Mrs. Cleary's killer, but our investigations are continuing. You are now free to move about the house and grounds. Should we need to speak with any of you further, we will summon you individually."

Alaric could almost see Stokes bite back the words *Rest assured we will do everything in our power to see the miscreant brought to justice.*

Despite Stokes's effort, all the assembled guests remained tense, almost on tenterhooks; far from being relieved or reassured, the guests cast suspicious glances at various gentlemen, and not all such glances were covert. Nevertheless, in the circumstances, no one's reaction seemed out of place. There were no guilty looks that Alaric could see.

Then Edward Mandeville, standing to one side of the mantelpiece, spoke. "If we might inquire, Inspector, what line of investigation are you pursuing?" Edward glanced around the company. "Is there any particular point you would like us, as a group, to try to recall?"

Stokes, reluctantly to Alaric's ears, replied, "The critical point we are endeavoring to ascertain is who Miss Johnson met in the shrubbery—indeed, why she went out there at all." Stokes paused and looked around, brows lightly arching in invitation, but while many frowned in transparent thought, no one volunteered any insights.

Alaric allowed his gaze to drift over the company; he glanced back at Edward in time to see him slant a strangely intent look at Percy. Following Edward's gaze, Alaric noted that, far from recovering from the shock of the murders, Percy seemed to be sinking deeper into...despondency? Ever-deepening gloom, certainly.

Could Percy be the murderer after all? Was that what Edward was worried about? Given Edward's reason for being at the Hall, Alaric could understand his concern; having a murderer in the family would play havoc with the family name.

Alaric considered Percy anew, but no matter how hard he tried, he couldn't see his old playmate committing such heinous acts. He could, however, see the pressure of Edward's continuing presence weighing heavily on Percy's weaker personality and worsening the remorse Percy was undoubtedly feeling over having invited both ladies to their deaths. That, Alaric could easily imagine Percy feeling guilty over.

"If no one has anything to add," Stokes said, "I repeat, you are free to move about the house and grounds as you wish."

Because he was watching, Alaric saw Percy haul in a huge breath, hold it, then make a valiant effort to rise to the occasion. "Thank you, Inspector. I'm sure I speak for all of us in saying we hope your investigations move forward apace."

"To a rapid and speedy resolution," Edward added in his usual, high-in-the-instep tone.

Others murmured agreement, and the guests rose and, in groups of three and four, filed out of the room.

Alaric glanced at Constance. She arched a brow at him, then rose; he came to his feet and offered his arm. She placed her hand on his sleeve, and they fell in at the rear of the company, dawdling behind Percy, Monty, and Edward.

They'd almost reached the door when Philpott intercepted them. "The inspector would like a word regarding your alibis." He directed them to where Stokes, who had retreated to confer with Barnaby and Penelope at the side of the room, was waiting to beckon them over.

Alaric realized that Philpott had spoken loudly enough for several of those ahead of them to have heard. Some glanced back, but then continued on their way, clearly seeing nothing odd in the summons.

Hiding a cynical smile—Stokes and his men were not to be underestimated—Alaric changed tack. He heard Philpott shut the drawing room door as he and Constance joined what was clearly an investigators' conference.

Stokes met Alaric's gaze. "That wasn't just a ruse." He shifted his gaze to Philpott. "Take a horse and go to the Tabard and check Miss Whittaker's movements with the staff there, then go on to Carradale Manor and speak with his lordship's staff—verify his movements on the nights of Monday and Tuesday. Then ride back via the bridle path his lordship uses to go back and forth—note how long it takes. We'll be speaking with the stableman along with the rest of the staff regarding the times his lordship came and went."

Philpott saluted. "Yes, sir."

"Wait." Carradale had hauled out his note tablet and had been scribbling. He tore off a sheet and handed it to Philpott. "Give that to my butler, Morecombe. I doubt he or the others will cooperate without that instruction."

Philpott read the note with Stokes peering over his shoulder.

Stokes humphed, and Philpott tipped a smiling salute to Alaric and departed.

"Right, then." From behind the lenses of her spectacles, Penelope's eyes gleamed. "We need to interview the staff, and despite our best efforts, it's already after eleven o'clock. We need to get on."

Stokes looked at Alaric and Constance. "As we're relying on members of the staff to alibi you two, you can't be present when we speak with them."

Along with Constance, Alaric inclined his head in acceptance.

"Is there anything we can do while you're busy with the staff?" Constance asked.

"I suggest you mingle with the other guests and continue to listen and observe," Barnaby said. "We have several questions we've yet to find answers to, and at some point, someone is going to let *something* fall."

Alaric looked at Constance, and both of them nodded. "Very well," Alaric said.

Constance's chin firmed. "We're happy to do whatever we can to help identify Glynis's and Rosa's killer."

CHAPTER 7

*I*n order to move things along as quickly as possible—and as they had no grounds whatever to imagine the murderer was one of the staff—Stokes, Barnaby, and Penelope elected to speak with the staff as a group in the servants' hall.

The staff duly gathered around the long deal table that ran the length of the room, sitting in what were no doubt their customary places, although Carnaby and Mrs. Carnaby forsook their positions at the table's head, leaving those for the investigators.

At Stokes's direction, they started at the beginning, with the arrival of the guests and, subsequently, the guests being shown to their rooms. Stokes and Barnaby questioned, while Penelope used the answers to draw up a rough sketch of the first floor and the position of the various wings and bedrooms. "So Miss Johnson followed Mrs. Macomber upstairs. Where, exactly, is Mrs. Macomber's room?"

Seated at Penelope's elbow, Mrs. Carnaby peered at the sketch. "At the start of the wing where we put the unmarried ladies and the matrons without husbands attending, ma'am. Close to the main stairs on the west side of the corridor"—she pointed—"just there."

"Good." Penelope scribbled that down. "And the unmarried gentlemen?"

"In the west wing, ma'am," Mrs. Carnaby said. "It's the long corridor leading to the master's room."

"I see." Penelope wielded her pencil. "Here?"

"More or less, ma'am." Carnaby added, "From the master's suite, what we call the family wing runs north."

"Are there any gentlemen with rooms there?" Stokes asked.

"Two," Carnaby replied. "Mr. Edward has one of the rooms toward the north end, and Mr. Alaric—Lord Carradale—now he's staying, has the room one door up from the west wing corridor."

They quickly filled in where the other unmarried gentlemen's rooms were situated; the married couples had been accommodated in yet another wing.

"And Mrs. Cleary's room?" Penelope asked.

"Just there, ma'am." Mrs. Carnaby tapped a spot toward the end of the ladies' wing. "She'd come before and liked that room, so we gave it to her again."

Barnaby glanced at the sketch; the gentlemen's rooms were on the opposite side of the house from the shrubbery, while the ladies' rooms lay more or less at the midpoint of the house. Two of the married couples' rooms overlooked the lawn before the shrubbery entrance, but the chances of anyone having glanced out at just the right moment to see the murderer cross the lawn were slim, and neither of the couples had mentioned any such sighting.

"Those of you who work in the stables." Stokes looked down the table. "What can you tell me about the times Lord Carradale came and went on Monday and, again, on Tuesday?"

It transpired that Carradale's gray gelding, Sultan, was a favorite among the stable staff; the stableman, Percy's groom, and the stable boy all verified the times Alaric had arrived at and had ridden away from the Hall.

With Morgan taking notes, Stokes turned his attention to Carnaby and the footmen who had been circulating among the guests at Monday evening's soirée. As they'd hoped, the staff were more acutely aware of who had been where, and through judicious questioning, Stokes pieced together a detailed account of Glynis Johnson's movements through the evening.

"So with Mrs. Collard, Miss Johnson approached Lord Carradale and the group he was chatting with," Penelope clarified. When one of the footmen and Carnaby nodded, she arched a brow at Barnaby.

Stokes caught her eye and arched a brow back.

She grimaced. "It could be nothing, but it does lend credence to

Carradale's suspicion that Glynis was using him as…well, cover, in some way. For some reason."

"Sadly," Barnaby dryly remarked, "that gets us no closer to comprehending that reason."

The footmen and Carnaby were very certain that no altercation, argument, or even disagreement had occurred among the guests during the course of the evening. "They all seemed very pleasant and civilized," Carnaby said.

Unfortunately, when it came to the critical time on Monday night immediately after the guests retired, when asked if they'd seen Glynis Johnson anywhere in the house or grounds, all the staff looked blank.

After a moment, they exchanged glances, then Carnaby volunteered, "We all assumed she'd gone upstairs with the other ladies."

"So no one saw her slipping outside to the shrubbery?" Stokes asked.

The reply was a circle of shaking heads.

Barnaby stifled a sigh. So often in cases such as this, the staff were the investigators' salvation; they'd almost grown to expect it. After a moment, he asked, "During Monday's events—earlier in the day or through the evening—did any of you see any interaction, any argument or discussion, between Mrs. Cleary and Miss Johnson?"

The staff clearly dredged their memories, but again, to no avail.

Barnaby glanced at Stokes, who pulled a glum face in reply. Stokes consulted the notebook Morgan held open for him to read, then looked around the table. "That's all the questions we have for the moment. If any of you remember anything to do with Miss Johnson or Mrs. Cleary that might mean something about their deaths—anything at all, no matter if you think it's not important—please come and find one of us. Don't think we won't want to know." He glanced around the table one last time, then pushed back his chair. He nodded to Carnaby. "Thank you for your time."

Getting to her feet, Penelope added, "We know you must be terribly rushed with so many guests in the house."

"Indeed, ma'am." Carnaby glanced at his wife, then looked back at Penelope. "We wondered, ma'am, if you and your husband and the inspector would prefer a light luncheon in the small parlor. We've a cold collation ready to go out for the other guests"—footmen and maids were already streaming past with dishes suitably laden—"but we thought you might perhaps prefer the privacy."

"Thank you, Carnaby." Penelope bestowed her most graciously approving smile. "That will, indeed, suit us better."

Pleased, the butler bowed. "If you will repair to the parlor, we'll bring in the platters momentarily."

Morgan indicated he would take his meal with the staff.

As she turned to follow Stokes, Penelope glanced at her sketch of the house, then paused and turned back. "Mrs. Carnaby."

The housekeeper turned from testing a jelly. "Yes, ma'am?"

"After luncheon, I believe we'll need to search the rooms of the deceased ladies. I have Mrs. Cleary's room marked, and I assume Miss Johnson was sharing the room with Mrs. Macomber."

"Oh no, ma'am. Miss Johnson specifically didn't want to share her chaperon's room. Quite put out about it, Mrs. Macomber was, but Miss Johnson held firm. Of course, the rooms had already been allocated, and the only other room in that wing with a spare bed was the one Mrs. Cleary preferred. Luckily, Mrs. Cleary said she didn't mind sharing, so Miss Johnson was in with her."

Penelope slowly blinked. They'd been searching for a connection between Glynis Johnson and Rosa Cleary, and there it was. A situation that would have allowed—nay, very likely encouraged—Glynis to share secrets with the more-experienced Rosa.

In a daze of whirling thoughts, Penelope thanked Mrs. Carnaby and followed Barnaby and Stokes, who had paused and looked back and had heard the exchange, to the small parlor.

Before they'd even had a chance to sit about the desk, which had been set with a cloth, plates, and cutlery, Philpott rejoined them. In a few short words, he confirmed that, according to several people's testimony, neither Alaric nor Constance could have murdered Glynis Johnson—"Neither of them could have been here at that time"—and Alaric also could not have killed Rosa Cleary. "Not unless he walked here and back through the wood in the dead of night, and even then, his people are attentive. They likely would have heard him leaving or returning to his house." Philpott shut his notebook.

Barnaby pulled a face. "That's a small step forward, but it's already lunchtime, and we're still left with seven possible culprits on our suspect list."

"Hmm. At this sort of house party, I would be surprised if more of the gentlemen didn't have an alibi, but getting the ladies involved to come forth with those alibis…" Penelope sighed and shook her head.

Stokes frowned. "Mrs. Gibson came forward without too much prompting."

"Ah," Barnaby cynically said, "but she's a widow."

"Mrs. Gibson," Penelope explained, "risked very little in alibiing Viscount Hammond. The other ladies, however, are all married. They are not going to—as they would see it—publicly admit to a liaison."

Stokes humphed.

The door opened, and Philpott stepped aside to allow three maids to ferry in various platters. He looked at Stokes. "Shall I join Morgan, then?"

Stokes nodded. "Go and eat. We'll want you both shortly." He arched a brow at Penelope. "I understand we have a room to search."

"Indeed, we do!" She felt much more enthused. The instant the maids finished laying out the platters and withdrew, she continued, "If Rosa and Glynis were sharing a room...well, that opens up all sorts of possibilities..." She paused, then grimaced. "Mainly as to why Rosa was killed. Still"—she was determined to remain optimistic—"there might well be something in the room that will cast light on what Glynis wore on that chain. Like a jeweler's box."

The three of them fell to. When they were served and eating, Barnaby glanced at Penelope. "Don't get your hopes up—remember, the murderer has been back in that room at least once since he killed Glynis. After killing Rosa, he might well have searched—in fact, that might have been his primary reason for killing her. To clear the way to search."

"Possibly." Stubbornness glinted in Penelope's eyes. "But I still say a search might turn up something—the murderer is a man, and men never know where to look. And even when they do, they often don't *see*."

Barnaby exchanged a glance with Stokes, then both addressed themselves to their plates.

Alaric was the first to reach the alcove off the gallery, where he and Constance had arranged to meet to share their thoughts and observations.

Sliding his hands into his pockets, he walked across to look out of the turret window. Spread out beneath him across the green sward of the croquet field, the rest of the company—virtually everyone including Mrs. Fitzherbert and Mrs. Cripps—were attempting to stoically get on with things by playing a tournament.

He scanned the heads, but as he'd hoped, Constance wasn't there; presumably, she was on her way.

At the thought of her—as her image formed in his head—his mind returned to their last moments in the drawing room when, apparently without any awareness of committing any solecism, she'd spoken for him. She'd used the royal "we" as if he and she were...if not an acknowledged couple, then certainly a team.

Partners in the pursuit of justice.

He'd found the moment faintly amusing—and also distinctly revealing.

Discovering that the Amazon was inherently bossy had come as no surprise; what he had found odd was that he didn't mind.

Not in the least.

As revelations went...

Quick footsteps sounded on the gallery floor, then Constance swept in. She was slightly breathless, and her cheeks were faintly flushed. "Mrs. Fitzherbert wanted chapter and verse as to where I was off to." Constance frowned. "I think she's feeling a touch guilty over the deaths—she's nominally Percy's hostess, after all—and is, in her way, attempting to shut the door after the horse has bolted, so to speak."

She'd spoken as she crossed the room; she fetched up beside Alaric and looked out, too. "Did you learn anything at all useful over luncheon?"

He returned his gaze to the scene below. "Nothing." He paused, then added, "While the ladies seem to be still chattering unreservedly, the men have become a touch more circumspect about what they say around me."

"Around us." She grimaced. "Hardly surprising, I suppose—none of them are idiots."

After a moment, she went on, "The one thing I did notice was your friend, Percy. He seems to be becoming steadily *more* maudlin, not less as one would expect." She cast Alaric one of her very direct looks. "Do you have any idea why?"

Partners. He and she were, indeed, partners—at least in this. Alaric grimaced. "I noticed, but no, I have no idea why Percy seems to be so... deeply affected. In terms of his usual resilience, I would definitely not cast this as normal."

She stared down at the lawn for several seconds, then drew breath and said, "I know he's your friend, and you don't think he could be the murderer—"

"I still don't think he is."

"That wasn't what I was about to suggest." She met his gaze as he looked at her. "But could Percy have guessed who the murderer must be and be in a funk over that?"

Alaric frowned, then he looked back down at those on the lawn. He picked out Percy's shining head. After a moment of consulting his instincts about Percy, he offered, "I don't think he's in a funk or anything like that. It's something else. It's as if the murder—and whether it's Glynis's murder, Rosa's, or both, I can't say—has affected him in some deep and fundamental way." After a moment, he added, "Percy's parents are alive, and so are all his siblings. I don't think that, as an adult, he's ever had to mourn the passing of someone near to him. That Glynis and Rosa were guests—in Glynis's case, invited specially, and Rosa was an old friend…it's possible he's weighed down with emotion, a mix of shock, grief, and guilt combined, and he simply doesn't know how to deal with it."

"He seems to be struggling." Constance's gaze touched Alaric's face. "Have you spoken to him about it?"

"No. I haven't had the opportunity." He set his jaw. "But if he continues this way, I will."

They heard footsteps in the gallery, passing the entrance on the way to the head of the stairs.

Constance whirled. "That's Pearl—my maid."

She rushed out into the gallery and around toward the stairs.

Alaric followed on her heels.

The maid—Pearl—heard them, looked back, and relaxed. "There you are, Miss Constance. I was wondering where you might be." The maid was about to go on, but then her gaze reached Alaric, and she paused.

Constance waved in his direction. "You can speak freely before Lord Carradale. What is it?"

The maid dragged her gaze back to her mistress's face. "It's Mrs. Macomber, miss. She's awake and—thank the stars—lucid at last. But when I said I was going to fetch you, she grew querulous and said she didn't think she was up to answering any questions."

Constance's face set. "Be that as it may, she will speak with me. We need to know what she knows, and we need to know urgently."

Without further ado, she strode for Mrs. Macomber's room. Alaric fell in alongside her. The maid, he noticed, hurried close behind.

Constance was glad—even a trifle relieved—to have Alaric with her; if Mrs. Macomber revealed anything of importance, Constance wanted an unimpeachable witness. But when they reached Mrs. Macomber's door, she paused; looking into his face—looking *up* into his face, something she rarely had to do—she felt compelled to warn him, "If you can, resist the urge to ask Mrs. Macomber questions, at least at the start. She was never what you might call a strong woman."

She saw his lips twitch, but he merely inclined his head, reached past her, opened the door, and held it for her.

Constance swept into the room and saw Mrs. Macomber, wearing a knitted bedjacket and with her hair in a cap, propped up by a mound of pillows in the bed. Alaric stepped around Constance, lifted the dressing table stool, and set it alongside the bed. She thanked him and sat, then focused on the chaperon's soft, lined face. Her color was still poor, and her eyes had grown round; she was staring at Alaric.

Constance reined in her impatience—barking questions at the timorous chaperon wasn't going to get them the results they needed—and calmly stated, "Lord Carradale is here because it's really quite urgent that we learn answers to certain questions. Please bear with us, Mrs. Macomber, but with an inspector from Scotland Yard in the house, we felt it would be easier for you if you spoke with us rather than be interrogated by him."

Alaric only just managed to hide his grin and assume a suitably concerned mien. His Amazon clearly thought quickly on her feet and was accustomed to dealing with difficult females.

Mrs. Macomber's old eyes had grown even rounder at the mention of Scotland Yard. At the word "interrogation," she shivered. "Oh! I hadn't realized things were that bad."

Constance nodded. "Sadly, there are constables in the house. So if you can tell us what you know about Glynis, we'll do what we can to keep the inspector from your door."

"Oh, thank you, dear. I never imagined..."

"First," Constance forged determinedly on, "why did Glynis accept Mr. Mandeville's invitation? She must have known her mother and the rest of the family would be horrified."

Mrs. Macomber blinked owlishly. "But it was because of the betrothal, of course. I thought, when Glynis told me of it, that there would be no question over her coming here...well, I thought the family would be delighted, you see."

Alaric appreciated the control Constance exhibited in keeping her "What betrothal?" to an even tone.

"Why, the one to Mr. Mandeville. Mr. Percy Mandeville. This visit was supposed to allow Glynis to meet his people—not his parents; that was to have come later—but his close friends and his old aunt. He felt sure his aunt would support him in taking Glynis to see his parents and gaining their approval of the match." Mrs. Macomber frowned. "Of course, when we got here, Percy told Glynis that because his meddling cousin had arrived out of the blue, that it was necessary—essential, even—to keep the betrothal a secret."

When Constance appeared to be struck dumb, Alaric softly asked, "As you know, I'm a close friend of Percy's, and I suspect he thought to gain my support for the match as well, and then had to conceal the betrothal instead. How long ago did Percy ask Glynis to marry him?"

Mrs. Macomber pursed her lips in thought, then replied, "At least three weeks ago. I can't be sure without consulting my diary."

"I see." Alaric exchanged a glance with Constance.

She looked at Mrs. Macomber and asked, "How did Glynis react to Percy's request to keep the betrothal a secret?"

"Well, she was put out, of course, but Percy convinced her it was only until his cousin Edward went away. Sadly, they both suspected that would mean the end of the house party, but still... As Glynis said, against spending a lifetime together, what were seven more days?"

Somewhat carefully, Alaric asked, "Miss Johnson was wearing a chain about her neck on Monday evening. Do you have any idea what she wore on it—there was a weight of some sort dangling from it."

Mrs. Macomber's expression grew puzzled. "I don't know—she didn't normally wear a chain. Indeed, I think she only put it on—the chain she had on that night—after we arrived here on Sunday."

When neither Alaric nor Constance immediately responded, Mrs. Macomber stretched out a hand and weakly gripped Constance's wrist. "My dear, I know I have no right to throw myself on the family's mercy, but I had no idea that accepting Mr. Mandeville's invitation would lead to this..." Her old eyes filled with tears. "I am truly, truly sorry."

Constance roused and patted the chaperon's hand. "Please—no one blames you for this. This was the fault of a dreadful murderer, and no one else is to blame."

"Thank you for saying that," Mrs. Macomber all but babbled, "but I know how others will see it."

"Nonsense!" Constance's tone switched to bracing. "I can assure you the family will not hold you in any way responsible. Now you must concentrate on regaining your strength."

"Oh, thank you." Mrs. Macomber produced a lace-edged handkerchief and blotted her eyes. Then she paused and said, "I really don't know much of the details of the betrothal, just the fact of it, as it were, but you could likely learn more from Percy's letters to Glynis. I know she kept every one."

Constance barely dared to breathe. "Where are they?" Who knew what clues might reside in the letters?

"Glynis kept them in her hatbox. It should be in the room she shared with Mrs. Cleary."

"Glynis and Mrs. Cleary shared a room?" That was news to Constance —and to Alaric and possibly the other investigators. She'd assumed Glynis's belongings had been in Mrs. Macomber's room, but in readying the room for Constance, the efficient maids had tidied Glynis's things away, and they were being held by Mrs. Carnaby; what with everything that had been going on, Constance hadn't seen any reason to collect them yet. She blinked. "I glimpsed a hatbox on top of the wardrobe in Mrs. Cleary's room. I thought it was hers." She was about to leap to her feet and race off in pursuit of the hatbox, but Alaric's hand on her shoulder held her down.

"One last question from me, Mrs. Macomber," Alaric said. "Have you mentioned the betrothal to anyone else—anyone at all?"

Mrs. Macomber reared back. "No—I haven't mentioned it to a single soul! I would never break such a confidence."

Alaric managed—how, Constance didn't know—to produce a reassuring smile. "I would expect nothing else, but we had to ask." He met Constance's eyes as she looked up at him, eyes wide, then said to Mrs. Macomber, "And now, we'll leave you to rest and recuperate."

As his hand left her shoulder, Constance surged to her feet. "Rest assured, Mrs. Macomber, that we'll speak with the inspector on your behalf."

"Oh, thank you, dear. That would be such a relief!"

Constance whirled to the door, but found Carradale before her. She joined him in the corridor, then turned, looked back into the room, and beckoned. "Pearl."

When Pearl slipped from the room, closing the door behind her, Constance said, "You are not under any circumstances to leave Mrs. Macomber alone."

"Great heavens, miss—is she in danger?"

"We hope not," Alaric said. "But better we take precautions and avoid any possible threat." He nodded at Constance in agreement and encouragement.

She looked back at Pearl. "I'll send someone else up shortly to spell you, but at all times, there needs to be at least one of you in the room."

Pearl looked as determined as her mistress. She bobbed a curtsy. "Yes, miss."

"If you need assistance in the meantime," Alaric added, "just ring. Someone will come up."

"Yes, my lord." Pearl bobbed another curtsy, this time accompanied by a curious glance, then she opened the door and went back into the room.

Constance locked eyes with Alaric. "At last—we have a real clue."

Grimly, he nodded. "And now I know why Percy's so wretched. He lost his fiancée, and the idiot hasn't said."

Constance frowned. "Why wouldn't he admit it?"

"That's easily answered," Alaric dryly replied. "Edward." He met Constance's gaze, hesitated, then explained, "Unless Glynis was the daughter of a viscount or better, Edward would insist the match was a mésalliance. It wasn't—wouldn't have been—but he would have described it in those terms to the wider Mandeville family. I'd take an oath Percy was trying to avoid that. But now, with Glynis gone..." Alaric's lips twisted. "I'm going to find him and talk some sense into him. This can't go on."

"Indeed. And I'll go and get those letters. I'll have to find Stokes first and get the key from him."

"I assume they'll still be interviewing in the back parlor."

"I'll go and fetch them—or at least the key."

Alaric hesitated. One part of him insisted that his need to find Percy should take second place to ensuring Constance didn't run into any danger in her quest to lay hands on the potentially revealing letters. He looked into her eager face—read her confidence and her self-assurance—and accepted that she wouldn't appreciate him hovering. And she was in a house swarming with servants and guests, and he had to be the one to find Percy.

And it was broad daylight.

He nodded. "Yes. All right. I'll find Percy and drag him to see Stokes —I'll meet you with the other three, wherever they might be."

Constance nodded and hurried off toward the stairs.

Alaric turned and headed for the stairs at the end of the gallery. The last he'd seen, Percy had been on the croquet lawn.

～

On quitting the small parlor, Stokes had decided that five people in a single room was too many to mount an effective search. Rather than waste Philpott's and Morgan's time, he'd sent the pair to watch and observe the guests gathered about the croquet lawn. "Covertly, of course. See if you can get a handle on anyone the gentlemen, especially, seem to suspect."

Stokes had glanced at Barnaby and Penelope. "Someone must at least suspect someone, even if they're keeping it to themselves."

Penelope and Barnaby hadn't disagreed. Penelope had led the way toward the front hall, but on passing a set of minor stairs leading upward, Stokes had suggested that to avoid the hall and the chance of encountering any of the guests, they go up that way. On arriving on the first floor, they found themselves in what Penelope's sketch identified as the married couples' wing.

She studied her rough map. "We have to go past the main stairs, on past the end of the gallery, then turn left into the first corridor. The room Mrs. Cleary and Glynis shared is toward the end."

Stokes squashed a cynical, world-weary smile; Penelope believed searching Rosa Cleary's room, which had also been Glynis Johnson's last abode, would yield some clue. In Stokes's jaded opinion, that was highly unlikely, yet nevertheless, the search had to be made.

"I really do think," Penelope said, bustling ahead, "that Rosa having shared a room with Glynis significantly increases the likelihood that Rosa knew something—enough, at least, to guess who Glynis's killer was." She paused, then added, "Mind you, it couldn't have been something Glynis directly told Rosa, given Rosa showed no immediate suspicion of anyone when Glynis was found dead."

"I agree." Barnaby sauntered in his wife's wake. "If Rosa had any firm idea of who the killer was, she would have said. Instead, she told Stonewall that she hadn't seen the gentleman well enough to recognize him. If she was going to speak and risk drawing the attention of the killer, why offer such inconclusive information if she knew who he was. She wasn't an inexperienced girl—she had to know she was putting herself at risk. She would have said if she'd known who he was or even had a strong suspicion."

Barnaby caught Penelope's eye as she glanced back at him. "I'm not sure we need to postulate that Glynis told Rosa anything. She sighted the gentleman in poor light, then—if I'm correctly interpreting what occurred in the corridor outside the billiard room—she saw him again in better light and recognized him then…" He paused, then tipped his head. "Or at least the possibility of who the murderer was occurred to her. She might not have been sufficiently sure, so she held her tongue, perhaps thinking to see him again to be certain before she made any accusation."

"Hmm." Penelope faced forward. After a moment, she said, "While all that is true, I still think two ladies sharing a room would have gossiped, and it's possible Glynis was sitting on some piece of prime, gossip-worthy material."

Stokes was content to let the couple bounce ideas back and forth; despite his years dealing with crimes in these circles, their grasp of society and the likely behavior of the people who moved within it was infinitely greater than his.

Yet in Stokes's experience, the minds and motives of villains didn't differ much class to class. "Viewing events from the killer's perspective, he didn't know Rosa had seen him leaving the shrubbery, so didn't immediately seek to silence her. He must have received a rude shock when, the next day, she revealed that she had—he must have nearly panicked then—but virtually in the same breath, she revealed she hadn't seen him well enough to identify him, making her no threat to him and not someone he needed to do anything about." He frowned. "His emotions had to have swung from smug assurance to panic and then back again, but no one noticed any overt reaction."

Barnaby nodded. "Our murderer is a very cool customer. For whatever reason, Glynis was his target. He wouldn't have harmed Rosa, except—"

"For that moment in the corridor." Penelope led them across the entrance to the gallery. "Something—something unexpected by both Rosa and our villain—opened Rosa's eyes. Or at least, she reacted in a manner that made the villain think so. That's why he killed her."

"And he did so quickly, coolly, and efficiently." Barnaby frowned. "I can certainly see Rosa noticing something that tipped her off as to his identity, but…" They paused at the head of the ladies' wing. Barnaby looked at Penelope, then glanced at Stokes. "What I'm not so clear about is how did he know? What caused him to think that Rosa had—or might have—realized who he was? She didn't join the company in the drawing room."

Penelope's eyes narrowed, and her chin firmed. "We need to ask more questions about what happened in that corridor."

Her frown deepened, then she humphed, swung on her heel, and led the way down the wing.

She glanced at her sketch as she went, then pointed to a door almost at the end. "That's the room."

She paused before the door. Instinctively, Barnaby reached past her and turned the knob.

Stokes was still reaching for the key in his pocket when Barnaby shot him a surprised look and sent the supposedly locked door swinging wide.

Their surprise wasn't half that of Percy Mandeville; he stood frozen, hovering over the open drawer of the nightstand beside one of the two beds. He'd obviously been searching.

Stokes, Barnaby, and Penelope remained clustered in the doorway, Stokes looking over Penelope's head; none of them said a word.

"Ah...er..." Percy stared at them much in the manner of a startled sheep. Then he straightened and swallowed and tugged at his cravat. "I say—I was just...well, searching. I realized you hadn't searched in here —for any clues or whatever there might be. Indications of who might have been in here...well, other than Rosa and Glynis, of course. And I suppose the maids, as well. But..." He hauled in a breath, then gestured, encompassing the room. "You know what I mean, of course. You're the experts." He stopped talking and stared at them, panic very close to his surface if the way he wrung his hands was any guide.

Penelope finally walked into the room. Her gaze on Mandeville, in a conversational tone, she inquired, "Did you find anything?"

"Er..." Percy looked around, as if hoping something useful might magically appear. "Ah, no. I mean"—he pointed to a slim volume on the nightstand by the second bed—"that's Rosa's address book, but I haven't looked through it."

Stokes took that to mean that Percy had been searching the nightstand Glynis Johnson had used.

"I...ah..." Percy gulped in a breath and, apparently, managed to engage his brain. "It occurred to me that as the host and owner of this house, I should make a greater effort to assist the police. Scotland Yard, that is." His gaze darted from Stokes to Barnaby, then settled on Penelope. "There's only so many of you, after all, and so many guests to interview. I thought I'd do my bit and see if there was anything to be found."

Barnaby shot Stokes a glance, then looked back at Percy and inclined his head. "For which we thank you. However, as we're here now, we'll take over the search. You have your guests to attend to, after all."

"Yes. Of course. I didn't mean to suggest..." Without looking down, Percy nudged the nightstand drawer closed with his knee, then edged toward the door. "And yes, I really should see to my guests. If you'll excuse me?" He bobbed and nodded to Penelope. "Mrs. Adair." He nodded vaguely toward Barnaby and even more vaguely to Stokes. "Adair. Inspector."

His expression impassive, Stokes stepped aside and allowed Percy to flee through the door.

The three of them stood and listened to his footsteps as he strode rapidly down the corridor. Then his steps faltered and halted, but after a second, started up again, even more rapidly than before. A moment later, they heard him clattering down the main stairs.

His brows rising, Stokes reached out and shut the door. "Evidently, Percy Mandeville should be a lot higher on our suspect list."

Barnaby wrinkled his nose. "Alaric's certain Percy isn't our man, and whether he acknowledges it or not, Alaric Radleigh is a very astute judge of character."

"Be that as it may," Stokes said, hands rising to his hips as he surveyed the room, "Mandeville was here searching for something. And while I admit we have nothing by way of motive linking him to either lady, I suspect that if we ransack this room, we might well find something."

Penelope arched her brows but, for once, didn't argue. The three of them exchanged a long glance, then they turned and set to.

Alaric reached the edge of the croquet lawn to discover that Percy had vanished.

"Think he went back to the house," Monty offered. "Said there was something he had to check."

Alaric stepped back.

"Aren't you going to take a turn?" Monty asked.

"No. I, too, have something to check."

With swift strides, Alaric strode back to the house. He entered via the front door. After the bright sunshine outside, he was, for an instant, almost blind.

Desperate hands seized his shoulders. "There you are! I've been looking for you everywhere!"

Alaric blinked. "Percy?"

"You have to help me—I don't know what to do!" White faced, Percy stared helplessly at Alaric. "They caught me searching Glynis's room, and now they think I killed her!"

"Slow down." Alaric caught Percy's wrists, breaking his near-death grip on Alaric's shoulders. "I was looking for you. Clearly, we need to talk."

When Alaric released him, Percy lowered his arms and nodded, looking more pathetic than Alaric had ever seen him.

Alaric glanced up the main stairs. "Let's go to the alcove off the gallery. None of the guests are likely to find us there."

"Yes. Good idea." Percy turned and rushed up the stairs.

After ascending the stairs more circumspectly, Alaric followed him into the deserted alcove.

Percy was waiting; he locked his gaze on Alaric's face. "I didn't kill Glynis—why would I have? We were hoping to marry..." Percy's face crumpled. "It's all gone so horribly wrong. I keep thinking this is all a bad dream, and I'll wake up and she'll be there, smiling at me..."

Before Percy could descend further into maudlin sorrow, Alaric commanded, "Tell me about this engagement. Especially tell me about why you suddenly wanted it kept secret."

Percy calmed, then snorted. "The latter should be obvious to you—Edward! He arrived without warning—I had no idea he intended to come."

When Percy all but weaved on his feet, Alaric pushed him toward the nearest window seat. "Sit."

Percy tumbled back onto the cushions. Alaric sat opposite, his gaze fixed on his erstwhile playmate's face.

Percy started speaking without further prompting, his tone that of one relating an occurrence that was now distant. "I met Glynis in London this Season. She and I...we simply got on. We felt...happy in each other's company." Percy wiped his hand beneath his nose and went on, "You know m'mother's always been at me to wed, and Glynis...she wanted to marry me. I thought it would be perfect—it would have been. When I proposed and she accepted, I explained about having to carefully manage our announcement, as my parents were up in Scotland until…" He broke off, then continued, "They should be getting home today, but that meant I couldn't do anything—couldn't speak with my father—straightaway.

"So instead, I invited Glynis and Mrs. Macomber here, to my party, and this year I only invited others I thought would be…well, appropriate. So the company wouldn't be risqué. I invited Miss Weldon and her chaperon, too, really just to lend verisimilitude, but as it turned out, Freddy Collins is keen on Holly Weldon…" Sadness seemed to wash over Percy, dimming what little animation panic had lent him.

After a moment, Alaric prompted, "Was there a reason you wanted to have Glynis here at the party?"

Percy gestured helplessly. "To introduce her to Aunt Enid. She—Aunt Enid—might be a crusty old soul, but she's always liked me, and Mama and even Papa listen to her, at least in matters such as family alliances. I also wanted to show Glynis the Hall. To let her see it and meet…well, friends like you. I told her that if she wanted to slip away from the crowd for a moment, that you were the one to ask—that you would be safe for her to get to know."

"I see." Alaric wasn't sure he appreciated being cast as a benign uncle, but that explained Glynis's request for his escort for their stroll on the terrace.

"But then Edward arrived, and you know as well as I that if he'd learned of our engagement, he would have done everything he could to scupper it. He would have declared it a mésalliance and would have immediately gone off and stirred up his father and brothers, and they would have descended on Papa—all before I could make our case."

Percy paused, then went on, "I wanted to get Aunt Enid and then Mama on our side first. Papa would have agreed, eventually, but if he'd first been pushed into a corner by Edward and Uncle Horace, there would have been no hope. You know how Papa gets once he's taken a position on something—it's as if it becomes carved in stone."

Alaric did, indeed, know the present Viscount Mandeville's tendency to adhere to a stated position in the face of all reason. Everything Percy said rang true. "So when Glynis and Mrs. Macomber arrived…?"

"I drew Glynis aside and explained about Edward and how things would play out if he heard of our engagement. I'm not sure she believed me at first, but then she met Edward and understood. We—she and I— had hoped to be more open about our engagement—we thought that once

Aunt Enid was won over, we could let it be unofficially known, at least among those here." Percy sighed—a bleak sigh of sorrow and loss—and raked his hand through his hair. "But that's all beside the point now."

"Did you or Glynis tell anyone here about your otherwise secret engagement?"

"No. Well, it wouldn't have been a secret then, would it? We both agreed to keep it to ourselves—we were set on marrying, and if that was what it took to have our best shot at it, then…we decided that's what we'd do." Percy paused, then amended, "I daresay she told Mrs. Macomber—I imagine in London before we realized we'd need to keep things under wraps here. Glynis must have said something to her about us keeping mum for the nonce. The old lady wouldn't have given us away—she's been a good egg throughout."

Alaric leaned forward, resting his forearms on his thighs and clasping his hands. His gaze remained locked on Percy's face. "Do you know why Glynis was outside in the shrubbery on Monday night after everyone else retired?"

Percy blinked and refocused on Alaric's eyes. "She came out to meet with me. That's what we were reduced to—meeting in secret in my own gazebo out by the long pool."

Alaric knew of the spot; he could see the sense in choosing it. "So she slipped away…from the drawing room?"

Percy nodded. "She went out via the terrace—no one but me saw her go. Then I went upstairs with the other men—well, I had to, because Edward was there, and his room is along the family wing, so I had to go into my room and wait until his door shut, then I came out again and went down the west stairs and around. Glynis was waiting for me in the gazebo."

"And later, when she left?"

"We left by different routes, just in case someone looked out and saw us leaving the shrubbery together. I went out via the shrubbery's rear entrance, the one the gardeners use, and circled around the hedges, then cut across the forecourt and walked around the house to the west door. Glynis went back toward the shrubbery's main entrance…" Percy's voice faltered; he drew in a long breath, then continued, "She intended to go back onto the lawn and return to the house via the front door." Percy looked at Alaric. "But some blackguard met her and murdered her."

Percy's head drooped, and he put up a hand to shade his eyes.

Alaric allowed several minutes to elapse, giving Percy a chance to compose himself. Then Alaric asked, "Do you know what it was that Glynis was wearing on the chain around her neck?"

Percy nodded. Looking down at his hands, now clasped between his knees, he replied, "I assume it was Mama's original engagement ring. Mama had given it to me—her fingers had swollen, and she'd had my father get her another ring, and she gave me the one he'd originally given her...to encourage me to find a suitable young lady on whose finger to place it."

That sounded exactly like the viscountess.

Finally, Percy raised his head and looked Alaric in the eye. All life seemed to have leached from Percy's face, replaced by deadening sorrow. In a flat tone, he said, "The last sight I had of Glynis, she was about to walk into the avenue leading to the shrubbery entrance. She turned and smiled at me and waved..." Percy's voice gave out, and he looked down.

After a long moment, he lifted bloodshot eyes to Alaric's face; he met Alaric's sharp gaze with absolutely no screens or veils. "And now she's dead, and they—the inspector and the Adairs—think I did it. And I must have been the man Rosa saw, and so they'll think I killed her, too. What am I to do?"

Alaric studied all he could see in Percy's eyes, then he straightened and rose and reached for Percy's arm. "Come with me." He drew Percy to his feet. "You need to tell Stokes and the others all you've just told me."

Percy looked frightened, but didn't resist as Alaric towed him out of the alcove.

CHAPTER 8

Constance had reached the small parlor to find it empty. For a second, she'd dithered, then she'd hurried through the busy kitchens and a neat kitchen garden to the stables. There, she'd found Vine, her grizzled groom, and towed him back into the house. Constance found Mrs. Carnaby in her room and requested a maid to conduct Vine to Mrs. Macomber's room, so he could assist Pearl in protecting the old lady.

At present, the tale of the secret betrothal rested on Mrs. Macomber's testimony.

Then Constance had begged the use of the housekeeper's master key and quickly climbed the back stairs.

After looking out of a window and confirming that the house party's guests were still engaged in knocking balls through hoops, Constance hurried into and down the corridor that served the ladies' wing.

On reaching the door of the room Rosa Cleary and Glynis had occupied, Constance inserted the key and tried to turn it, but the mechanism wouldn't shift. She frowned, then eased the key the other way and felt resistance; the door was already unlocked. Carefully and silently, she withdrew the master key and gently gripped the knob. When it turned, she held her breath, then, having no idea who she would find, she drew in air, opened the door, whisked inside, and shutting the door, placed her back to the panel and stared across the room—

"Oh." She took in Stokes's, Barnaby's, and Penelope's curious faces.

At least they aren't laughing. She straightened. "I looked for you down-stairs, then borrowed the housekeeper's key." She held it up.

"Searching this room is one of those must-do things on our investigation list," Stokes dryly said. "Especially after we learned that Rosa and Glynis shared it."

"Alaric and I just learned the same thing." Constance glanced from Stokes to Penelope and Barnaby. "Have you found the letters?"

"What letters?" Penelope's eyes lit, and eagerness infused her expression.

Constance opened her mouth to answer, but before she could speak, a sharp rap on the door had her stepping smartly away.

The door opened, and Alaric entered—dragging Percy Mandeville after him.

"Ah," Constance said. "This should explain all."

Alaric had focused first on her, then he looked at Stokes, Barnaby, and Penelope. "There are several things Percy has to tell you that you need to hear."

Alaric stepped back and closed the door, leaving Percy exposed to the interested—and at that point, unthreatening—gazes of Stokes, Barnaby, and Penelope. Indeed, if there was any emotion visible in their faces, it was encouragement and curiosity—a willingness to listen.

Percy, apparently, saw that. He drew himself up, seemed to search for words, then confessed, "I...ah, haven't, I regret, been entirely forthcoming"—Percy glanced at Constance and warily dipped his head—"regarding my relationship with Miss Johnson."

Constance listened without comment as Percy falteringly—with the occasional prompt from Alaric—explained the circumstances of his engagement to Glynis and the reasons he had asked and she had agreed to keep their understanding a closely guarded secret. None of the others interrupted, either; given Percy's rambling style of explication, any question risked delaying the moment when they would have it all clear in their heads.

The one point above all others that struck Constance was Percy's quite evident pain. She had to agree with Alaric's assessment that Percy was definitely not Glynis's murderer; he had patently been one step away from worshipping the ground on which Glynis trod.

While Percy's attempts to smooth their way with his family made him appear weak in Constance's eyes, she could easily see Glynis having no argument with Percy's approach; it was one Glynis herself would unquestionably have used had the shoe been on the other foot. Even to the imposed secrecy.

"So, you see, it was my mama's original engagement ring that Glynis wore on the chain. I gave it to her as a sign of my unwavering intentions on Sunday, when we spoke and she agreed to keep our engagement secret. The ring was here, so I hadn't been able to give it to her earlier—having to hide it spoiled the moment somewhat, but Glynis was pleased with it regardless. She said she didn't mind hiding it, as that was the best route for us to get to the altar." Percy looked around rather blankly. "That was what I was searching for when you found me. I couldn't be sure that Glynis was wearing the ring on the chain on Monday night, so I came to see if it was here."

"It isn't," Barnaby said. "We've searched thoroughly and found no ring."

"Moreover," Penelope added, "we suspect that the chain, with the ring, was around Glynis's throat when she was killed, and the murderer took it."

Percy frowned. "Whatever for?" Then he blinked. "I suppose it does have monetary value—it was a very pretty sapphire surrounded by diamonds set in gold."

Constance remembered her goal. "What about the letters?"

Penelope pushed up her glasses. "I ask again, what letters?"

Constance glanced at Percy. "You wrote to Glynis, and she kept the letters."

Percy blinked. "She did?"

"Yes. According to Mrs. Macomber, she kept them in her hatbox." Constance turned and pointed to the hatbox perched on top of the armoire at her back. "I'm fairly sure that's it."

Alaric crossed to the armoire, lifted down the box, and handed it to Constance.

Stokes sighed. "I looked in there already. There are no letters there."

Constance had opened the box. She looked down at the contents. Penelope drew close and peered in, too.

"Empty, as reported," Penelope said. "But see"—she put her hand into the box and waved it—"there's a space here, between her scarves, where the letters must have been."

Constance stared at the empty spot, then she closed the hatbox. Alaric took it and set it back on top of the armoire.

Meanwhile, Penelope had turned and directed a meaningful look at Barnaby.

Barnaby glanced at Stokes. "We need to talk this through, but not here." He looked at Percy. "We need somewhere where we can be absolutely certain we won't be overheard."

They adjourned to the south lawn, to the green room created by the sprawling branches of an ancient oak. The leaves screened them from curious eyes, yet allowed them to scan through the foliage in all directions. If anyone approached, they would see them long before they got close enough to hear anything short of a shout.

Stokes's first order of business was to take Percy through the where, the when, and the substance of his private exchanges with Glynis, both in London prior to the house party and after her arrival at Mandeville Hall. Percy had, by then, regained some of his composure; he answered Stokes's probing questions readily and with increasing clarity.

Eventually, having realized Stokes's direction, Percy stated, "I honestly don't think anyone could have overheard us. We were careful from the first. I recognized the necessity of presenting the match to my parents in the best possible light—in the right way—and Glynis supported that."

Alaric mentally conceded that, in the matter of marrying Glynis Johnson, Percy had acted with quite astonishing circumspection—the very opposite of his usual recklessness.

"And it must be said," Penelope stated, "that unless all the ladies here are lying, Glynis successfully concealed what she wore on her chain. Trust me—a ring like that would have caused a great deal of whispered comment, not to say speculation."

Percy frowned. In the green-tinted shade beneath the leafy canopy, with his pallor deepening, he appeared increasingly bilious. He looked at Stokes. "You said the murderer had ripped the chain from about Glynis's neck and taken the ring." Percy's expression turned devastated. "Good God! Was she killed because she'd accepted me?"

It was an appalling question to have to face. Sadly, no one had an answer—and none of them could bring themselves to offer Percy false assurances, either.

After a moment, Barnaby shifted. "Percy—did you keep the letters Glynis sent you?"

Lost in some nightmarish vision, Percy blinked, then with an effort, seemed to focus. After several seconds, he slowly shook his head. "No—I burned them. I'm not...tidy. I didn't want any lying around where someone from the family—like Edward—might see. It was important I be the first to raise the marriage with my parents."

Barnaby gently said, "You've stated several times that it was important to present the marriage to your parents in the correct way, but you haven't explained why. You're a second son, and Miss Johnson is surely eligible enough—I would have thought your parents would have been glad that you wished to settle down."

"They would have been." Percy raked a hand through his hair. "But trust me—if Edward or his father, or even one of his brothers, had heard of my choice before I'd gained my father's support, they would have kicked up such a fuss the marriage would never have happened." Percy glanced at Constance. "It wasn't so much that Glynis was below me socially as that her rank wasn't high enough for them."

Alaric said, "Even though they are not the primary line, Edward's branch of the family hold a highly elevated notion of the family's station. Calling them high in the instep doesn't come close to the reality." He paused, then added, "Had I been in Percy's shoes, having to deal with his parents and relatives, I might well have done the same."

"I see." Constance glanced around the circle, then asked, "When did Edward arrive? And why did he come?"

"I hadn't expected him," Percy said. "He simply turned up at lunchtime on Sunday. He's never attended my house parties before, but apparently, he heard stories from some acquaintances of mine about what had gone on in years past and decided his presence was required to ensure nothing of a scandalous nature occurred. As he put it, 'Nothing that might reflect adversely on the family name.'" Percy's expression reflected his distaste for his cousin. "He's nothing but a prig, but he cloaks his priggishness in supercilious, holier-than-thou arrogance, and frankly, it's always proved easier to simply put up with him and wait for him to go away." Percy met Barnaby's eyes. "That was the tack I took this time, too. Concealing what I didn't want him to know and waiting for him to go away."

Constance glanced around again, then voiced the question that had to be hovering in everyone's brain. "Could Edward have learned of your betrothal?"

Percy's eyes widened, and he paled to a ghastly shade. "Good God, no!" After a second, he added, "Take it from me—if he had, I wouldn't have heard the end of it. He would have badgered me night and day—that's how he operates. He batters at one until one gives in and does as he wants. He's relentless." Percy blinked, then more calmly went on, "But he hasn't said a word to me about the betrothal or Glynis."

Given her experience of Edward, Constance found the assurance convincing; from the faint grimaces she caught on the others' faces, they thought so, too.

For several moments, the six of them stood in the cool shade and grappled with all they'd heard, turning around this fact and that supposition, trying to piece what they now knew into a cohesive, understandable picture.

Eventually, Stokes stated, "While it's tempting to put Edward at the top of our suspect list, there's no evidence linking him to either crime."

"No more than we can link any of the other gentlemen to the murders," Alaric said.

Percy looked taken aback at the suggestion that his cousin might be the murderer, but from the others' expressions, it was obvious to Constance that the rest of them were thinking along similar lines.

Barnaby humphed. "At least with Edward, we have a solid, established motive. One that potentially covers both murders."

"Hmm." Penelope wrinkled her nose. "I'm not sure about that. Consider—Edward came here to ensure no scandal occurred to blot the family escutcheon, and instead, he commits two murders."

Stokes grunted. "His intention in coming here is virtually an antimotive. If he'd learned of the betrothal, he might have wanted to disrupt it and ensure no marriage took place, but murdering the prospective bride to achieve that end would surely defeat his principal purpose."

Penelope sighed. "I know it's dangerous to make judgments of this type, but you have to admit that Edward is such a stuffy, finicky sort, it's hard to see him coolly plotting and carrying out not just one murder but two. And if his motive was to end Percy's betrothal, then we're talking about premeditated murder—plotted, planned, and executed." She shook her head. "That just doesn't seem like Edward."

"You also need to know," Alaric said, "that Edward is deeply religious. His father's a clergyman—"

"The Bishop of Lincoln's right-hand man," Percy glumly put in.

"—and Edward's mother is a very pious lady."

Stokes grunted. "If Edward's not our man, and we discount Radleigh and Percy, that still leaves us with four gentlemen on our suspects list." He looked at Percy. "You asked if Glynis could have been killed because she'd accepted your suit. Did she have any other suitors? Could she have been killed out of jealousy?"

Percy blinked. "I—I don't know." He looked lost. "I didn't meet Glynis until late in the Season—it was at one of Lady Islay's events." Percy frowned, then his expression clouded. "Lady Islay is Guy Walker's aunt, and I gathered that she'd invited Glynis at Guy's suggestion."

"Indeed?" Penelope looked at Alaric. "Didn't you mention that Mr. Walker was known not to take rejection well?"

Stokes had his notebook out and open. "In fact," he said, "you hypothesized that Mr. Walker was the sort who 'might have bailed up Miss Johnson over a suspected liaison with some other man, and given her inexperience, she might well have said or done something that caused him to lose control.'" Stokes looked at Alaric. "Any further thoughts?"

Alaric grimaced. "I concede that scenario is possible. How probable…I can't say."

Percy looked sickly pale again. "Both Henry and Guy showed interest in Glynis early on. Before…" His expression grew stark. "I didn't pay much attention, of course, especially after Glynis accepted my offer. But as we had to keep our engagement a secret, both Henry and Guy were still attentive, sniffing around… Glynis mentioned on Sunday night that she had to keep discouraging them and didn't quite know how. That's why I suggested Alaric as a gentleman she could safely cling to if she had need of an escort or to help put off Henry or Guy if they became too persistent."

Alaric looked at Barnaby and Penelope. "That's what I detected when Glynis approached me—that her request of my escort on the terrace was with the intention of sending a message to some man." His lips twisted self-deprecatingly. "It just wasn't the message I'd assumed it was."

"Both Wynne and Walker are on our list," Stokes said. "Neither has an alibi—Wynne claimed Mrs. Cleary was his, but that won't hold."

Percy was slowly shaking his head. "Surely not. I've known both of them for years."

Constance had been following her own train of thought. "But where are Glynis's letters?" She looked around the faces. "It seems the murderer must have taken them, but why?"

"Presumably because they held some clue to his identity." Barnaby frowned. "We've been talking of Percy's letters to Glynis, but there's no reason to assume she hadn't received letters from other gentlemen and kept those as well—especially any missives of a romantic nature."

"I can imagine the murderer might have suspected she could have kept them and searched, then simply taken the lot rather than pick through them and risk missing one," Stokes said.

"If he took them," Alaric said, "by now he'll have burned them. He's too clever to hold onto something so incriminating."

"So one would suppose," Penelope said, rising excitement in her voice. "But if he's burned them, we might still have a major clue." She looked around the circle. "It's late August, and it's been unusually hot— no fires have been lit for weeks. There should be no ashes in any of the grates—I think we can rely on Mrs. Carnaby to have seen to that. So if ashes suddenly turned up in some grate, I'm sure the maids would have cleaned them up—but that should have stuck in their minds as odd. Who had burned what and why?"

Stokes nodded, Penelope's eagerness infecting him. "That's something we can check."

Barnaby mused, "Against Alaric's assumption the murderer would have disposed of the letters, sometimes murderers do unexpected things. He might have taken the letters for some other purpose." Barnaby glanced around and lightly grimaced. "And no, I can't at the moment think of what."

"There's also the possibility," Constance said, "that Glynis herself took the letters from the hatbox and hid them somewhere else. She was sharing the room with Mrs. Cleary—perhaps, in light of having to keep the betrothal a secret, she decided to put the letters somewhere out of Rosa Cleary's orbit."

Stokes was busily jotting. He inclined his head. "That's possible, too." He looked up. "Regardless, the letters—or evidence of their disposal—is something we can search for. We could mount a search of all the gentlemen's bedchambers. I can't see a murderer using any of the reception rooms to dispose of incriminating evidence."

"I could help with that." Percy's eyes shone with a fanatical light. "If anyone sees us searching, they won't question it if I'm with you."

To Constance, and she suspected the others, it was clear that Percy needed to be doing something to actively help find Glynis's—his fiancée's—murderer. Anything to assuage the guilt riding his shoulders, to soothe the cauldron of his emotions. The nervy energy that had him in its grip cried out for action.

Stokes saw it. He dipped his head in acceptance. "That will help. We can search for the letters or any sign of them and also for the ring and chain." He grimaced. "Although that's easier to conceal—he might even have decided it's safer to keep that on him."

Stokes closed his notebook, slipped it away, and drew out his watch. His expression darkened. Tucking the watch back, he glanced around. "There are several points we need to follow up. It's already after three o'clock, and as we only have until tomorrow morning before this investigation starts to hit rocks, I suggest we split up. Penelope and Constance— if you'll come with me, I need to interview Mrs. Macomber. After that, we should search the married couples' rooms."

"Meanwhile," Barnaby said, "Percy, Alaric, and I will search the gentlemen's rooms." He nodded at Percy. "We'll start with yours. Not that we expect to find anything, but we need to be thorough, and starting there will quash any protest."

Stokes looked around the faces, then nodded. "Right, then. In this case, time is not on our side—we need to make the next hours count. Let's get to it."

The determination in his voice—and the sense of finally having something definite to pursue—resonated with them all.

Unfortunately, Stokes made Mrs. Macomber nervous. And when she grew nervous, she grew dithery—even more dithery than she generally was.

"I really don't know anything about Glynis's letters." Mrs. Macomber attempted to look haughty, but the effect was more like a cornered rabbit. "I didn't feel it was my place to pry. I was her chaperon. Mrs. Johnson herself was with us through virtually all of the Season. My role was merely to guide Glynis socially, and…and…"

The older lady's eyes started to fill with tears…

Stokes looked at Constance with widening eyes.

Recognizing the danger, Constance briskly asked, "Do you think Glynis might have hidden her letters somewhere else?" Stokes retreated, stepping back from the armchair in which Mrs. Macomber sat swathed in shawls, and Constance went on, "She was sharing a room with Mrs. Cleary, and the hatbox was on the armoire, where Mrs. Cleary could have looked…"

Distracted from her incipient weeping, Mrs. Macomber looked puzzled. "Glynis didn't mention any reservations about Mrs. Cleary. Indeed"—Mrs. Macomber fluffed up like an indignant chicken—"it was Glynis who refused to share a room with me— *me*, who was hired purely to support her!" Mrs. Macomber sniffed, and her spurt of energy faded. "All I know is that Glynis always put her precious, sentimental things in her hatbox."

Constance inwardly sighed and looked at Penelope.

Penelope leaned forward and gently said, "We appreciate your help, Mrs. Macomber—any help you can give us. Can you tell us if the letters were tied up in some way?"

Mrs. Macomber nodded. "Yes, Mrs. Adair, they were. Glynis kept them neatly tied up with a canary-yellow ribbon. A pretty color on her, it was…"

"Although we understand you didn't pry," Constance carefully said, "do you happen to know if Glynis had received letters from any gentleman other than Mr. Mandeville?"

Mrs. Macomber frowned. "I can't say that she did, but she might have. Mr. Mandeville hove on our horizon rather late in the Season, and Glynis was doing well attracting the attention of suitable gentlemen prior to his appearance, so"—Mrs. Macomber lightly shrugged—"it's possible one of those gentlemen wrote to her, but as to whether she kept his letters or not, I'm sure I couldn't say."

"I spend each Season in town," Penelope said, "so I'm acquainted—in a distant fashion—with most of those here. I can appreciate that it would have been quite a coup for Glynis to have attracted the attention of any of the available gentlemen presently at the Hall. Which of them showed interest?"

Constance sat back and admired a master; Penelope had hit just the right note to elicit confidences from a hired chaperon.

Mrs. Macomber leaned closer to Penelope and lowered her voice. "It's depressing to speak of it now, of course, with poor Glynis gone— and in such a hideous fashion—but at one point, I had great hopes she would attach Mr. Henry Wynne, Mr. Guy Walker, or Mr. Robert Fletcher. All were vying for her smiles at that time."

Mrs. Macomber's expression lightened, as if she was looking back on a remembered near-triumph, then her face fell. "Of course, that was before Mr. Mandeville. Once he appeared, Glynis didn't look at any other man."

Constance and Stokes shared a glance.

Penelope patted Mrs. Macomber's hand. "It is terribly sad. You came so close to seizing the prize."

Mrs. Macomber nodded; she lowered her head and applied her lace-edged handkerchief to her eyes.

Penelope arched a brow at Stokes, clearly asking if he had more questions.

Stokes shook his head.

Constance turned to Pearl and spoke in a low murmur. "Stay with her. I'll tell Vine to remain on guard outside the door. Until we have the murderer by the heels."

"Indeed, Miss Constance," Pearl grimly replied. "You can count on us to keep the old lady safe." Pearl glanced across the room at the chaperon. "A sniffly thing, she is, but she's got a good heart, and she's not a pea-brain, either—she just sometimes sounds like one."

That was a ruthlessly accurate observation. Constance kept her response to a nod. She turned to find Penelope taking her leave of Mrs. Macomber.

From beside the door, Stokes gravely inclined his head to the chaperon. "Thank you for your time, Mrs. Macomber. We'll leave you in peace."

"Thank you, Inspector." Mrs. Macomber spoke with greater strength than she'd displayed to that point. "I hope you find your man in short order."

On that note, Stokes, Penelope, and Constance quit the room.

In the corridor, Constance paused to tell Vine that his services as guard were still required.

"Aye, miss. I'll stay right here." Vine grinned. "The maids bring me up my tea and dinner, so all's right in my world."

Constance arched her brows at him in affectionate warning, then walked to where Stokes and Penelope had halted a few paces along the corridor.

"We should look in on the others," Stokes said, "and let them know they need to keep an eye out for a canary-yellow ribbon—wrapped around letters or not. And that they should check any letters they find to make sure they aren't addressed to Glynis."

To Constance, Stokes seemed edgy. Not nervous but restless—wanting to get on. She nodded and pointed. "Percy's room is that way. They were going to start in there."

❧

Barnaby and Alaric were searching the antechamber of Percy's room in a rather desultory fashion. The activity was, after all, all for show; they didn't expect to find anything—they just had to go through the motions before they moved on to the other gentleman suspects' rooms.

Percy's room was the master suite of the Hall. It was a long room with a partition dividing it into an antechamber with armchairs before the hearth and various pieces of furniture, such as a wardrobe and sideboard, dotted about the walls. A door in the left wall led to a relatively recently constructed bathing chamber. Alaric knew that on the other side of the partition, the large four-poster bed sat in all its glory, facing tall windows. There were more chests and tallboys and the nightstands in there, yet to be searched.

Percy had assisted by opening the wardrobe to the left of the door and leaving Barnaby to search it, while Alaric went through the drawers and cupboards of a sideboard against the wall to the door's right. Percy stood in the middle of the antechamber, watching them and looking around. Alaric noted that Barnaby was watching Percy from the corner of his eye. As was Alaric; why, he didn't know. He knew Percy wasn't the murderer and felt confident Barnaby did, too.

Percy looked at Barnaby, then at Alaric, both industriously searching, then Percy shrugged and walked to the archway that led into the bedroom. "I don't suppose it matters if I help, does it?"

From where he stood, Alaric couldn't see Percy, but Barnaby turned and, with his gaze, followed Percy as he vanished into the bedroom.

Barnaby continued to watch. Alaric went back to sifting through the papers Percy had shoved into the sideboard's drawers.

The sound of a drawer being opened in the bedroom reached his ears.

"Oh my God!" came from Percy.

Alaric looked up to see Barnaby striding for the bedroom.

"I say!" Percy exclaimed.

Quitting the sideboard, Alaric followed Barnaby. He found him with

Percy in front of a tallboy against the wall. Both were peering into the top right-hand drawer.

As Alaric joined them, Barnaby reached into the drawer and drew out a bundle of letters tied with a bright-yellow ribbon.

Percy was gabbling, "But—but—they weren't there! They weren't there this morning." He wrung his hands.

Barnaby and Alaric exchanged a look. They believed Percy; his horrified shock was all too genuine.

Then Alaric frowned and looked at Percy. "How can you be sure?"

His nonaccusatory, matter-of-fact tone drew Percy back from the brink. He immediately replied, "Because I swapped my cravat pin this morning." He pointed into the drawer; Alaric looked inside and saw the wooden box of cravat pins and shirt studs and sundry fobs sitting at the front of the drawer, with the rest of the drawer stuffed with loose letters and notes. Percy pointed to one particular pin—a diamond set in gold. "That's the one I've been wearing lately—I had it on yesterday. But this morning, I switched it for this one." Percy jabbed a finger at the black onyx head of the pin currently anchoring the folds of his gray silk cravat. "As a sign of mourning."

Barnaby nodded in a decisive fashion that signaled his unqualified acceptance of Percy's explanation. "Remember I mentioned that the murderer might not burn the letters but use them for something else? He did." Barnaby held up the sheaf of letters. "He put them in your drawer, thinking to implicate you." Barnaby glanced at the general detritus in the drawer. "Most men don't change their cravat pins every day—or even every week. He wouldn't have expected you to have looked in this drawer this morning."

"But," Alaric said, following the same line of thought, "that means he must have put the letters here sometime between when you left the room this morning and now."

The main door opened.

Barnaby and Alaric walked back to the archway and saw Stokes follow Penelope and Constance into the room.

Three pairs of eyes locked on the bundle in Barnaby's hand.

Stokes humphed. "We were coming to tell you the letters were tied with yellow ribbon."

"Canary-yellow ribbon, to be precise," Penelope said. "But you've already found them."

Constance came forward and took the letters from Barnaby, who handed them over without quibble. Constance pulled the ribbon bow undone, then started flicking through the letters.

Alaric went to look over her shoulder. When she glanced at him, he explained, "I know Percy's hand."

Stokes and Penelope outlined what they'd learned from Mrs. Macomber. "So there's definitely the possibility of letters from Wynne, Walker, and Fletcher. Those were the three Mrs. Macomber said were most attentive prior to Percy capturing Glynis's interest."

"Except," Constance said, looking up from the sheaf of letters she'd made her way through, "these are all in one hand."

"They're all from Percy," Alaric verified.

Constance hesitated, then she gathered the letters, retied the ribbon, and offered the bundle to Percy. "Here. Best put them somewhere else."

Percy took them and thanked her in a choked voice.

Barnaby then explained how Percy—under Barnaby's eye—had discovered the letters and what the timing of their appearance in the tallboy drawer meant.

Stokes looked enthused. "This is a chance we can't afford to pass up. Clearly, those letters were placed in Percy's room by the murderer to divert our investigation and paint Percy as the killer. If we can find which guest came up to this floor, to this room, between the time Percy left it and now, we'll either have our man or at least reduce our suspect list substantially."

No one argued.

Penelope narrowed her eyes. "The critical time period is, in fact, shorter than that." She looked at Barnaby and Stokes. "We held all the guests in the drawing room for most of the morning—from the time we arrived, which was nine-thirty, more or less on the dot."

"True." Barnaby looked at Percy. "What time did you go down this morning?"

"Just after eight o'clock," Percy replied. "And Carnaby can tell you that most of the guests were already down and at breakfast when I reached the dining room."

Constance and Alaric both murmured agreement. "Most came down in good time," Constance said.

"They wanted to speculate on how your interviews would be run and what they might expect," Alaric dryly added.

"So if our murderer wasn't among those already down, he had an hour or so's opportunity then," Penelope said. "We didn't release the guests from the drawing room until after eleven o'clock, and luncheon was served at twelve-thirty, so that was another hour during which he might have slipped up to Percy's room."

"After that, however," Alaric said, "everyone went outside. Most if not all congregated on the croquet lawn, and they're still there."

"So," Stokes said, busily jotting in his notebook, "we have two approximately hour-long windows of opportunity during which the murderer might have planted the letters in here. Beyond those times, he would have had to slip away from the assembled guests—which would increase the likelihood of him being observed leaving or having his absence noted."

"Yes, and since the guests repaired to the croquet lawn, Alaric and I, and more recently you four as well, have been rushing about the corridors up here," Constance pointed out. "Yet we haven't glimpsed anyone—especially not any gentleman—slinking about."

"He wouldn't slink," Stokes said. "As cool as he is, he would stride along as if his purpose was completely innocent."

"There was that half hour while we were out under the oak," Percy put in. "Whoever he is, he could have noticed us, slipped away from the others, and planted the letters then."

The others all looked at him, then Stokes grunted. "Good point." He made another note.

"This room is at the end of the gentlemen's wing," Alaric said. "And only my room and Edward's are in the cross-wing—the family wing. Anyone approaching Percy's door would be in full view of anyone in either corridor and even by someone at the head of the stairs. There's a clear line of sight."

"So it was difficult and risky," Barnaby said, "yet he managed it."

"But was he seen?" Penelope asked. "That's the critical question."

Constance looked at Alaric. "Am I right in thinking that to get to the main stairs, Edward would have to pass Percy's door, but in doing so, he would be visible to others farther up the corridor?"

Alaric met her eyes, then nodded. "Yes."

Stokes paused in his writing to look at Alaric. "So if Edward had come from his room with the letters in his pocket, he could have walked into the gentlemen's corridor close by Percy's door, looked up the corridor and checked if there was anyone to see him, and if there wasn't, he could have slipped into Percy's room unseen?"

"Yes, but why would he?" Penelope answered. "If Edward's

misguided motive in killing Glynis and subsequently Rosa was to protect the family name, then surely returning the letters to Percy runs counter to that."

"Unless he was simply returning the letters to Percy as the safest option," Barnaby said. "From the state of that drawer, he might have thought Percy wouldn't look in there in the next few days, and Edward might have realized that burning anything in the grates at this time of year would be noticed. He had no way of knowing that we would learn of the letters and search."

"That still puts Edward's principal motive at risk," Stokes said. "Better he hide the letters somewhere in the house where they're unlikely to be found and dispose of them later."

Penelope grimaced. "True." After a second, she added, "And more, the person with the letters, presumably the murderer, doesn't have to be Edward. Just because the letters placed in Percy's drawer were all from Percy, that doesn't mean there weren't other letters—ones from the murderer—that he needs to get rid of."

Stokes grunted. "We're going around and around inventing possibilities. The truth is we know far too little of our possible suspects to find success by that route."

Penelope sighed. "You're right. And I don't have my usual supporters to appeal to. Finding out about anyone is much easier in London."

"Yes, but," Barnaby insisted, "we can still advance our cause by asking around and seeing if we can get a bead on who put the letters in here. It's a house party, and all the guests know they have a murderer in their midst. They'll be keeping their eyes open for any unusual behavior." Barnaby looked at the others. "We need to ask." He glanced at Penelope and Constance. "And aside from the guests, surely there would have been maids scurrying about, making up beds and so on?"

Both ladies nodded. "Indeed, there should have been," Constance said, "at least during some of those windows of opportunity."

"All right." Stokes was getting restless, no doubt conscious of time running out. "We need to act immediately, so let's divide the obvious next tasks." He looked at Constance and Penelope. "You ladies are best qualified to extract information from the maids and the housekeeper—we need to know whether any of them spotted one of the gentlemen in the upstairs corridors or even on the stairs during our stipulated times. Also, whether they've noticed any unexpected ashes in some grate."

Stokes shifted his gaze to Barnaby and Percy. "Meanwhile, we'll interview the male staff on the same topics." Stokes looked at Alaric. "I don't want to call my constables off their assignment watching the guests. They're likely to be more use to us by keeping track of who is where at this moment."

Alaric nodded. "I'll let them know what's going on, and while I'm downstairs, I'll find Monty. In general, his talents are unimpressive, but Monty has one peculiar trait—he observes in remarkable detail and can usually remember everything. It's how his memory works."

Stokes arched his brows. "Is that so? Then by all means, see what he can recall of the gentlemen's movements during the day."

Barnaby had been consulting his fob watch. He tucked it back into his waistcoat pocket. "Time is ticking on. Let's tackle our respective tasks and meet under the oak in an hour, at which time it'll be close to five o'clock."

CHAPTER 9

Five minutes later, Constance and Penelope were seated in comfortable chairs in the housekeeper's room. Mrs. Carnaby stood before her small fireplace, and the maids of the house were assembled in serried ranks before Constance and Penelope.

"Now, girls," Mrs. Carnaby said. "Please listen carefully to these ladies, and if you have an answer to their questions, speak up." To Constance and Penelope, Mrs. Carnaby added, "I know I speak for all the staff in saying that we hope this nasty murderer is clapped in irons by the inspector and soon!"

"We sympathize entirely," Constance replied.

"Indeed." Penelope focused on the maids. "Our first question may seem strange, but have any of you noticed any ashes in any grate—any suggestion of papers being burned?"

The maids looked at each other, then at the youngest, a girl of about fourteen. She looked mortified to have been singled out, and blushed, then vehemently shook her head.

"Mitzy—speak up," Mrs. Carnaby instructed. "No ashes in any grate?"

"No, ma'am," Mitzy whispered.

"Good." Penelope bestowed a smile on the tweeny, then looked at the maids as a whole. "Now, to those of you whose duties took them upstairs this morning—did you see any gentleman slip into your master's room?"

The reply was a general shaking of heads and an eventual "No, ma'am" from the senior maid.

"At any time between eight o'clock this morning and when luncheon was served," Constance said, "did any of you notice any gentleman walking about the upstairs corridors—the west wing and family wing in particular? Or even simply going upstairs?"

But that, too, was met with shaking heads and a "No, ma'am."

Penelope met Constance's eyes briefly, then changed direction. "Have any of you seen a sheaf of letters tied with yellow ribbon in any of the gentlemen's rooms?"

After another exchange of looks and many heads shaking, the senior maid concluded, "No, ma'am."

Constance shared a resigned look with Penelope; it had been a long shot to hope the murderer had left the letters lying about before he'd slipped them into Percy's tallboy drawer. Then, recalling how literal staff sometimes were when being questioned by their betters, she looked at the maids and asked, "Did anyone see a gentleman carrying such a bundle of letters?" More shaking of heads. "No sighting of such a bundle of letters tied with yellow ribbon at all?"

One of the upstairs maids shifted. When Constance and Penelope focused on her, she offered, "If you mean Miss Johnson's letters, then I did see them in her room."

"Yes, those are the letters we're interested in." Penelope sat straighter. "When did you see them?"

The maid shot a look at Mrs. Carnaby; after the housekeeper nodded encouragingly, the maid replied, "I was assigned to help Mrs. Cleary and Miss Johnson, ma'am. She had the letters out a few times when I was in the room—that would be on Sunday evening and again on Monday after-noon—just reading or looking at them, but she always tucked them away in her hatbox, the one she kept on top of the armoire."

"Did Mrs. Cleary know about the letters?" Constance asked.

The maid frowned. After a moment of inner debate, she said, "I can't be sure, ma'am, but she was there on the Sunday evening when both ladies were dressing for dinner, and Miss Johnson had the letters out then, so Mrs. Cleary would most likely have noticed them, but I can't say that she ever read them, ma'am."

"I see." Constance paused, then asked, "Did you notice what Miss Johnson was wearing on the chain around her neck?"

The maid nodded. "A ring it was, ma'am. Not sure what it meant to her, but she kept it hidden under her bodice, most times. I only saw it when I was helping her into or out of her gowns."

"Do you think Mrs. Cleary knew about the ring?" Penelope asked.

The maid thought, but this time shook her head. "I shouldn't think so, ma'am. Miss Johnson used the dressing screen, so unless she showed Mrs. Cleary the ring deliberate-like, I don't think Mrs. Cleary would have known anything about it."

Penelope suppressed a grimace. "Thank you." She exchanged a glance with Constance, then surveyed the maids once again. "While we have you all here, is there anything any of you noticed about Mrs. Cleary—anything at all out of the ordinary? Anything that struck you as even mildly odd."

"Anything you can tell us might be helpful," Constance added, "no matter how trivial it may seem. As both ladies are dead and we're trying to catch their murderer, this is not the time to hold your tongue."

"Just so," Mrs. Carnaby agreed.

Several elbows nudged one of the younger maids. Blushing furiously, she darted a glance at Mrs. Carnaby, then cleared her throat and timidly offered, "On Monday night...well, more like early Tuesday morning, I was out the back, in the kitchen garden, talking with Ben—he's one of the grooms."

Penelope nodded encouragingly. "That was the night Miss Johnson was killed."

"Aye." The maid's voice gained in strength. "I was on my way back to the house when I saw Mrs. Cleary on the terrace. Just standing there, looking out, she was. She didn't do anything that I saw."

"Where on the terrace, exactly?" Penelope asked.

"Right at the end, ma'am, where the balustrade goes across." The maid waved to the east side of the house. "She was standing out from the wall in the corner of the balustrade. She looked to be just taking the air."

A frown had formed in Constance's eyes. "I can't recall—was there moonlight that night? You said you saw Mrs. Cleary..."

"Oh no, ma'am—it wasn't bright at all. The moon wasn't anywhere near full. But it was a clear night, and I could see her..." The maid tipped her head, clearly reviewing what she'd seen. "Well, I didn't know it was her then, of course, but I could see it was a dark-haired lady standing there, looking out. I could make out that much easily enough."

Constance's eyes lit, and she nodded graciously to the maid. "Thank you." When Constance glanced Penelope's way, brows arched, asking if she had more questions, Penelope shook her head. Constance turned and graciously thanked Mrs. Carnaby and the maids for their time and their help.

Sensing a rising impatience in Constance, Penelope fell in with her co-investigator's transparent wish to end the interview. They waited while Mrs. Carnaby dismissed her staff, then followed her from the room.

Stepping into the corridor leading to the servants' hall, they heard the rumble of male voices; obviously Stokes, Barnaby, and Percy were still questioning the male staff.

Constance's hand closed on Penelope's wrist, and Constance halted, then she met Penelope's eyes and tipped her head toward the rear door.

When Penelope arched her brows in query, Constance said, "I know we'll be early to the oak, but unless you can think of something else to pursue, there's a scenario I'd like to go over with you—away from here."

Penelope inclined her head. "I can't think of anything worth our while. A juicy scenario sounds promising—and it was pleasant under that oak."

~

Barnaby surveyed the footmen, grooms, gardeners, and assorted boys Carnaby had assembled in the servants' hall. It had taken more than fifteen minutes to gather all the male staff, but at last, they were all there, standing around the long table; from beside Stokes at the table's head with Percy on Stokes's other side, Barnaby listened as Stokes outlined the thrust of their questions—whether any gentleman of the house party had been seen going upstairs to the master suite during the day.

Stokes detailed the critical time periods during which gentlemen would have been free to slip upstairs. He concluded by running his gaze around the faces about the table. "So—did any of you see any of the gentlemen upstairs during those hours?"

Barnaby stirred. "Or even heading up the stairs."

Carnaby and the footmen exchanged glances. As one, the footmen shook their heads, and Carnaby looked at Stokes. "No sir. But we're rarely upstairs during those hours—only if called, and I don't remember anyone ringing. Also..." Carnaby paused, then offered, "In the matter of tracing gentlemen visiting upstairs, I should point out that there are three staircases the guests might use to access their rooms, and we only monitor the front hall and the main staircase."

Barnaby shot Stokes a look, which Stokes met. Both were recalling the secondary stairs they'd used earlier; apparently, there were more and doubtless several servants' stairways as well.

Stokes returned his gaze to the assembled men. "Thinking back to those hours I mentioned and where you were during those times, did you notice any gentleman walking alone, either through the house, back to the house, leaving the house, or returning to the rest of the guests on the croquet lawn?"

Although the outdoor staff had been scattered here and there, weeding beds, digging a drainage ditch, and in the shrubbery, no one had seen any gentleman on his own. But even that came with a caveat. The head gardener pointed out that they'd all been busy and not looking about, keeping watch. Gentlemen may have come and gone, and they wouldn't necessarily have noticed.

Stokes acknowledged that with outward good grace, but Barnaby could read his underlying frustration. Time was running out, and every lead they'd pursued had led to a dead end. Although Stokes tried several more questions regarding the movement of the male guests, there was clearly no pertinent knowledge to be extracted.

Finally accepting that, Stokes glanced at the clock. Barnaby followed his gaze—they still had more than half an hour before their meeting under the oak.

Doubtless fired by a dogged desire to have something positive to report, Stokes switched tacks. "Considering Mrs. Cleary, the second lady who was killed, is there anything—anything out of the ordinary at all—that any of you noticed about her?"

A pause ensued, then one of the older footmen volunteered, "I was in the conservatory corridor—the one that runs past the billiard room—on the evening before the lady died. I was there—close—when she came over faint."

Along with Stokes, Barnaby looked as encouraging as he could, and the footman went on, "I noticed it particular because she stared straight ahead, as though she'd seen a ghost right there in the middle of the corridor." He glanced at his mates. "T'tell the truth, it gave me quite a turn—the way she stared—but then the other ladies gathered around, and she seemed to come out of it all right."

Carnaby put in, "I'd sent Mark to put the billiard room to rights given the gentlemen were leaving and heading back to the drawing room."

Barnaby studied the footman's face; he didn't look to be the fanciful sort. A picture of what might have happened in the corridor took shape in Barnaby's brain. "The gentlemen came out of the billiard room ahead of Mrs. Cleary and the other ladies—correct?" When Carnaby and Mark nodded, Barnaby went on, "Could Mrs. Cleary have been staring at one of the gentlemen walking away down the corridor ahead of her?"

Mark blinked, then frowned. "Aye," he allowed, "she could've been." He grimaced. "If that was so, whoever he was, just the sight of him gave her a nasty turn. Went white as a sheet, she did."

Stokes leaned forward. "Do you have any idea which gentleman it might have been? The one she reacted to?"

Mark shook his head. "No, sir. I was looking at her, not at the gentlemen. They were all together, walking in twos and threes up the corridor."

Barnaby said, "At the moment in time when Mrs. Cleary reacted and you looked at her, had all the gentlemen left the billiard room?"

Mark looked at Barnaby and didn't hesitate. "Yes, sir. They were all out. I was standing directly opposite the billiard room door, my back to the wall, waiting for the ladies to pass so I could go in."

Percy, who, after instructing Carnaby to gather the male staff, had kept mum, cleared his throat and said, "I led the gentlemen out of the billiard room. I and those around me—Carradale and others—were at the head of the pack, as it were. We didn't notice the ladies, and we'd no idea anything had happened until we heard later, in the drawing room."

Stokes stared at Percy for a moment, as if juggling the positions of people in the corridor, then turned Barnaby's way; Barnaby was waiting to catch his gaze and tip his head toward the door.

Stokes looked at Carnaby and the assembled men. "I believe that's all we need for the moment. Thank you for your assistance." Stokes cocked a brow at Barnaby.

"Let's go." Barnaby led the way out of the servants' hall, but instead of heading for the front of the house, he turned toward the rear, eventually halting in the small foyer by the back stairs and the rear door.

"What?" Stokes said as he halted.

Barnaby turned to Percy as he joined them. "I'm not sure I have this right, but bear with me. From the rear end of the terrace, Rosa saw a gentleman leaving the shrubbery. You assumed the man she saw was you, but what if it wasn't? Let's say it was another gentleman—specifically the man who murdered Glynis. Am I correct in thinking that from where Rosa stood at the end of the terrace, her view of any man leaving the shrubbery and walking toward the front of the house would have been more or less from the back? At an angle, true, yet mostly from the back? That essentially, she saw the man walking away from her?"

Percy frowned. "I hadn't really thought of it, but if Rosa was standing at the *end* of the terrace, then yes—if anyone came out of the shrubbery heading directly for the front of the house, unless they turned and looked squarely at the house or looked back toward where Rosa stood, she could only have seen their back."

Barnaby met Stokes's eyes. "We've just heard that Rosa nearly fainted at the sight of the gentlemen leaving the billiard room—where she again saw men from the back."

Stokes's eyes narrowed. "She recognized him—and he must have realized she had."

Grimly, Barnaby nodded. "That's why Rosa Cleary died."

Stokes grunted. "That still doesn't tell us which man she saw, but with luck, it will narrow the field." He stepped forward and opened the back door. "Let's see if the others have found anything to help with that."

Penelope managed to bridle her curiosity until they reached the oak on the south lawn, but immediately they passed into the shade beneath its widespread branches, she demanded, "So what is it—this scenario of yours?"

Constance halted and faced Penelope. "Percy assumed it was him Rosa saw, when he was crossing from the front edge of the shrubbery to the forecourt. But Percy has a mop of bright fair hair—even in poor light, Rosa wouldn't have missed that. More, Rosa said she saw the man *leaving* the shrubbery—not just coming from the direction of the shrubbery. So all distractions aside, it now seems clear that Rosa definitely saw the murderer leave the shrubbery via the main entrance."

With one hand, Penelope made a "go on" motion.

Constance drew breath and rapidly ordered her arguments. "We've focused on why Glynis was murdered and not so much on Rosa."

Penelope nodded. "But Rosa was killed by the same man, presumably because he feared she'd seen him."

"Precisely. But when she saw him leaving the shrubbery, Rosa didn't see him well enough to identify him—she consistently said so, and the testimony of the maid we just heard confirmed that the light wasn't good enough to see features."

"But it was good enough to see hair coloring, at least to distinguish between bright blond and brown, so it wasn't Percy Rosa saw." Penelope paused, then went on, "I accept that's now certain."

"Indeed." Constance beckoned. "Now come over here and look." She led Penelope to the other side of the oak, closer to where they'd stood earlier. Constance halted and pointed through the leaves. "See—from here, we have much the same line of sight as Rosa had when she was standing at the rear corner of the terrace. You can see the shrubbery entrance. If a man came striding out making for the front door, Rosa would have seen him at a sharp angle to his left side—mostly just his left arm and his back. She would have seen what she reported—the cravat and all the rest—but no real profile. Mostly, what she saw was his back."

Penelope peered through the foliage; she had to stand on her toes—she was far shorter than Constance—and shift this way and that to get the right angle. Eventually, she allowed, "All right. I agree—Rosa saw the gentleman mostly from the back."

"Rosa wasn't lying in saying she didn't recognize him from that sighting, but later..." Constance met Penelope's eyes. "She recognized him—at least well enough to raise a real question in her mind—when she saw him leaving the billiard room and walking away from her."

"You're saying her turn was—as we'd earlier hypothesized—because recognition struck."

"And struck hard—enough to make her giddy and faint. Something must have happened to trigger the realization." Constance closed her eyes. She felt Penelope's gaze on her face and said, "I'm reliving the moment in the corridor. I was there—I must have seen something."

"Replay the memories slowly." Penelope's voice was almost hypnotic in tone, but with an undercurrent of eagerness. "Don't force things, just observe as if from a distance. Start from where you left the conservatory." After a moment, she asked, "Where are you in relation to Rosa Cleary?"

"Behind and to her left. There were six of us all told, three ladies walking in front—Rosa in the middle, with Mrs. Collard on her left and Mrs. Finlayson on her right—and Mrs. Cripps was to my right with Miss Weldon beyond her, behind Mrs. Finlayson."

"Good," Penelope said. "So you started walking along the corridor. What happened next?"

"We strolled, as one does, in the direction of the drawing room. None of us were in any hurry. Then the door to the billiard room, which was farther up the corridor on the right, opened, and the gentlemen started streaming out. I think all of them had been in there." Constance paused, the recollection now vivid in her mind. "They didn't see us—I suspect we were just far enough away that they didn't glimpse or sense us as they came through the door. I could only see the tops of heads over those of the ladies before me, but I'm sure none of the gentlemen paused or looked back—not then. They turned out of the door and strode on, making for the front hall and the drawing room."

"Did Rosa react straightaway—as the men streamed out?"

Constance frowned. "No. She didn't." Of that she was now sure. "In fact...it was after the last of the men had stepped into the corridor. They were in groups of three or four, so fell in much as we were, two or three abreast." Constance paused, wracking her memory of the relevant moment. "As to the timing...I'm sure it was after all the men had stepped into the corridor and the last had taken at least a few steps. *Then* Rosa gasped and stopped and clutched Mrs. Gibson's arm."

Penelope waited, then prompted, "And...?"

"We all gathered around Rosa." Constance concentrated, trying to focus on every little detail of who and what and in what order. "She'd gone as white as the proverbial sheet. The expression on her face...she didn't look horrified so much as...well, uncertain. Shaky and shaken. That's why we all so readily accepted her word that she'd come over faint and thought no more about it at the time. But..." Constance pored over one little snippet of memory, then her lips firmed. After a second of replaying, yet again, the relevant second, she said, "Reviewing what I saw as we crowded around, just before Rosa looked down, drew in a breath, and seemed to regain a little of her composure, she was looking straight ahead, and her eyes were wide. From where I stood, I couldn't see all of her face, her full expression, but I did see that."

Constance's description was sufficient to allow Penelope to envisage the scene. "So as we suspected, she was staring at one of the men who had just left the billiard room."

"But given her height—she was only average at most—and the timing of her reaction, the man who triggered it had to have been one of the last to leave the billiard room. Indeed, he was almost certainly in the last three or at most five or six—the men who made up the rear of the pack." Constance opened her eyes and met Penelope's. "He must have done something to trigger Rosa's recognition. She'd been among the guests all day without realizing who he was."

Penelope thought for a second, then raised her arms and mimicked closing them around the invisible throat of someone shorter than herself. "Strangling a lady." Then she changed position. "Playing billiards." She pantomimed leaning over a billiard table and striking a ball with a cue.

She straightened, shrugging her bodice into place—then she looked at Constance, and with dawning wonder, they chorused, "She saw him resettling his coat!"

Penelope felt the upsurge in confidence that told her they'd got it right. Then she realized, "He must have a particular way of doing it—some idiosyncrasy that marked him definitively as the murderer."

Constance considered. "I suspect many men have a particular way of doing it—it's one of those little actions they do constantly, so it becomes a habit."

"One almost impossible to change." Penelope's eyes gleamed. "Rosa may be dead, but she's left us with one solid clue to the murderer's identity."

Constance thought, then sighed. "Sadly, he now knows that, or at least he should." She met Penelope's disgruntled gaze. "If you're imagining getting all the men to take off their coats, then put them on again, just to see who stands out as having a memorable way of resettling his coat's shoulders and sleeves, I can't say I favor your chances."

Penelope made a disgusted sound. "Sadly, you're correct. However"—she held up a finger—"we do know that the murderer was among the last gentlemen to exit the billiard room. After all our floundering—and given time is running out—it's something definite at last. Surely we can use that to winnow our suspects." Her expression turned grimly determined, and behind her spectacles, her eyes glinted. "We need to learn which of our four candidates was walking at the rear of that gentlemanly pack."

The company of guests had, at last, quit the croquet lawn and retreated to the morning room. Alaric had to smile and exercise his considerable charm and the social skills learned through a decade and more of consorting with society's raciest elements to cut Monty from the horde; his cousin was a gregarious soul and tended to be in the thick of animated gatherings—very often featuring as the center of attention—which was part of what made him so useful.

Finally, Alaric had Monty by the elbow, gripping hard enough for his cousin to understand his attention was required and that resistance was futile. Relentlessly, with nods and aloof smiles to others who might have waylaid them, Alaric steered Monty out of the morning room and across a hall into the rarely used—and currently helpfully deserted —library.

Once inside with the door shut, Alaric released Monty. Rubbing his abused elbow, his cousin turned to him, his face a mask of puzzlement. "What is it?"

Alaric waved to a setting of two armchairs. Ever obliging, Monty sank into one while Alaric rather more elegantly claimed the other. "I need you to cooperate and pick through your memories."

It was something of a family secret that Monty had well-nigh perfect recall; if society ever learned of his unexpected talent, he'd be shunned.

Monty heaved a put-upon sigh. "Very well. What do you want to know?"

"We need to know which gentlemen went or could have gone upstairs, alone and separate from the other guests, during the day. Start from the period immediately after breakfast ended and before the guests were gathered together in the drawing room at Inspector Stokes's direction. Did any of the gentlemen leave the general group of guests—on any pretext, for any reason—and possibly go upstairs?"

Monty frowned, his attention going inward. After a moment, he said, "I'm assuming other than you and Percy?"

"Yes."

"Guy Walker slipped upstairs immediately after breakfast to change his cravat—bit of egg, don't you know?"

When Monty fell silent, Alaric prompted, "Anyone else?"

Monty shook his head. "Not before we were all cooped up in the drawing room."

"Go on to after, once we'd been released."

Monty's gaze grew distant. "Wynne went up to fetch a book he said he would loan Prue Collard—they'd been discussing it while we were waiting for our interviews with the inspector. Then came luncheon, and just after we'd risen from the table, before we headed out to the croquet lawn, Fletcher went up. No idea why, but he was back down within a few minutes. Then, just as we were about to head out of the house, Edward excused himself and went upstairs to change his coat. He was wearing a morning coat, and it did look a trifle too tight across the shoulders for wielding a croquet mallet—and you know Edward. He always takes any competition seriously, and we'd already settled on a round-robin tournament."

"And did he rejoin you in a less-restricting coat?"

Monty nodded. "He was back soon enough in a herringbone jacket. Quite nice."

"Anyone else?"

Monty sighed again and closed his eyes.

Alaric waited with what patience he could muster; he knew better than to try to rush Monty's mind.

Finally, his eyes still closed, Monty said, "Those four, I'm sure of." He opened his eyes and looked with some asperity at Alaric. "But as to whether there might have been others…you'll have to remember that you hadn't asked me to keep track, so I wasn't counting heads. Someone could have slipped away, and I didn't notice. F'r instance, the colonel and Captain Collins ambled off during the tournament. That was to enjoy a cheroot, I'm certain, but they didn't return for quite a while. For all I know, they might have gone upstairs, either together or separately."

Alaric released a frustrated breath; he'd hoped Monty's memory would help shorten the list of suspects. Lips thin, he slumped back in the chair and eyed Monty. "So we have Walker, Wynne, Fletcher, and Edward who definitely went upstairs."

Monty nodded and earnestly added, "There might have been others." He shrugged. "I simply can't say."

Alaric swallowed a growl, pushed up from the armchair, and nodded to Monty. "Thank you."

Monty huffed. "I won't say it was my pleasure."

Alaric uttered a short laugh. He dropped a hand on Monty's shoulder as he moved past, then strode to the French windows, opened them, stepped out onto the terrace, and headed for the south lawn.

Alaric walked around the rear corner of the house and made for their meeting place. Situated partially behind the walled kitchen garden and backed by the wood, the south lawn was rarely used by guests, and as Alaric strode onto the sward, heading for the old oak, he confirmed that today was no exception.

Instead, he spied Barnaby, Stokes, and Percy ahead of him and jogged to catch up with them.

He fell in beside Percy. "Any advance?"

Barnaby waggled his head. "In a way—yes."

"But in general," Stokes grumbled, "no."

Alaric looked inquiringly at Percy, but he only grimaced and shook his head.

Barnaby glanced at Alaric. "You?"

He raised his brows in frustrated resignation. "Yes and no sums it up all too aptly."

Stokes snorted.

As they neared the oak, they spotted the two ladies waiting in the deep shade. The four men ducked under the branches and immediately saw from both Penelope's and Constance's expressions that they had had better luck.

"What?' Stokes asked.

Penelope all but jigged with eager earnestness; Constance, Alaric noted, was rather more contained, yet was also distinctly enthused.

"First," Penelope said, "did anyone learn anything regarding who might have put the letters in Percy's room? We didn't—not the faintest hint of a clue."

Stokes grunted. "We, too, got nowhere as to the letters." He looked at Alaric. "You?"

"Since breakfast, at least four men left the rest of the company at some point and went upstairs alone. Walker immediately after breakfast, Wynne later, after you'd released the guests from the drawing room, then Fletcher immediately after lunch, and lastly Edward just before the company went outside." Alaric paused, then disgruntledly continued, "That said, as Monty pointed out, at various times, others drifted here and there—some off to smoke a cheroot, for instance—and they could have gone upstairs unnoticed by the other guests." Alaric looked around the circle of faces. "Trying to identify who put the letters in Percy's room is—"

"Not really a viable way forward," Penelope concluded.

Several gave vent to frustrated sounds, but no one disagreed.

Stokes glanced at Alaric. "While I agree with our general consensus, those four definites—Walker, Wynne, Fletcher, and Mandeville—keep cropping up."

"If only one of them would crop up without the others," Barnaby dryly observed, "we might have a chance of solving this case."

"Hmm. Yes, well, on to what else we discovered." Behind the lenses of her spectacles, Penelope's eyes gleamed. "From one of the maids, we learned more about what Rosa must have seen in the night." She glanced at Percy. "Incidentally, what we heard makes it impossible that it was you Rosa saw. She definitely saw the murderer."

Percy frowned. "Are you sure?"

Penelope lifted her gaze to his hair. "As sure as you are a very fair blond. Despite the poor light, Rosa would have seen your hair and recognized you. None of the other gentlemen have such fair hair—the closest is a mid-brown, which would look darker, not lighter, in poor light. We also went over all Rosa herself said, and one thing we can now be sure of is that Rosa saw the murderer leave the shrubbery.

"Then," Penelope continued, "adding everything together—what Rosa might have seen of the murderer and what Constance can remember of the incident when Rosa turned faint after seeing the gentlemen leave the billiard room, presumably inadvertently alerting the murderer so that he realized she had—or was close to—recognizing him, we're now as certain as we can be that the murderer *must* have been one of the last men to quit the billiard room. He had to have been at the rear of the group—and we believe Rosa recognized him, or suspected it was he, based on the way he resettles his coat."

"We think," Constance said, "that in the corridor, she saw him perform the exact same action as he had when he left the shrubbery after strangling Glynis—settling his coat's shoulders and sleeves in some distinctive way."

"But the most important actual fact," Penelope stated, "is that given the timing of Rosa's reaction and her relative height, then the man she reacted to had to have been one of the last to walk out of the billiard room."

"They—the men—were walking two and three abreast," Constance said. "So say the last five or six. He had to have been one of them."

Stokes studied Constance's and Penelope's eager faces, then humphed. "As it happens, that's much the same conclusion we reached after speaking with the footman who was in the corridor at that time, waiting to go into the billiard room."

"Although you've narrowed it down further," Barnaby said. "We assumed it was a man toward the rear of the group, but from what you say, I agree he's likely to have been one of the last five or six."

Alaric exchanged a look with Percy.

Percy deflated. "I was at the head of the pack—and you were with me, weren't you?"

Alaric pulled a face. "I was." He looked at Stokes. "And I have absolutely no idea who was at the rear."

Penelope exhaled, then arched a brow at Constance. "Do you think there's any chance the ladies flanking Rosa—Mrs. Collard and Mrs. Finlayson—might have noticed which gentlemen were at the rear of the pack?"

Alaric watched as Constance closed her eyes and—like Monty—appeared to consult a visual memory. After a moment, she shook her head, opened her eyes, and looked at Stokes. "I sincerely doubt those two ladies will be of any help. They were discussing some lily and how best to grow it, right up until the moment Rosa gasped. Once she did, we all looked at her." Constance met Penelope's gaze. "As I said, Rosa was staring straight ahead when she gasped, but by the time I noticed—by the time any of us got a clear look at her face—she'd looked down, and the revealing moment had passed."

"Did the men halt and look back?" Barnaby asked.

Briefly, Constance closed her eyes, then opened them and said, "Yes. At least a few of them paused and glanced back, but it was just the usual cursory glance. The instant they saw us all gathering about, they presumably assumed we had everything in hand, and they faced forward and continued on. I'm afraid I didn't focus on their faces—I just know they were there, looked back, then went on."

Stokes and Barnaby shared a long glance, then Stokes said, "If we don't get a bead on this murderer by morning, we might have to sit all the gentlemen down, one by one, and ask them to say who was where as they left the billiard room."

"And," Barnaby stated, his features hard, "who paused and looked back." Grimly, he regarded the others. "That's one of the few things we know about our murderer—like Lot's wife, he absolutely has to be one of those who looked back."

CHAPTER 10

*A*ll the investigators—among whom Constance now included herself, Alaric, and even Percy—had remained under the oak, discussing how best to address what were now their critical questions: Which gentleman had Rosa been staring at when she'd come over faint? Which gentleman had left the billiard room at the rear of the gentlemanly pack and then paused and looked back at Rosa?

As Barnaby had pointed out, the trigger, as it were, for Rosa's murder had to lie there. The murderer had to have seen with his own eyes that Rosa was a threat to him; that was why he'd killed her.

Their first thought had been to round up the guests and, in whatever way, press ahead, but that impulse had swiftly been tempered by caution; if their actions tipped their hand to the murderer and he felt that they were closing in, he might well flee—or worse. Although what worse he might do, no one had defined. But of even greater concern was Stokes's assessment that identifying the murderer as the man Rosa had stared at was, as evidence went, too flimsy to obtain a conviction. As Stokes had explained, "We need to know who he is, and then we need to build a case, either through his reactions to being accused or by finding solid evidence linking him to one or both murders."

Barnaby had looked around their circle and gravely stated, "In this case, identifying the murderer will only be the start of building a prosecutable case against him."

"But," Penelope had said, "as long as we can be certain we know which gentleman he is by tomorrow morning, Stokes can hold him and prevent him from leaving, and then we'll have time to build our case."

Evidently, bringing Glynis's and Rosa's murderer to justice all hinged on learning his identity beyond question by midmorning the next day.

Consequently, despite the feeling that they were starting to find their way through the morass created by the house party—with at minimum four suspects, a large and rambling house, and people wandering here and there at will—an uncertain mood had enveloped them; the prospect of failure had hovered oppressively beneath the branches of the oak. As they'd debated their options for reducing their list of suspects to one, the knowledge that tomorrow morning was their last opportunity—that they had to succeed over just those few hours before the party broke up and everyone, including the murderer, left—had weighed on them all.

Eventually, they'd realized the afternoon was waning. Alaric had checked his watch and discovered it was already six o'clock; despite nothing being decided regarding their next steps, together with Alaric and Percy, Constance had hurried back to the house to change for dinner. Heads together, still discussing potential ways to unmask the killer, Barnaby, Penelope, and Stokes had ambled off to the stable, ultimately to return to the Tabard Inn.

As Constance held up her arms and allowed Pearl to slide her evening gown over her head and draw it down, she wracked her brains, going over all the happenings again in the hope of stumbling on some clue they'd missed.

"You'll be late if you don't concentrate," Pearl admonished as she wrestled closed the buttons down the back of the gown. "Woolgathering, you are. And you rushing up at the last minute to change."

"We're on the hunt for this murderer." Constance wriggled, settling the bodice, then reached for her pearl earrings. "We still don't know who he is—and we need to know by tomorrow midmorning, before everyone leaves."

Pearl humphed. "You're a lady—leave searching for murderers to those paid to do it."

Constance smiled. "Mrs. Adair is far more of a lady than I am, and she's in the hunt up to her eyebrows."

Pearl's only reply was another humph. She finished with the buttons and prodded Constance toward the dressing stool. Once Constance sat, Pearl started on her hair; the activities of the day had freed myriad curls from her originally neat chignon. Working swiftly, Pearl loosened the thick, wavy mass, brushed it out, then wound it up into a knot.

Constance secured her string of pearls about her throat, then glanced about the room and belatedly realized the other occupant was absent. "Mrs. Macomber went down?"

"Mmm." Pearl had pins between her lips. She set them in place, anchoring the knot of Constance's hair, then said, "I finally got her courage up, and she toddled off near half an hour ago. I saw that Mrs. Cripps take up with her, and the two settled into chatting, so I think she'll be fine."

"Good. I was worried she'd take to life as a recluse."

"I think she considered it, but she likes a good chat, and recluses don't get much of that."

"True." The instant Pearl set the last pin in place, Constance shot up from the stool. She whirled, grabbed the evening reticule Pearl had left out for her, and headed for the door.

Sliding the strings of the beaded reticule over one wrist, Constance strode up the corridor. The rooms she passed were silent, all the other guests already downstairs.

She stepped into the wide hall where the corridors from the various wings converged before the head of the main stairs. She glanced to her left, down the corridor leading to the gentlemen's rooms, and almost involuntarily slowed.

They hadn't searched for the chain and ring.

She glanced at the stairs. Everyone else would be downstairs by now. She listened, straining her ears, but heard nothing; the rooms all about her were deserted.

Swiftly, she debated. She couldn't search every gentleman's room, but she could search the rooms of the critical four.

She'd seen Penelope's sketch of the house; closing her eyes, Constance called it to mind. Edward's room was the farthest away, around the corner at the end of the gentlemen's wing and along the family wing. She'd start there.

She didn't have time to reassess; if she was to do this, it had to be done now.

Quickly and quietly, she walked down the corridor. Nearing the corner around which she'd intended to turn, she saw that the door to Percy's room—which faced directly up the corridor—was ajar.

She halted and stared at the slightly open door.

It was possible a maid or footman hadn't closed it properly.

She debated for a second more, then crept closer. She put out one hand and gently eased the door farther open. It swung noiselessly; she poked her head around and peered inside.

And saw no one and nothing out of place.

The tension that had gripped her abruptly drained away.

Then she heard the scrape of a drawer.

Someone was in Percy's bedroom. Given the hour, it wouldn't be him.

Caution tugged at her, urging her to back away, but she couldn't leave without knowing…

Stealthily, she edged around the door. Holding her breath, she crept across the carpet; placing her slippered feet with care, she crossed the anteroom to where she could see past the dividing wall and into Percy's bedroom.

To the tallboy against the wall. The same tallboy in which they'd found Glynis's letters in the top right-hand drawer.

Edward Mandeville stood with that same drawer open, peering inside.

The mirror sitting on top of the tallboy gave Constance a clear view of Edward's face. He was frowning down at where the letters had been.

From the fingers of his left hand, a gold chain hung, a lady's ring dangling pendant-like on the chain.

Constance's lungs seized. She took a step back.

Edward looked up—into the mirror. His eyes clashed with hers.

For a split second, they both froze.

Then Constance whirled and fled.

She ripped open the door and raced into the corridor.

Her full skirts tangled about her legs. She drew in a breath.

Then Edward was on her. He slapped a hard palm across her lips, yanking her head up and back against his shoulder, smothering her scream. His other arm wrapped like a steel band around her waist, and despite her height and robust strength, Constance couldn't escape.

She tried kicking back at his legs and frantically squirming.

Edward proved far stronger than she'd imagined. He held her easily.

"You fool," he hissed into her ear. "Now, it'll have to be you, too."

Constance heaved forward, but he countered the movement. Then he started to drag her back down the west wing.

Furious—and increasingly terrified—Constance fought every step of the way. One of her arms was clamped to her side, the other hampered by her reticule; she violently shook her wrist to make the reticule's strings slip over her hand. Finally, the reticule fell, and she had one hand free.

She tried to tug Edward's hand from her lips. Unfortunately, being a practical lady, she kept her nails neat and short—they were useless for scratching and inflicting damage, at least damage enough to make Edward let go.

She tried to reach up and back, hoping to find his face and his eyes, but he sensed the movement and jerked his head away from her clawing hand.

Silently swearing, she lowered her hand and tried—equally futilely—to pry away the arm about her waist. If she could twist to the side, she might break his hold...

With one hand clamped painfully across her face and the other clutching her waist, Edward grunted and tugged, wrestling to keep her moving. Despite her best efforts, step by step, he forced her feet to move in the direction he wished. To her relief, he didn't make for Percy's room but hauled her down the family wing.

Wildly glancing around, she glimpsed the maw of the minor staircase for which Edward was making.

He intended to take her out of the house before murdering her.

Of course. If she—her body—wasn't found for days, he could leave tomorrow and fly free.

It was already late; the gong for dinner would soon sound. Alaric and Percy would be expecting her to appear. When she didn't...

Desperation lent her clarity. Alaric would come to find her; she had to leave a trail. Because of her size, Edward had to drag her; she was too heavy for him to lift, even to the extent of getting her feet off the ground. He had no way to straighten the runner the heels of her shoes had rucked up; glancing back, she saw the rippling and the drag marks left by her shoes—and dug her heels in even more.

Edward growled, but didn't halt.

She realized he couldn't risk freeing either hand to strike her into acquiescence if not insensibility. She wasn't going to be as easy a victim as Glynis and Rosa had been.

Constance hooked her heels into the runner with every step, leaving the long strip rumpled and askew—hopefully as obvious as a painted arrow.

Then they were at the stairs, and Edward all but pushed her down them.

Fear clutched at Constance's throat; with Edward's weight behind her, she couldn't stop her feet from descending.

$\sim$

Alaric and Percy had no idea who was at the rear of the gentlemen when, as a group, they'd quit the billiard room, but it was possible that Monty, with his habit of noting every little fact regardless of consequence, knew the answer.

Monty might even know who Rosa had stared at.

Sadly, it was equally possible that Monty had been just behind Alaric and had noticed no more than he.

Consequently, Alaric hadn't mentioned to the others the possibility that Monty might know, not wanting to get their hopes up only to dash them.

Especially given the somewhat fraught tension that had prevailed under the old oak.

Over the day, they'd followed several promising leads, and every one had fizzled out and left them with, at best, only a tantalizing snippet more of information regarding the murderer.

The pre-dinner gathering in the drawing room dragged on interminably. Alaric kept one eye on the door, waiting for Constance to appear. He'd intended to have her with him when he questioned Monty; however, she was taking her time. Admittedly, they'd been late going upstairs to change.

He was also watching Monty, who, as usual, was surrounded by others and chatting animatedly.

Alaric glanced at the clock. Dinner would soon be served, and he couldn't question Monty at the table.

Then Monty smiled and stepped back from the knot of guests with whom he'd been conversing; he paused by the wall, presumably catching his mental breath before joining the next group of guests.

Alaric glanced once more at the doorway—still empty—then walked to Percy's side, dipped his head, and murmured, "We need to speak with Monty."

Percy glanced at him, met his eyes, then rapidly made his excuses to Mrs. Finlayson and the colonel and followed Alaric as he cut across the room and cornered Monty.

Monty regarded Alaric warily. "What now?"

"A simple question," Alaric said as Percy joined him, halting by his side so that Monty was largely screened from the company. "On the night Rosa was murdered, when we—all the gentlemen—left the billiard room and headed for the drawing room, where in the scrum were you?"

Monty's brows rose. "You and Percy here were in the lead. I brought up the rear."

Thank God.

Alaric's heart leapt. He tried not to let himself hope too much—not yet. "Who was with you at the rear of the column?"

"Edward, Henry, Guy, and Robert."

All four of their principal suspects; Alaric felt his burgeoning hopes start to deflate.

"I don't suppose," Percy asked, "that you saw whether Rosa stared at a particular man before she came over faint."

Monty shot Percy a supercilious look. "Of course I did. It was Edward. No idea why she should turn so green at the sight—he's not bad looking, all in all, and he was turned out well enough—but she took one long gawp, then looked quite bilious."

"Edward?" Alaric fought to keep his voice down. "You're sure?"

Monty frowned as if offended. "Of course I'm sure. I was standing next to him."

"Good God!" Percy breathed.

Alaric swung around and scanned the guests. After a second, Percy copied him.

"Edward's not yet down, if that's who you're after," Monty informed them.

"He must have done a bunk." Percy sounded faintly panicked.

"Why?" Monty asked.

"Because he's the murderer," Percy hissed. "My God, I can barely believe it!"

Alaric was silent. Premonition stroked his nape with icy fingertips, and with increasing desperation, he scanned the guests again... "No. He hasn't left yet—Constance isn't here, either."

He didn't want to put the two circumstances together and make them one, but every instinct he possessed was screaming that was the case.

"I have to find Edward." Abruptly, he started for the door.

He had a terrible fear that when he found Edward, he'd find Constance as well.

Alaric forged a path through the guests, dimly aware of the surprise on many faces as he passed without the slightest hint of a smile. He strode into the hall. A swift glance back showed Percy hurrying after him and Monty—insatiably curious—trotting behind.

Jaw setting, Alaric reached the main stairs. His heart a stone lump in his chest, he took the steps three at a time.

He hit the first floor at a run, making for the ladies' wing. As he passed the mouth of the corridor leading down the west wing, he caught a glimpse of something out of place and turned his head and looked.

The door to Percy's room was wide open. Judging by the state of the runner, there'd been a struggle in the corridor before the door.

Alaric skidded to a halt, changed directions, and charged down the west wing. He barreled straight into Percy's room. The antechamber was empty. He rushed into the bedroom and wildly looked around, but it was empty—devoid of life—too.

Everything appeared undisturbed...except for the top right-hand drawer of the tallboy, which was hanging open.

Percy and Monty had piled into the room in Alaric's wake.

Like Alaric, they both looked around, then Monty pointed to a spot on the floor. "What's that?"

Alaric stalked over, bent, and swiped up a gold chain with a ring hanging from it.

Percy gave a cry. "That's the ring I gave Glynis."

Alaric dropped chain and ring into Percy's reaching hands. Panic was a drumbeat in his blood. Where was Constance?

All rational and irrational thoughts insisted Edward had her, yet...

Alaric stalked back into the anteroom and headed for the corridor. He should check her room just in case his instincts had it wrong.

He stepped out of Percy's door—and instantly saw the beaded reticule lying beneath a side table. Even more telling, the rucking of the runner was more extensive than he'd thought. The struggle had gone around the corner and all the way down the family wing to the rarely used west stairs.

He swore as Percy and Monty joined him. He pointed at the runner. "Edward seized Constance, and he's taken her that way."

He broke into a run, heading for the stairs.

He'd taken three strides when Monty called, "There they are!"

Alaric pulled up, swung around, and saw Monty staring out of a window. Alaric rushed to a closer window and looked out.

Edward was heaving and wrestling Constance along, pushing her before him onto one of the many paths that led into the surrounding woods. Seeing Edward manhandle Constance sent a surge of fury through Alaric, an emotion more intense than he'd experienced in decades.

Possibly ever.

Percy and Monty hurried up to look out of the same window.

"What the devil does he think he's doing?" Monty demanded.

Neither Percy nor Alaric answered. Alaric's mind was racing, thinking, considering... He glanced at Percy. "Does Edward know the woods?"

Grim faced, Percy nodded. "Not as well as you or I, but he's been visiting since he was a child."

Alaric looked back at the struggling figures. "She's slowing him down." Constance was no lightweight, and Alaric thanked God for it.

He hauled in a breath and fought to batten down his impulses. He had to think—quickly and clearly. He had to rescue Constance—yes!—but he also had to approach Edward and his captive in the right way; he couldn't —wouldn't—fail Constance, and rushing after the pair with no plan would risk doing precisely that.

The driving thud of his heart in his ears made it difficult to think, but... "Edward won't risk killing her too close to the house."

"*Killing her?*" Monty paled. "Good God!"

Alaric made up his mind. He swung to Percy and Monty. "Percy—I'll need you with me. Monty—go and send a groom hell for leather to the inn to fetch Stokes and the Adairs back. Whatever happens, we'll need them."

Monty boggled for a second, but then nodded and dashed off. He rounded the corner, and his footsteps were swallowed by the thunder of heavy feet determinedly marching closer.

Henry Wynne swung into sight; he was followed by Walker, Fletcher, Collins, and Viscount Hammond—all the unmarried gentlemen. In the lead, Wynne said, "We left the others to watch over the ladies. What's afoot?"

Alaric wanted to race after Constance, but there were lots of paths through the woods. It was possible he might lose Edward and Constance; he couldn't afford not to accept any and all help.

Impatience yanked at him; ruthlessly, he held it back. "Edward Mandeville is the murderer, and he's seized Miss Whittaker and dragged her into the woods. Obviously, we have to go after him—Percy and I know these woods like the backs of our hands, so we'll take point. It would help if you lot could follow as quickly *and* as quietly as you can. Unless we spook him, Edward won't kill Miss Whittaker too close to the house—he'll be thinking to ensure her body isn't quickly found so he can get away tomorrow. Once Percy and I figure out where he's heading— where he thinks to hide her body—we'll need the rest of you to fan out and then close in. Stopping Edward from killing Miss Whittaker...the only way might be through persuading him there's no longer any point to it."

Henry Wynne grimly nodded. "Understood. You go—we'll follow."

Alaric didn't wait a moment longer; he turned and raced for the stairs at the end of the wing. He plunged down, leaping down four steps at a time, Percy at his heels, just as when they'd been children.

There was nothing childish about what drove him now. Fear, urgency, and something much more powerful compelled him. He pushed through the half-open door at the bottom of the stairs and burst onto the lawn. He put his head down and raced, flat out, for the opening to the path along which Edward and Constance had gone.

The shadows of the wood closed around her, and still, Edward forced her on. She didn't make it easy for him but fought and made him battle for every step, ignoring the obscenities he hissed in her ear.

Despite the fear that clogged her throat, she vowed she would not give up—not in any way. She wouldn't be dead until she was; she could give up then. Right now, she had far too much to live for—to fight for.

Avenging Glynis.

Seeing her grandfather and her aunts again.

Alaric. And the possibility she'd sensed between them, the easy cama- raderie, the gentle light in his eyes.

She'd never had a man look at her as he did. He saw not just the large physique but the mind and soul her body sheathed.

From the first moment of meeting his eyes, she'd felt a connection, a link that had allowed her to be herself unrestrainedly, unreservedly.

Like now; she used her height and her weight and, for once, rejoiced in both. The combination made it impossible for Edward to easily manage her, not that any man ever had.

She doubted screaming now would do much good, so she didn't care that Edward still had his hand clamped over her lips. Forcing him to leave it there meant she could keep him, if not off balance, then without the purchase and leverage he would otherwise have had.

Indeed, from his mutterings, he seemed to have realized that killing her was going to be significantly more difficult than killing Glynis and Rosa had been. Apparently, the risk that she might break free and escape had led him to conclude he needed to take her farther away than he'd first intended... She hoped that would work in her favor, allowing Alaric and the others time to catch up with them.

She continued to hold panic and even fear at bay by concentrating on slowing their progress along the woodland paths. Edward seemed to know where he was going, but as he turned onto less-frequented ways, the uneven surfaces made it even easier for her to gain traction with her feet and deny him the next step—and make him grunt and heave to force her on, just for one step.

He remained determined, but so was she.

At one point, a tiny niggle of doubt found a gap in her armor and slipped into her mind, raising the question of why Alaric would race to rescue her. Somewhat to her surprise—in reality, she had no call on Alaric's protection—her inner self remained adamantly steadfast in believing that he would come. That he would follow them and seize her back. That he would rescue her from death at the hands of a madman—she who had never in her life needed rescuing by anyone, much less that anyone had offered.

Somewhere buried deep inside her lay the conviction that she could rely on Alaric Radleigh. That all the shared looks of complete comprehension and the apparently idle brushes of their hands over the past days had, indeed, meant something. Something both of them had set to one side to deal with Glynis's and then Rosa's murder.

Because ultimately, murder threatened them all, just as it threatened her now.

What she felt about Alaric burned strong and true inside her. She drew strength from the certainty, placed her trust in him, and continued to force Edward to fight for every foot of path.

She hoped she could keep him sufficiently busy wrestling with her that he didn't glance back and notice the trail he and she were leaving.

CHAPTER 11

*A*laric and Percy raced along the woodland paths. In the deepening twilight, they slipped and slid, but didn't slow. Courtesy of the scuffing left by both Constance's and Edward's shoes, the pair was easy to track.

Then the path veered onto rockier ground, and the trail became less certain.

His lungs working like bellows, Alaric forced himself to slow, to search for broken twigs and crushed leaves to make certain of the way. These woods were riddled with paths, intersecting and connecting in a complex web; he couldn't afford—Constance couldn't afford for him—to lose the trail.

Percy helped, wordlessly pointing the way if Alaric hadn't already picked it out. They passed through countless intersections, leaving twigs and rocks as markers for those following as they pressed deeper and deeper into the old woods.

Alaric fought to block out the thought of how far Edward would go—how long he would wait—before closing his hands about Constance's throat and choking the life from her. The image the thought conjured... If he allowed it to gain purchase in his mind, it would bring him to his knees.

How, exactly, he was going to seize Constance back, he didn't know —he only knew that he would. He had no idea what the price might be; he only knew he was ready to pay it.

"He's definitely heading somewhere," Percy panted from behind Alaric.

"Yes, but where?" That was the question. If they could guess, they might be able to skirt around and get there first... Alaric's jaw set. "He might know these woods, but he doesn't know we're in pursuit. He doesn't even know we know he's taken Constance." He was speaking as much for himself as for Percy. "He'll think he has time to stage Constance's death and concoct some believable tale to cover his absence and allow him to drive away tomorrow."

Twenty paces later, they came to a point where the path they were following split into three. The intersection lay on a rocky shelf worn smooth by the years; they searched in the waning light, but this time, they found nothing to say which way Edward and Constance had gone.

Alaric and Percy turned in slow circles, listening for all they were worth, but no sound—of birds startling into flight or annoyed by intruders —came to show them the way.

Eventually, with panic pricking beneath his skin, Alaric looked at Percy. They were on Mandeville land, and Percy knew it better than anyone. They were both breathing rapidly, both nursing stitches in their sides. Alaric bent over, bracing his hands on his knees. Percy dropped into a crouch opposite.

Alaric caught Percy's gaze. "We have to think like Edward." He paused, then went on, "He's displayed remarkable sangfroid throughout —he hasn't panicked prior to this, and I doubt he's panicking now. Instead, he's focused on his goal. He's obviously got some place in mind, some place where no one lives and that no one normally visits. And possibly where no one will think to look for a missing lady's body."

Percy nodded. "Edward's cold and calculating—he always has been."

"All right. So he's come this far." Alaric waved a hand to indicate the woods around them. "Think. What hidden-away place is he making for, one where considerable time will elapse before Constance's body is found?"

Alaric stared at Percy.

Percy looked back, then bit his lip. His expression said he'd thought of somewhere that fitted Edward's bill, but was too frightened to say—to take the responsibility.

Between them, Alaric had always been the leader and Percy the follower. This time, Alaric had to make Percy understand that he trusted

Percy's judgment, that in this instance, Percy's judgment was better than his own.

"Percy—we have to get this right. It'll be dark soon. Regardless, we're not going to have time to come back and try a different path." Alaric waved at the three paths before them. "You know these woods better than anyone, and I trust you in this. Which way do you think he's gone?"

His gaze meeting Alaric's, Percy hesitated for a moment more, then quietly said, "I think he's making for the old woodcutter's cottage—not the one they use now but the one from my grandfather's day. Do you remember it?"

Alaric blinked, dredging memories from early childhood. "Vaguely... and yes!" He straightened. "I think you're right." With renewed certainty and burgeoning vigor, Alaric swung to face the right-hand path. "It's this way, isn't it?"

"Yes." Percy rose from his crouch. "It's about a hundred, maybe two hundred yards on. The place is rickety and partly overgrown."

Perfect for Edward's purpose.

"Come on—and keep quiet." Paying attention to his own admonition, Alaric hurried on.

Resolve filled him; determination buoyed him.

At last, they were close. All he had to do now was reach the old cottage in time—before Edward succeeded in ripping from this world a treasure Alaric had only just found.

Despite Alaric's renewed hope, fear increasingly got the upper hand as he pounded along the path. The light was failing. Even though his lungs were burning, he pushed himself to go faster.

Instinct pricked like spurs, insisting he had to get there— *now!*—or risk losing Constance.

She wasn't even his, but he didn't care; she now stood in his mind as too precious to lose.

People loved her.

So did he.

Then ahead, the dark shadows fell away, revealing a clearing bathed in the last light of the dying day.

Fifty yards ahead, he saw Edward and Constance, stationary but still struggling.

A modicum of relief swept over Alaric; Constance still lived and breathed—and was still fighting.

She and Edward stood face to face in the clearing of beaten earth before the ruins of the tumbled-down cottage. Edward gripped Constance's wrists, one in each hand, while Constance was using her arms and Edward's hold on her wrists to fend him off.

Alaric's gaze had locked on the wrestling pair.

He saw Edward's jaw clench, then he exerted ferocious strength and overwhelmed Constance's spirited defense; a snarl curling his lips, Edward pushed close, released her wrists—and clamped his hands about her throat.

Alaric burst full tilt into the clearing.

Edward jerked back, head swinging toward the intrusion. He saw Alaric. Edward's jaw dropped, his features registering utter shock.

Relishing Edward's incredulous stare, Alaric, his gaze flicking only briefly to Constance, slowed to a halt.

Constance seized Edward's momentary distraction and wrenched free. Gasping, one hand rising to her throat, she staggered to the side, then stumbled and sank to the ground.

Free and out of Edward's reach—free of immediate danger; Alaric tracked her in his peripheral vision and deemed her safe where she was. He kept his eyes on Edward.

His hands now empty, Edward lowered his arms. His expression stated he was stunned to have been found, let alone caught in the act.

His own expression the definition of implacable, Alaric started forward again, his gait a predatory stalk.

Evidently reading his fate in Alaric's eyes, Edward snapped his jaw shut, took one step back, reached into his coat pocket, and whipped out a pistol.

Alaric halted—truly surprised—as Edward trained the barrel on his chest.

For an instant, absolute silence reigned.

"Don't take another step," Edward ordered. His aim was steady; even now, he wasn't panicking.

To Alaric's right, Constance scrambled to her feet. "Don't be a fool."

Edward swung the pistol her way. "Stay back!" Immediately, he retrained the barrel on Alaric.

"What are you going to do?" Constance's tone dripped contempt. "You can't kill both of us with a one-shot pistol."

Alaric inwardly groaned; he wished she'd refrained from pointing that out.

Edward's gaze flicked to her, then returned to Alaric. "I've discovered I'm rather good at improvising."

Alaric knew Percy had been behind him on the path, yet Edward hadn't even glanced toward the path's opening. Without shifting his gaze, using only his peripheral sight, Alaric scanned the edges of the clearing— and saw a bush to the left quiver. A few seconds later, branches farther around the clearing shifted, then stilled.

He hoped it was Percy creeping around to come up behind Edward and not just a curious deer. Alaric wasn't sure what his old friend might be planning, but it would obviously be wise to keep Edward's attention fixed on him.

Locking his gaze more definitely with Edward's, Alaric took one deliberate step closer.

Edward's eyes darkened. His grip on the pistol tightened. "Not one more step," he rapped out. He was starting to sound a tad tense.

Given Constance had already mentioned it... Alaric arched his brows. "So which of us are you going to shoot?"

The answer was obvious. Edward's eyes shifted from Alaric to Constance, then back again. Despite his masklike expression, Edward was clearly starting to work out a plan.

Not wanting him to get too far with that, Alaric manufactured a sigh. "Regardless, tell me why. Why did you strangle Glynis? That's hardly the sane thing to do if your intention was to keep the family escutcheon unblemished."

The mention of Edward's abiding obsession served to remind Alaric —and he hoped Constance and Percy as well—that Edward would do damned near anything to protect the family name.

For a moment, Edward plainly struggled—either against the urge to explain or simply to find the most acceptable words with which to justify his actions; he was so rarely off balance that in any other circumstances, the sight would have been priceless.

Regardless, Edward couldn't resist Alaric's invitation. "The stupid chit!" Edward's lip curled. "That night, I heard Percy go down the west-wing stairs—naturally I followed, and I saw him meet her in the gazebo. From what happened, it was plain she had her claws sunk into him, so I waited until they parted and stepped into her path—literally and figuratively. I told her she would never be permitted to marry Percy—and the twit pulled out the ring Percy had given her and brandished it in my face! It was the viscountess's ring the idiot had given her—the Lord only knows what he was thinking. Or if he thought at all. He couldn't have married her—a flighty girl from a no-account family. Obviously, I had to save him from himself. I demanded she give me the ring, but she refused. I grabbed it, but the silly bint started screeching. I had to shut her up—" Edward broke off.

A silent second passed; Alaric wanted to look at Constance, but didn't dare shift his gaze from Edward's.

Then Edward shrugged. "And then she was dead."

Alaric didn't hide his contempt. "So you left her there for anyone to find."

"It was better that way. Anyone could have killed her. Because I left her where she fell, her death was no threat to anyone."

"But it was you, Edward, who killed her—a perfectly innocent, blameless young lady."

"What gave you the right?" Constance's voice grated with suppressed fury.

Edward sneered. "It's perfectly obvious. The Mandevilles are an old family with a revered name. She couldn't be allowed to reach so high— she shouldn't have even thought of it. You and your family should have managed her better—kept her under better control. A chit like her couldn't expect to marry into a family like the Mandevilles."

Constance's eyes had narrowed to shards. "So it's *her family's* fault that you murdered her?"

Alaric almost smiled; in terms of dishing out excoriating scorn, Edward was well and truly outclassed. But Alaric could now see Percy; he was creeping out of the wood directly behind Edward, but Percy was still too far away to make any difference.

Alaric focused on Edward. "What about Rosa? She recognized you, so you killed her, too?"

"I would have let her live if she hadn't realized who she'd seen leaving the shrubbery. But in the corridor outside the billiard room, she saw something that told her the mystery man was me." Edward paused, then amended, "At least, I think she realized, although she didn't say anything then. But I couldn't take the risk that she would speak to Sir Godfrey in the morning. He might not have believed her, but others might have. So she had to die, too—in the scale of such things, her life didn't weigh against the honor of the Mandevilles."

Constance choked. *"Honor?"*

"Yes, honor." Edward's expression grew even more supercilious. "It's not something you or Miss Johnson would know anything about."

Percy had reached the side of the ruined cottage; Alaric saw him bend and carefully—silently—lift a stout log from the debris.

"So now," Alaric said, "in the name of the Mandeville honor, you're going to kill me and Miss Whittaker." Percy was drawing closer. Alaric had to keep Edward's every sense locked on him. He conjured a puzzled expression. "How do you justify that, Edward? The Radleighs are older than the Mandevilles by a century or more, and the families have been allies forever."

Edward frowned and shifted his weight. "You shouldn't have butted in. No one asked you to meddle in the investigation. If you hadn't, the deaths would have been accounted for by now—that fool Stonewall would have happily done as I wished, and we wouldn't have Scotland Yard poking their noses in and threatening scandal for everyone."

"One thing puzzles me," Constance said; Alaric realized she could now see Percy creeping up behind Edward. "If it was the family you wanted to protect, why did you put the letters—and later intend to put the ring—into Percy's drawer?"

Edward's eyes were shifting from Alaric to Constance and back again, assessingly, measuringly; he replied rather vaguely, "I assumed he would have the sense to hide them, and if they were found…well, if one of the family had to be convicted, better him than me. After all, it was his fault all of this happened."

Alaric couldn't hide his disgust.

Edward straightened and raised his head. "I've made up my mind." Something flared in his eyes. "I'll shoot you, then strangle Miss Whittaker, and arrange things to look like you killed her, then shot yourself."

Alaric could see the increased tension in Edward's arm; the hand holding the pistol had started to shake, the barrel wavering. "Why would I kill her?"

Edward cut a swift glance at Constance. "Because she spurned your advances. I've seen the way you look at her, and I'm sure others have, too, but she's a virtuous lady and wouldn't welcome the attentions of a rakehell like you."

Constance snorted. "Much you know." Her scorn was once again given full rein.

Alaric noted that, but distantly. Percy was nearly close enough…

They needed Edward's full attention trained on Alaric for just a few seconds more.

Alaric fabricated a massive, transparently resigned sigh. "Very well. But at least have the goodness to take the time to calm down and make it a clean shot. I have no wish to die messily."

Edward blinked, but then nodded. "All right." He drew in a deep breath and settled to sight along the barrel. "I'm glad you're taking this so well—"

Using two hands, Percy heaved up the log and brought it down on Edward's head.

The pistol discharged.

Edward's eyes rolled up, and he crumpled to the ground.

Her heart in her throat, Constance flung herself at Alaric.

Wonder of wonders, the man stood his ground and caught and steadied her; he didn't even stagger.

Her senses registered those facts, but her mind was awash with fear—for him. And that she might lose him—lose any chance she might have had…

His arms had come up to hold her. She pulled back and gripped his upper arms. "Are you all right?" Without waiting for a reply, she ran her hands frantically over his face, shoulders, and chest. "Where did the shot go?"

Even she heard the frantic note in her voice.

His lips curved gently, and he caught her hands, trapping them between his. "Into the trees to my left." For a moment, he looked into her face, his gaze searching her eyes.

What she saw in his…

Her heart swelled. She threw caution to the winds, freed her hands, and framed his face and kissed him.

Passionately. With all the pent-up emotion in her soul.

Then his arms locked her to him, and he was kissing her back…

For the first time in her life, she understood what it felt like to swoon.

Confident and assured, his lips moved on hers, then his tongue stroked languidly over her lips and, when they parted, slid within to caress and claim and subtly conquer.

Sounds penetrated the fog of joy and rising desire that held them, reminding them of where they were—that they weren't alone.

Together, they eased back—then she remembered and broke the kiss and glared at him. "You blithering idiot! Couldn't you think of any other way to distract him besides offering yourself for target practice?"

His slow grin reminded her that he saw her far more clearly than any other ever had. "I love you, too."

She blushed and fell into his eyes again.

Reading her expression—open and direct as it always was—Alaric felt as if his heart had taken flight. He bent his head and brushed her lips with his. When, reluctantly, he raised his head, he couldn't miss the stars in her eyes.

He wondered what his looked like.

He tightened his arms around her for a second, then they drew apart and looked to where Percy stood over Edward.

Edward was unconscious, sprawled on the ground. Percy still held the log in his hands, hefting it as if considering…

Alaric stiffened. "Percy?"

Gently, Constance said, "You don't need to hit him again."

Percy's gaze was locked on the back of Edward's head; his expression was tortured and torn. "He killed Glynis." The words were condemnation and sentence.

"Yes. But you don't need to descend to his level." Alaric glanced toward the path to see Stokes and company approaching. "You can leave retribution to the law and Scotland Yard."

Still, Percy stared down at Edward and gripped the log, his hands shifting as he adjusted his hold.

"And one murderer in a family is enough," Constance said.

That seemed to penetrate Percy's emotion-driven brain. He blinked and eased back. Then he glanced at Stokes, who, with Barnaby and Penelope, was nearing. Percy lowered the log, then opened his hands and let it fall to the ground. He stepped away from the now-groaning Edward. "You're right." He glanced contemptuously down at Edward. "As it is, my uncle and aunt will never live this down."

Stokes halted beside Alaric, and Constance asked, "How did you get here so soon?"

"We never left," Penelope said as she and Barnaby joined them. "Stokes and Barnaby wanted to hear the maid's evidence for themselves, and I wanted to hear the footman's testimony. We'd only just started for the stable when Mr. Radleigh raced up. We followed the trail as quickly as we could, then we caught up with the other gentlemen, and they explained Alaric's instructions, so we fell in with them." She waved at the four gentlemen who were stepping into the clearing from various directions. "When we got here, Edward already had his pistol out. We could see Percy sneaking up, and we didn't want to push Edward into seizing a hostage, so we hung back."

"Thank God you did." Alaric looked at Stokes. "Edward Mandeville isn't all that good at planning or even thinking things through, but as he himself said, he's proved surprisingly adept at improvising. God alone knows what might have happened had you shown yourselves."

Stokes clapped Alaric on the shoulder. "You seemed to have everything in hand."

"Although," Penelope said, head tipping consideringly to one side, "for my money, you cut things a little too fine."

Constance snorted.

Alaric waved at Edward, who was starting to regain consciousness. "Did you hear?"

His expression grimly satisfied, Stokes nodded. "More than enough." He glanced at the other men who, led by Monty, had gathered around Percy, some with words and others wordlessly offering support. "And if required, we have witnesses galore."

Barnaby shifted. "To tell the truth, despite the drama—which we would all rather have done without—this has worked out for the best. There simply wasn't and never would have been enough evidence to bring Edward to book for the murders. Everything we could gather was circumstantial. He had to do or say something—only through his own words or actions could we hope to convict him." Barnaby's smile wasn't humorous. "And now we will."

Stokes walked forward, bent, and retrieved the spent pistol. He showed it to Percy. "Is this his, or did he filch it from the Hall?"

Percy peered at the pistol, then shook his head. "It's not one of mine."

Stokes's grin was lethal. "Even better." He looked around. "Philpott? Morgan?"

"Here, sir." The two constables came jogging up.

Stokes tipped his head at Edward, who was slowly dragging himself up to sit, one hand held to the back of his head. "Put the shackles on him and take him away. The Tabard will most likely have a cellar you can lock him in. Make sure he hasn't anything he might use to do himself in."

"Yes, sir!" Philpott, assisted by Morgan, quickly had Edward up on his feet, his wrists locked before him in heavy cuffs.

Stokes, with Barnaby and Penelope flanking him, told Edward what would be done with him.

Sullen, Edward made no reply, but he was still weaving on his feet.

"Once he recovers enough to find his tongue," Constance observed, "I'm sure he'll be claiming all sorts of justifications for what he's done."

"Much good will it do him," Alaric said. He doubted he would ever forget the sight of Edward with his hands locked about Constance's throat.

The other gentlemen were ready to head back to the Hall. Several, including Monty, urged Percy to go with them, and as host, Percy acquiesced.

Percy paused beside Alaric and met his eyes. "Thank you for letting me hit him."

Alaric inclined his head. "Thank you for doing it in time."

Percy glanced at Constance, but she only dipped her head in agreement.

Percy nodded and clapped Alaric on the shoulder. "I'll see you both back at the house."

The gentlemen and Percy led the way. The constables with their prisoner stumbling between them followed, and Stokes, Barnaby, and Penelope fell in behind them.

Hand in hand, Alaric and Constance brought up the rear, both content to amble slowly through the thickening shadows and let the evening peace of the woods enfold them, easing all lingering tensions.

After a while, catching a glimpse of Percy and the gentlemen ahead on the path, Constance murmured, "Do you think Percy will be all right? That he'll recover?"

Alaric had been turning that very question over in his mind. After a moment of searching for the right words, he answered, "Marrying Glynis would have been good for him—I don't think anyone who knows him and had ever been even acquainted with her could doubt that. But being married to her wouldn't have changed him—he would still have been the old Percy we all know. However"—he paused, then went on—"I have an inkling that having Glynis taken from him—ripped from his arms, so to speak—might well be the making of Percy."

They walked on for a moment, then he glanced down, met her eyes, and gently smiled. "We'll see."

Constance pondered his words, then she leaned her head against his shoulder. "Thank you. If Glynis's death does even that much good…that will be some small comfort to the family."

Alaric glanced at her head, resting against his shoulder, then he bent his head and placed a kiss on her curls.

And as night fell about them, they walked on—back to the Hall, back to society, back to lives that had changed forever.

When Alaric and Constance reached the Hall, they found Stokes, Barnaby, and Penelope facing a demanding audience in the drawing room. All those who had remained—the ladies and the married couples—wanted to know the details of all that had transpired.

Barnaby took the lead, with Penelope assisting, while Stokes spoke only when it was necessary to insert the gravitas now accruing to Scotland Yard.

Alaric and Constance hung back by the door and watched and listened. At one point, Constance murmured, "I'm remembering all the less-than-complimentary remarks made earlier regarding the police."

Alaric smiled cynically. "Stokes has done well by his office. None of those here will cast such aspersions again."

"And they'll spread the word," Constance added.

When Penelope outlined their speculation that, on quitting the billiard room, Edward Mandeville's manner of settling his coat had been idiosyncratic enough to jog Rosa Cleary's memory and identify him as Glynis's murderer, Monty spoke up and agreed, saying that Edward invariably jerked both lapels to settle his shoulders, stiffly tweaked his right sleeve, then his left, and finally passed his right hand over his hair before patting down the back of his collar.

Several others confirmed Monty's description, which pleased Stokes as well as Penelope.

Eventually, the story of Edward Mandeville's latest attempt at murder and his subsequent capture was exhaustively told.

Those of the company who hadn't previously heard the complete accounting of his doings sat back and exchanged wide-eyed looks.

"I can't believe it was *Edward*!" Mrs. Collard shook her head. "My parents know his parents—they're so very stuffy and strict, it's all but impossible to imagine Edward, of all people, committing such atrocious acts."

"I don't know." Henry Wynne looked at Percy. "Edward was always rabbiting on about the Mandeville family and how dashed superior they were—above all of us, certainly. When I heard him in that clearing... well, it seemed all of a piece."

Monty nodded gravely. "All the pieces fitted neatly together. It was Edward first to last."

"Indeed," Stokes said. "And as Mr. Mandeville has helpfully confessed in the hearing of a great many witnesses, I can assure you all that this case will be closed, and he will stand trial and be convicted in due course."

"Where is the fiend now?" Mrs. Cripps rather anxiously asked.

"Locked up beneath the Tabard Inn," Stokes replied. "We'll be taking him to London tomorrow. You won't see him again."

People turned to each other, and the sound of avid chatter rose as they exclaimed and speculated on the likely social repercussions.

Monty had been standing along the wall beyond Constance; he came up to her and Alaric. "I say!" Monty looked thoroughly chuffed. "Quite exciting, that chase through the woods and then the action in the clearing. Mind you, I'm glad it wasn't me looking down the barrel of Edward's pistol."

Alaric laconically arched his brows.

Constance humphed, but without heat. Everything had worked out, no one else had been harmed, and the murderer was in shackles.

And she was leaning on Alaric's arm.

Guy Walker and Mrs. Gibson strolled up to ask whether Alaric would be heading back to London soon.

While they had Alaric's attention, Monty tugged Constance's sleeve. When she looked his way and arched a brow, he leaned closer and murmured, "Just wanted to say how pleased I am." His gaze shifted to Alaric and back to her, his eyes wide, his gaze warm. "And to let you know how delighted the whole family will be—they'll welcome you with open arms. You can take my word on that—they've been waiting for years for Alaric to make his choice."

Constance felt Monty might be rushing his fences, yet rather than saying so, curiosity prompted her to ask, "But aren't you his heir?"

Monty grinned. "Yes, but the last thing I or anyone else in the family would ever want to see is me inheriting. Good Lord—that would be a disaster!"

She had to smile at the comical look on Monty's face. As it faded, she touched his arm. "Thank you for your vote of confidence." She glanced at Alaric. "I don't know what might come to pass, but…thank you."

Monty gave her a strange look, then grinned again. "Trust me— there's no doubt at all about his direction. Take it from one who's known him from birth." He paused, then added, "Mine, that is—he's older than me."

Constance couldn't help but laugh.

Smiling, Monty tipped his head to her and moved off to speak with Henry Wynne and Mrs. Humphries.

Constance surveyed the company. Many were discussing their arrangements to leave the next day. Most, she suspected, would make a beeline for their favorite center of gossip to gleefully relate the scandalous details of the murders at Mandeville Hall.

For herself…

She'd seen Glynis avenged and her murderer brought to justice; that had been her goal in remaining at the Hall.

There really wasn't any other reason for her to stay.

Except…

She looked at Alaric—to find him waiting to catch her eye. Mr. Walker and Mrs. Gibson had moved on, leaving Alaric and Constance in their own quiet spot in the room.

She couldn't drag her gaze from his—from the promise she could see in the hazel brightness.

He smiled, reached for her hand, closed his fingers about hers, and gently tugged. "Come with me." His voice had lowered to a tone meant solely for her. His eyes held hers. "There's something I want to show you."

There was a great deal more behind the simple words.

A great deal more she wanted to explore.

She nodded, gripped his hand, and placed her trust in him. And knew, in her heart, that she could and always would.

CHAPTER 12

$\mathcal{W}$hat Alaric wanted to show her was a view of his home by moonlight. The moon had waxed over the past days; now it bathed Carradale Manor in a silvery light.

"This," he said, halting and drawing her to stand before him and wrapping his arms about her waist, "is my favorite sight. Daylight does it justice, but moonlight…"

"Turns it magical." She could see it—sense it. She relaxed against him, and it felt natural. Normal. As things should be—feeling the strength of his body against hers, supporting her, protecting her. Something no other man had ever presumed to do.

She could laugh at that now, at her prickly former self. Accepting this sort of protection from a man like him—an instinctive protection offered with no thought of recompense—was no weakness.

Indeed, she was starting to view partnership as a strength.

And heaven knew she'd always been attracted to strength.

It was a quality he had in abundance—not just physical strength, not just mental acuity, but that inner strength that defined the true mettle of a man.

"This sight," he said, his voice low but clear, "embodies my life. My home, my estate, my responsibilities. My future." He paused, then went on, "I know we only met days ago, but I wanted to show you this…and ask you not to leave. I wanted to beg you to come and live with me here, through peace and prosperity and whatever else comes."

"And are you? Asking me? Begging me?"

"Yes."

She found she couldn't breathe, then his hands shifted at her waist, and she turned within his arms to face him.

To look into his face, the planes sharp and defined, chiseled by an artist's hand.

To fall into his eyes, shadowed though they were, into the depths that tempted and held her.

To understand that he spoke from the heart when he said, "Marry me, Constance, and stay."

She felt as if her heart leapt—reaching for him, for the future he offered. Challenges there would be, but there was no question in her mind or her soul that this was what she wanted. What she had always craved.

"Yes." The word fell from her lips.

Her gaze locked with his, she could think of no more she needed to say; the magnitude of what he had so simply proposed and she had, equally simply, accepted lay manifestly clear between them. They weren't the sort of people to broach such matters lightly, on a whim.

All of that passed between them, borne on the near-tangible link of their gazes.

Then his lips lightly curved, and he bent his head, and she stretched up, just an inch, and their lips met.

Fused as they kissed; now they no longer needed to exercise restraint, the kiss burgeoned and deepened, and desire flowered.

It was she who stepped closer and pressed her body to his, then his arms tightened, and he crushed her to him. Her senses sang as their tongues tangled, as he explored and she welcomed, and the kiss spun on.

When they eventually drew back, their lips parting by the merest fraction—hungry still—they were both breathing rapidly.

He touched his forehead to hers. "Come to the manor." The words whispered over her lips, then he took them again, confident, assured, demanding, yet not overwhelming. "Come and be my lady, tonight and forevermore."

She didn't answer with words. Instead, she framed his face and replied with a kiss laden with her own brand of passion.

Eventually, they drew apart and, with their senses alive and their bodies thrumming, walked hand in hand through the moon-dappled darkness of the wood to the house on the rise—to Carradale Manor. They approached from the stable; the house lay slumbering, wrapped in peace, as they walked around it to the front door. He opened it with his latchkey and drew her inside.

He led her up the stairs and around the gallery to the room above the front door.

He bowed her in, and with a smile, she walked into the room. She halted four paces inside, in the middle of a space before a set of windows flanking a French door that gave onto the semicircular balcony above the front porch, and took stock. A luxuriously large bed lay to her right, while to her left, two armchairs sat angled before a huge fireplace. Minor doors flanked the fireplace; she assumed they would lead to a bathing chamber and a dressing room.

She turned to him as, having followed her inside and closed the door, he joined her.

Whether he drew her into his arms or she went to him was moot. The hunger they'd incited in the depths of the wood had simmered, swelled, and grown; it invested their kiss, turning it demanding, commanding—driving them on.

Hunger deepened to need and infused each caress, prickling their skins, turning each touch increasingly urgent. Spreading through their veins, that heated desire lured, captured, and whipped them on.

Her gown slid to the floor on a susurrating sigh. His coat, cravat, and waistcoat followed. Her petticoats and his shirt.

His hands closed about her heavy breasts, still shielded by the silk of her chemise. She moaned as his fingers, strong and sure, closed, massaging, then framing the aching peaks, and he uttered a guttural growl.

She'd thought she'd known what lovemaking was—what it entailed, what it felt like. He opened her eyes.

To the thrills of desire, to the tactile joys of passion harnessed and wielded with skill.

He was beyond experienced; to say he played her body like an instrument would be no lie. His hands stroked her skin until it burned. His fingers found nerves she hadn't known she possessed and set them afire. As for his mouth and his wicked tongue... She gasped, clutched, and clung—and urged him on in every possible way.

He lavished untold delight and near-unimaginable pleasure upon her, with an unstinting devotion that struck to her heart.

Never before had her senses soared beyond the earthly realm.

Never before had she felt so alive—so worshipped, so beloved, so blessed.

So filled with heat, passion, and joy that she had to share—wholly and completely. Without reservation or reticence.

And he, sophisticated and worldly, let her—let her have her turn at touching, stroking, and caressing, and using her lips and tongue and her mouth to storm his senses.

Need escalated and passion flamed, and finally, he rolled her to her back in the rumpled sheets and came over her, stretching his long body the length of hers and parting her thighs with his. On a near-frantic gasp, she wrapped her arms about him and urged him on, and at last, he joined them; eyes closed the better to savor the moment, she felt him thrust deep and fill her.

No sensation had ever felt so exquisite. So necessary and needed.

To her senses, no star in the heavens had ever burned as brightly as they did in that instant.

She opened her eyes and stared into his and saw all she felt reflected back at her. Then, palms locked, fingers entwined, body to body, their lips again seeking each other's, they started to dance, and the age-old rhythm caught them. With every thudding heartbeat, they moved faster, pushed harder; the friction between them became a searing whip, and they strove, racing and plunging and seizing and wanting.

Until in a rush of dizzying splendor, they were there, teetering on the cusp of fulfillment, and with one last long thrust, one last sobbing moan from her and a low groan from him, they touched heaven and fell.

Senses shattering, fragmenting, their bodies consumed in sensation's furnace, they clung and gloried.

Then passion's starburst faded; held safe in each other's arms, they spiraled back to earth.

To the rucked sheets and disarranged covers of his bed.

In the aftermath, they lay wrapped in peace and contentment, the glow of satiation still warm beneath their skins.

She lay on her back, staring in something like awe at the ceiling, her mind still submerged in the fading sensations.

He'd disengaged and slumped beside her, one heavy arm thrown over her waist, his face half buried in the pillow beside her head.

After several long moments, he shifted his head and brushed a kiss to her temple. "You weren't a virgin." Statement, not a question.

She thought before she replied, "Does it bother you that I wasn't?"

It was his turn to think; his silence suggested it was a point he'd never before considered. Eventually, he humphed softly. "Not really. After all, I definitely wasn't."

She chuckled, then offered, "There was just one—a young man long ago. He was a soldier and was posted overseas. He was killed before we could wed."

"In that case, I can pity him—to have found heaven and then lost it."

She smiled and tipped her head to touch his.

After a moment, he turned on his side and somewhat disgruntledly said, "I'm discovering that when it comes to you, I'm more...possessive than I ever thought to be. Just as long as he truly is in your past, and you're willing to give your present and future to me."

She heard the underlying vulnerability in his tone—not an emotion she associated with him. Beneath his arm, she wriggled around to face him so she could look into his eyes and say, "I am, and I have."

He read the commitment in her eyes, and his expression eased. A second later, the ends of his lips kicked up. "I suppose I'll have to be on my mettle then, to ensure that what we share transcends the joys and pleasures of first love."

She held his gaze and confessed, "I wasn't in love with him. I thought I was, of course, but I now know that what I felt for him wasn't truly love. It was hope and expectation at best. I know that now—now that I know what love truly is."

His brows rose; his expression remained serious, his gaze intent. "And what is love to you now?"

She raised a hand and cradled his lean cheek. "Love is powerful. Strong. It's impossible to deny, impossible to turn away from, and equally impossible to mistake."

He covered her hand with his, then turned his head and, lids lowering, pressed a kiss to her palm. "And you haven't mistaken this?"

"No." As he looked back at her, she caught his eyes. "I love you. Even had you not spoken—even had I departed still alone—I would still love you. I will until I die."

His slow smile, the one she'd realized was always genuine, curved his lips. His hazel eyes seemed to brighten. "Good. That's only fair. Because I love you, Constance mine, and will until the stars collide and the earth is no more."

She laughed—more joyous and carefree than she could remember being since childhood. Then she shook her head at him. "I can't think of words to trump that."

"Never mind." He shifted onto his back, lifted a muscled arm over her head, and tucked her against his side. "We can keep a running tab. We'll have years to continue the competition before we need to tally it."

She chuckled, spread one hand on his chest, and settled her head in the hollow of his shoulder.

Alaric sighed. Contentment of a degree he'd never known before slid through him. Along with the realization that she was his perfect mate—his counterpart, the lady who made him whole and complete—and that she would be with him forevermore.

"I'm thirty-seven. I never expected to find love." He didn't know where the words came from; the depth of his contentment had, apparently, loosed the reins on his tongue. "I never truly believed in it, not even as a concept. Moving through the ton as I did, I saw too much to place any faith in what is commonly held to be love. The few genuine cases I stumbled across—like the Adairs—I viewed as aberrations, the exceptions that proved the rule." He paused, then said, "You have to admit that the Adairs as a couple are singularly unconventional."

"Yes and no—it depends on your perspective." Constance tapped his chest. "But go on—you were saying…"

"That being thirty-seven—and you've met Monty, so you'll understand the necessity—I'd accepted that I needed to find a bride. Over the last weeks, while organizing everything in preparation for making an offer, I've been trying to define what sort of lady would be the ideal wife for me." He paused, then said, "Don't laugh, but I'd concluded that the right sort of wife for me would be a sweet, gentle, and compliant lady. Then I met Glynis. After I spoke with her, I realized she would have fitted the bill I'd drawn up, but that she or any like her would, in short order, bore me to tears. On Monday night, after I left Mandeville Hall and returned here to my cold bed, I discovered that I had absolutely no idea what criteria I should look for in my perfect wife."

He waited, but she neither moved nor spoke; knowing she couldn't see, he allowed his lips to curve. "Then I met you, and I knew. I didn't need to cudgel my brains further. And despite my past skepticism, once Cupid struck, I—like you—discovered that I couldn't deny what I feel. Not just what it is, but that it's so much more than simply a *feeling*."

After a second, she said, "Love is a connection."

"Yes. Just that. I felt it the first time I laid eyes on you—even over Glynis's dead body with you all but accusing me of having killed her."

"I know. I felt it, too. It was as if a link clicked into place, and thereafter, whenever anything at all happened, the very first thought to pop into my head was what you would think of it."

He tightened his arms around her, gently squeezing, and dropped a kiss on her curls. "Sharing. Love is sharing."

"And partnership—like the Adairs, but scripted for us. Working together."

"Learning of each other and exploring life together."

"Trusting." Constance knew she'd finally put her finger on what was, for her, the most vital aspect. She turned in Alaric's strong arms and raised her head to look into his eyes. "Love is trusting implicitly and never fearing to be betrayed."

His hazel eyes held hers. "Love is belonging, heart and soul, to the other. You are my other half, and as long as we live, no power on earth will set us asunder."

Constance read that truth—that vow—in his eyes, then stretched up and set her lips to his.

They sealed their troth—pledged their future and their lives—in a kiss that came from the depths of their souls.

Alaric and Constance would have happily spent the following day entirely at the manor, putting the necessary arrangements in place for the announcement of their betrothal and for the wedding they were determined would follow soon after.

But both had unstated commitments at Mandeville Hall, and neither was the sort to let such matters slide.

In midmorning, they walked back through the woods. They walked around the Hall, passing the entrance to the shrubbery with a single long glance.

The front door stood wide, and when they stepped into the front hall, they found it abuzz with maids and footmen running this way and that, and a faintly harassed-looking Carnaby directing the gathering and sorting of the guests' luggage.

Luckily, there were no guests hovering to see Constance arrive in the same gown she'd worn the previous evening.

Alaric met her eyes. "I'll find Percy and see how he's faring. And I need to speak with Monty as well."

She arched a brow. "To tell him our news?"

Alaric smiled and inclined his head. "That and other things."

"I'll come and find you after I've changed and spoken with Mrs. Macomber and given Pearl and Vine instructions to decamp."

They parted at the base of the stairs, Constance going swiftly up, dodging a pair of footmen heaving a traveling trunk down to the hall, while Alaric strode for the drawing room.

Constance found Mrs. Macomber in the room they'd shared. The older woman was in a despondent, dejected state—no doubt worrying over what was to become of her—and, on seeing Constance still in her evening gown, clearly didn't know whether to be openly scandalized or whether perhaps she should pretend she hadn't leapt to the obvious conclusion.

Pearl was there, too, packing Constance's things into her trunk; at the sight of Constance, Pearl's eyes had widened, and as her gaze lingered on Constance's face, they widened even more.

Closing the door, Constance smiled—radiantly. After a swift glance at Pearl, who was starting to relax and look pleased, Constance turned to Mrs. Macomber and put the elderly chaperon out of her misery. "Lord Carradale and I are to marry."

Mrs. Macomber's eyes flew wide, and her mouth fell open. Abruptly, she sat on the edge of her bed.

Pearl's smile was almost as brilliant as Constance's.

Before Mrs. Macomber could gather her wits and speak, Constance rolled on, "However, given the sudden nature of our betrothal, we—Carradale and I—wondered if you would consent to extending your service to the Whittaker family and act as my companion for at least the next weeks. We plan to remain in Hampshire"—Constance waved toward the woods—"at Carradale's house nearby, for the next week or two, while we make arrangements to travel north to visit my grandfather so Carradale can formally ask for my hand."

Mrs. Macomber gaped, but then gathered her wits and, after offering her congratulations, declared that she would be honored to act as Constance's companion for however long her services were required.

Pearl was even more chuffed. She whisked out a fresh walking dress and helped Constance out of her creased evening gown and into the nicely fitted forest-green dress. "Carradale's a right one—anyone can see that. I did wonder, what with him charging out to rescue you. So now you're to be a lady and all." Pearl grinned cheekily. "I've always wanted to be a proper lady's maid."

Constance laughed.

As soon as Pearl finished brushing out her hair and refashioning it into a chignon, Constance gave her orders to Pearl, who volunteered to carry the good news to Vine and oversee the transfer of their luggage, as well as Mrs. Macomber and her boxes, to the manor. "We'll take the coach and drive around. Someone in the stables here will tell us the way."

"Excellent." Constance turned for the door. "I have to rejoin Carradale. The staff at the manor are expecting you. The butler is Morecombe, and his wife is the housekeeper, and the other one you'll meet is Carradale's man, Johns. Tell Vine the stableman is Hilliard."

"We'll manage." Pearl shooed. "Go. Go."

Mrs. Macomber, almost overcome, gave her a bright if watery smile.

Feeling as giddy as a girl buoyed on happiness, Constance rushed back to the stairs and went down. Alaric was standing beside Percy inside the open front door. Most of the guests appeared to have congregated in the hall as well.

Inspector Stokes and the Adairs had, apparently, just arrived and were greeting Percy and Alaric.

As Constance joined the small group, all three Londoners welcomed her with a smile. The other guests, she noted, were keeping a polite distance.

"We're about to head back to London." With a wave, Stokes indicated the coach drawn up before the door. His gaze returned to Percy. "I wanted to formally inform you that I've reviewed the charges and the evidence, and I'm confident of making our case against Edward Mandeville. My constables are escorting him to the Yard to be charged —they started off at first light. In due course, he'll be tried, and there's no reason to doubt that he will be found guilty and, eventually, will hang."

"We thought you might like to know," Barnaby said, "so that you can prepare your family."

His expression contained, Percy inclined his head. "Thank you. I intend setting off later today to speak with my father. I'll leave it to him to pass the news on to Edward's parents." Percy hesitated, then asked, "Did he—Edward—show any remorse?"

Stokes met Percy's gaze and, stoically, shook his head. "No." Stokes paused for a heartbeat, then added, "In my experience, his sort rarely do. They believe their end justifies any means."

After a second's silence, Penelope said, "But for the rest of us, our lives go on." She turned to Constance and smiled. "And at least for now, we must make our farewells."

They proceeded to do so, the men shaking hands and Penelope and Constance being bowed to and having their fingers bussed.

As Alaric straightened from kissing Penelope's fingers, she widened her eyes and said, "Incidentally, we will be expecting an invitation to the wedding." She caught Alaric's eye, an intrigued and inquiring look in hers.

Alaric laughed and drew Constance to him. "The wedding is already in train, although we haven't addressed the guest list yet."

Beaming smiles and congratulations ensued.

Barnaby told Constance, "You and Carradale must call on us when next you're in London. Number twenty-four Albemarle Street."

Penelope seconded the invitation, then Stokes and the Adairs took their leave on a tide of good wishes.

Then the other guests—who, of course, had overheard—gathered around to congratulate Alaric and Constance.

Alaric accepted the accolades and the inevitable ribbing with his usual languid charm, but throughout he remained aware of Percy, quiet and reserved on the edge of the crowd.

In organizing this house party, Percy had imagined standing in Alaric's shoes. Instead, his betrothed was dead.

Yet Percy had congratulated Alaric and Constance with genuine feeling—with affection and sincere wishes for their future; with Edward's capture, Percy seemed to have found his emotional feet and patently had his demeanor under strict control—a greater degree of control than Alaric had previously observed in him.

Indeed, to Alaric, Percy seemed to have aged overnight, not so much physically as in the way he looked on the world. In the way he saw his own place in it. His intention to travel to his father's house immediately wasn't a decision the old Percy would have made; the old Percy would have prevaricated and found excuses to put off the difficult task for as long as he possibly could.

Instead, it seemed that Alaric's comment of Glynis's murder being the making of Percy might not be far wrong.

Carriage wheels rattled on the gravel outside, and in twos and threes, the guests departed. Alaric and Constance remained beside Percy and waved them all away.

Monty was the last to leave. He hung back until the other guests were rolling down the drive, then came forward and thanked Percy with his usual easy address.

Then Monty turned to Alaric and Constance and, with a beaming smile, wished them well.

Shaking Monty's hand, Alaric dryly told him, "Naturally, you'll be one of my groomsmen. We'll let you know the date."

"What?" Monty's eyes lit. "Oh, I say—yes, of course! You can count on me."

Constance and Alaric laughed.

Then Monty leaned closer and in a hushed voice said, "I just wondered if you would allow me to be the bearer of your glad tidings to the rest of the family." He opened his eyes wide. "Quite a coup, what, if I'm the first with the news?"

Alaric laughed again and clapped Monty on the shoulder. "Go forth and spread the word far and wide, but as an as-yet-unofficial understanding. It'll be a week at least before I can present myself before Constance's grandfather, so the official notice won't appear until a few days after that."

"Right-ho!" Monty beamed at Constance, then leaned in and bussed her on the cheek. "Welcome to the family, m'dear. Unofficial or not, everyone's going to be thrilled at the news."

After waving Monty away, Alaric and Constance farewelled Percy and headed back to the manor.

As the dappled shade of the woods closed around them, Alaric glanced back at Mandeville Hall. "Percy coped better than I'd expected." He met Constance's inquiring gaze. "I spoke with Carnaby—I wondered what had been done with Rosa Cleary's body. But Carnaby said Percy had learned from Mrs. Collard who Rosa's next of kin was and had notified them and paid for the undertaker to transport her body home."

"I take it Percy hasn't had to…well, be head of a household before."

"No. Although Mandeville Hall was made over to him some years ago—when his father inherited the title from a cousin and moved to live at the viscounty's principal estate in Lincolnshire—Percy simply went on as he had before, as if he was merely a son of the house with little to no responsibility for what, in essence, is now his estate." Alaric paused, then said, "His father and mother will be pleased to see the changes in him."

"You know them?"

"Reasonably well. And yes, I rather think I'll drop them a note"—

smiling, he met Constance's eyes—"by way of confirming that what they see is real."

"And perhaps making it clear what brought about the change? I suspect Percy will gloss over that."

Alaric nodded, unsurprised to find her mind following the same track as his. He glanced at her. "You've managed a household for some years, haven't you?"

Her smile was fond, but tinged with resignation. "When my parents died, I went to live with my grandparents, and shortly after that, my grandmother died. I was fourteen, but…" She waved at herself. "I was always on the large side, and many thought I was older. My grandfather had never managed anything in the house—he'd relied on my grand-mother for that. So I picked up the reins, and as my grandfather aged, I became his right hand in all things, including running the estate."

Alaric tightened his grip on her hand. "I thought as much."

They reached the spot where the trees fell away to reveal Carradale Manor, and they paused to study it.

After a moment, Alaric glanced at Constance and tipped his head at the house and fields. "Are you ready to become mistress of that?"

She met his eyes. She hesitated, then said, "You told me of the lady you imagined marrying. As for me, after my fiancé was killed, I decided that I would never wed. That I had no need of a husband, that I had all I could want being my grandfather's chatelaine."

She looked at the manor.

After a second, Alaric prompted, "But?"

Her gaze warm and loving, she met his eyes and smiled. "You proved me wrong. But it's having you as my love that's the heart of my desire. However"—she waved at the manor, and her smile deepened—"as the manor is clearly an integral part of you, yes, please—lead on."

Alaric laughed and settled her hand in his, then did as she asked, and side by side, they walked on—the rakehell and his Amazon—into the future Fate had designed for them, the perfect shared life for them both.

≈

In the carriage bowling along the highway to London, Penelope leaned her head against Barnaby's shoulder. On the seat opposite, Stokes had fallen asleep and was quietly snoring. She smiled at the sight.

"He deserves a rest." Barnaby nodded across the carriage. "Solving this case—which I suspect will cause quite a stir when the news gets out —and doing it in just a few days will be a significant feather in his cap."

Penelope hummed in agreement, then murmured, "Regardless, you have to admit that nothing ends a murder investigation better than having a wedding to look forward to."

Barnaby glanced down at her. "But you guessed Alaric and Constance would marry from the first, didn't you?"

"Of course! It was obvious—at least to a journeyman matchmaker such as I. However, in this case, I didn't need to interfere. They managed perfectly well on their own."

Barnaby humphed. "Strange to say, I suspect they had a bit of help— definitely a push—from Edward Mandeville."

"Hmm. You might be right." After a moment of cogitation, Penelope opined, "Indeed, they might not even have met were it not for Edward. If he hadn't killed Glynis, Alaric and Constance would have, at best, only seen each other in passing. And I doubt that would have done the trick."

"Fate moves in mysterious ways, her wonders to perform," Barnaby said.

Penelope sighed contentedly. "True." She turned an impish smile on her husband. "After all, Fate led me to you."

∽

Dear Reader,

When I completed writing *The Murder at Mandeville Hall*, I realized how much of the characters' actions were driven by one motive, namely, to protect—either a family member or a romantic interest. Constance journeyed to Mandeville Hall seeking to protect Glynis. Alaric felt protective of Glynis, too, as well as Percy, his childhood friend, and also soon added Constance to that list. Meanwhile, Percy sought to protect Glynis, and Edward sought to protect Percy. Although I didn't know it when I started writing, *The Murder at Mandeville Hall* became a study in what people might be driven to doing in order to protect those, who for whatever reason, they care for. I hope you enjoyed the result.

THE CASEBOOK OF BARNABY ADAIR series is one I continue to add to. The volume immediately preceding this one, the sixth installment, *The Confounding Case of the Carisbrook Emeralds*, was published just 2 months ago. More information about earlier volumes—*Where the Heart Leads*, *The Peculiar Case of Lord Finsbury's Diamonds*, *The Masterful*

Mr. Montague, The Curious Case of Lady Latimer's Shoes, and *Loving Rose: The Redemption of Malcolm Sinclair*—can be found following, along with details of my other upcoming and recent releases.

Barnaby, Penelope, Stokes, Griselda, and their friends continue to thrive. I hope they and their adventures solving mysteries and exposing villains will continue to entertain you in the future just as much as they do me.

Enjoy!

Stephanie.

For alerts as new books are released, plus information on upcoming books, exclusive sweepstakes and sneak peeks into upcoming novels, sign up for Stephanie's Private Email Newsletter
http://www.stephanielaurens.com/newsletter-signup/

The ultimate source for detailed information on all Stephanie's published books, including covers, descriptions, and excerpts, is Stephanie's Website www.stephanielaurens.com

You can also follow Stephanie via her Amazon Author Page at
http://tinyurl.com/zc3e9mp

Goodreads members can follow Stephanie via her author page
https://www.goodreads.com/author/show/9241.Stephanie_Laurens

You can email Stephanie at stephanie@stephanielaurens.com

Or find her on Facebook
https://www.facebook.com/AuthorStephanieLaurens/

COMING SOON:

The second volume in
Lady Osbaldestone's Christmas Chronicles

LADY OSBALDESTONE AND THE MISSING CHRISTMAS CAROLS
To be released on October 18, 2018.

A heartwarming tale of a long-ago country-village Christmas, a grand-mother, three eager grandchildren, one moody teenage granddaughter, an earnest young lady, a gentleman in hiding, and an elusive book of Christmas carols.

Therese, Lady Osbaldestone, and her household are quietly delighted when her younger daughter's three children, Jamie, George, and Lottie, insist on returning to Therese's house, Hartington Manor in the village Little Moseley, to spend the three weeks leading up to Christmas participating in the village's traditional events.

Then out of the blue, one of Therese's older granddaughters, Melissa, arrives on the doorstep. Her mother, Therese's older daughter, begs Therese to take Melissa in until the family gathering at Christmas—otherwise, Melissa has nowhere else to go.

Despite having no experience dealing with moody, reticent teenagers like Melissa, Therese welcomes Melissa warmly. The younger children are happy to include their cousin in their plans—and despite her initial aloofness, Melissa discovers she's not too old to enjoy the simple delights of a village Christmas.

The previous year, Therese learned the trick to keeping her unexpected guests out of mischief. She casts around and discovers that the new organist, who plays superbly, has a strange failing. He requires the written music in front of him before he can play a piece, and the church's book of Christmas carols has gone missing.

Therese immediately volunteers the services of her grandchildren, who are only too happy to fling themselves into the search to find the missing book of carols. Its disappearance threatens one of the village's most-valued Christmas traditions—the Carol Service—yet as the book has always been freely loaned within the village, no one imagines that it won't be found with a little application.

But as Therese's intrepid four follow the trail of the book from house to house, the mystery of where the book has vanished to only deepens. Then the organist hears the children singing and invites them to form a special guest choir. The children love singing, and provided they find the book in time, they'll be able to put on an extra-special service for the village.

While the urgency and their desire to find the missing book escalates, the children—being Therese's grandchildren—get distracted by the potential for romance that buds, burgeons, and blooms before them.

Yet as Christmas nears, the questions remain: Will the four unravel the twisted trail of the missing book in time to save the village's Carol Service? And will they succeed in nudging the organist and the harpist they've found to play alongside him into seizing the happy-ever-after that hovers before the pair's noses?

Second in series. A novel of 62,000 words. A Christmas tale full of music and romance.

ALSO AVAILABLE:
The first volume in Lady Osbaldestone's Christmas Chronicles
LADY OSBALDESTONE'S CHRISTMAS GOOSE

#1 New York Times *bestselling author Stephanie Laurens brings you a lighthearted tale of Christmas long ago with a grandmother and three of her grandchildren, one lost soul, a lady driven to distraction, a recalcitrant donkey, and a flock of determined geese.*

Three years after being widowed, Therese, Lady Osbaldestone finally settles into her dower property of Hartington Manor in the village of Little Moseley in Hampshire. She is in two minds as to whether life in the small village will generate sufficient interest to keep her amused over the months when she is not in London or visiting friends around the country. But she will see.

It's December, 1810, and Therese is looking forward to her usual Christmas with her family at Winslow Abbey, her youngest daughter, Celia's home. But then a carriage rolls up and disgorges Celia's three oldest children. Their father has contracted mumps, and their mother has sent the three—Jamie, George, and Lottie—to spend this Christmas with their grandmama in Little Moseley.

Therese has never had to manage small children, not even her own. She assumes the children will keep themselves amused, but quickly learns that what amuses three inquisitive, curious, and confident youngsters isn't compatible with village peace. Just when it seems she will have to set her mind to inventing something, she and the children learn that with only twelve days to go before Christmas, the village flock of geese has vanished.

Every household in the village is now missing the centerpiece of their Christmas feast. But how could an entire flock go missing without the slightest trace? The children are as mystified and as curious as Therese—and she seizes on the mystery as the perfect distraction for the three children as well as herself.

But while searching for the geese, she and her three helpers stumble on two locals who, it is clear, are in dire need of assistance in sorting out their lives. Never one to shy from a little matchmaking, Therese undertakes to guide Miss Eugenia Fitzgibbon into the arms of the determinedly reclusive Lord Longfellow. To her considerable surprise, she discovers that her grandchildren have inherited skills and talents from both her late husband as well as herself. And with all the customary village events held in the lead up to Christmas, she and her three helpers have opportunities galore in which to subtly nudge and steer.

Yet while their matchmaking appears to be succeeding, neither they nor anyone else have found so much as a feather from the village's geese. Larceny is ruled out; a flock of that size could not have been taken from the area without someone noticing. So where could the birds be? And with the days passing and Christmas inexorably approaching, will they find the blasted birds in time?

First in series. A novel of 60,000 words. A Christmas tale of romance and geese.

RECENTLY RELEASED IN THE CASEBOOK OF BARNABY ADAIR NOVELS:

THE CONFOUNDING CASE OF THE CARISBROOK EMERALDS

The sixth volume in
The Casebook of Barnaby Adair mystery-romances

#1 New York Times *bestselling author Stephanie Laurens brings you a tale of emerging and also established loves and the many facets of family, interwoven with mystery and murder.*

A young lady accused of theft and the gentleman who elects himself her champion enlist the aid of Stokes, Barnaby, Penelope, and friends in pursuing justice, only to find themselves tangled in a web of inter-family tensions and secrets.

When Miss Cara Di Abaccio is accused of stealing the Carisbrook emeralds by the infamously arrogant Lady Carisbrook and marched out of her guardian's house by Scotland Yard's finest, Hugo Adair, Barnaby Adair's cousin, takes umbrage and descends on Scotland Yard, breathing fire in Cara's defense.

Hugo discovers Inspector Stokes has been assigned to the case, and after surveying the evidence thus far, Stokes calls in his big guns when it comes to dealing with investigations in the ton—namely, the Honorable Barnaby Adair and his wife, Penelope.

Soon convinced of Cara's innocence and—given Hugo's apparent tendre for Cara—the need to clear her name, Penelope and Barnaby join Stokes and his team in pursuing the emeralds and, most importantly, who stole them.

But the deeper our intrepid investigators delve into the Carisbrook household, the more certain they become that all is not as it seems. Lady Carisbrook is a harpy, Franklin Carisbrook is secretive, Julia Carisbrook is overly timid, and Lord Carisbrook, otherwise a genial and honorable gentleman, holds himself distant from his family. More, his lordship attempts to shut down the investigation. And Stokes, Barnaby, and Penelope are convinced the Carisbrooks' staff are not sharing all they know.

Meanwhile, having been appointed Cara's watchdog until the mystery is resolved, Hugo, fascinated by Cara as he's been with no other young lady, seeks to entertain and amuse her...and, increasingly intently, to discover the way to her heart. Consequently, Penelope finds herself juggling the attractions of the investigation against the demands of the Adair family for her to actively encourage the budding romance.

What would her mentors advise? On that, Penelope is crystal clear.

Regardless, aided by Griselda, Violet, and Montague and calling on contacts in business, the underworld, and ton society, Penelope, Barnaby, and Stokes battle to peel back each layer of subterfuge and, step by step, eliminate the innocent and follow the emeralds' trail...

Yet instead of becoming clearer, the veils and shadows shrouding the Carisbrooks only grow murkier...until, abruptly, our investigators find themselves facing an inexplicable death, with a potential murderer whose conviction would shake society to its back teeth.

A historical novel of 78,000 words interweaving mystery, romance, and social intrigue.

Praise for *The Confounding Case of the Carisbrook Emeralds*

"(An) alluring mystery brimming with red herrings, lots of intrigue, and that perfect touch of romance for which Laurens is rightly revered."
Angela M., Copy Editor, Red Adept Editing

"Laurens crafts a story as elegant as the gentlemen and women who populate it." *Kim H., Proofreader, Red Adept Editing*

"I really enjoyed this well-written historical mystery novel! The characters unravel exciting plot twists and turns as they investigate the disappearance of a famous set of emeralds." *Kristina B., Proofreader, Red Adept Editing*

ALSO RECENTLY RELEASED:

The first volume in THE CAVANAUGHS
THE DESIGNS OF LORD RANDOLPH CAVANAUGH

#1 New York Times bestselling author Stephanie Laurens returns with a new series that captures the simmering desires and intrigues of early Victorians as only she can. Ryder Cavanaugh's step-siblings are determined to make their own marks in London society. Seeking fortune and passion, THE CAVANAUGHS will delight readers with their bold exploits.

An independent nobleman

Lord Randolph Cavanaugh is loyal and devoted—but only to family. To the rest of the world he's aloof and untouchable, a respected and driven entrepreneur. But Rand yearns for more in life, and when he travels to Buckinghamshire to review a recent investment, he discovers a passionate woman who will challenge his rigid self-control...

A determined lady

Felicia Throgmorton intends to keep her family afloat. For decades, her father was consumed by his inventions and now, months after his death, with their finances in ruins, her brother insists on continuing their father's tinkering. Felicia is desperate to hold together what's left of the estate. Then she discovers she must help persuade their latest investor that her father's follies are a risk worth taking...

Together—the perfect team

Rand arrives at Throgmorton Hall to discover the invention on which he's staked his reputation has exploded, the inventor is not who he expected, and a fiercely intelligent woman now holds the key to his future success. But unflinching courage in the face of dismaying hurdles is a trait they share, and Rand and Felicia are forced to act together against ruthless foes to protect everything they hold dear.

AND FOR HOW IT ALL BEGAN...

Read about Penelope's and Barnaby's romance, plus that of Stokes and Griselda, in

The first volume in
The Casebook of Barnaby Adair mystery-romances
WHERE THE HEART LEADS

Penelope Ashford, Portia Cynster's younger sister, has grown up with every advantage - wealth, position, and beauty. Yet Penelope is anything but a typical ton miss - forceful, willful and blunt to a fault, she has for years devoted her considerable energy and intelligence to directing an institution caring for the forgotten orphans of London's streets.

But now her charges are mysteriously disappearing. Desperate, Penelope turns to the one man she knows who might help her - Barnaby Adair.

Handsome scion of a noble house, Adair has made a name for himself in political and judicial circles. His powers of deduction and observation combined with his pedigree has seen him solve several serious crimes within the ton. Although he makes her irritatingly uncomfortable, Penelope throws caution to the wind and appears on his bachelor doorstep late one night, determined to recruit him to her cause.

Barnaby is intrigued—by her story, and her. Her bold beauty and undeniable brains make a striking contrast to the usual insipid ton misses. And as he's in dire need of an excuse to avoid said insipid misses, he accepts her challenge, never dreaming she and it will consume his every waking hour.

Enlisting the aid of Inspector Basil Stokes of the fledgling Scotland Yard, they infiltrate the streets of London's notorious East End. But as they unravel the mystery of the missing boys, they cross the trail of a criminal embedded in the very organization recently created to protect all Londoners. And that criminal knows of them and their efforts, and is only too ready to threaten all they hold dear, including their new-found knowledge of the intrigues of the human heart.

FURTHER CASES AND THE EVOLUTION OF RELATIONSHIPS CONTINUE IN:

The second volume in
The Casebook of Barnaby Adair mystery-romances
THE PECULIAR CASE OF LORD FINSBURY'S DIAMONDS

#1 New York Times *bestselling author Stephanie Laurens brings you a tale of murder, mystery, passion, and intrigue – and diamonds!*

Penelope Adair, wife and partner of amateur sleuth Barnaby Adair, is so hugely pregnant she cannot even waddle. When Barnaby is summoned to assist Inspector Stokes of Scotland Yard in investigating the violent murder of a gentleman at a house party, Penelope, frustrated that she cannot participate, insists that she and Griselda, Stokes's wife, be duly informed of their husbands' discoveries.

Yet what Barnaby and Stokes uncover only leads to more questions. The murdered gentleman had been thrown out of the house party days before, so why had he come back? And how and why did he come to have the fabulous Finsbury diamond necklace in his pocket, much to Lord Finsbury's consternation. Most peculiar of all, why had the murderer left the necklace, worth a stupendous fortune, on the body?

The conundrums compound as our intrepid investigators attempt to make sense of this baffling case. Meanwhile, the threat of scandal grows ever more tangible for all those attending the house party – and the stakes are highest for Lord Finsbury's daughter and the gentleman who has spent the last decade resurrecting his family fortune so he can aspire to her hand. Working parallel to Barnaby and Stokes, the would-be lovers hunt for a path through the maze of contradictory facts to expose the murderer, disperse the pall of scandal, and claim the love and the shared life they crave.

A pre-Victorian mystery with strong elements of romance. A short novel of 39,000 words.

The third volume in
The Casebook of Barnaby Adair mystery-romances
THE MASTERFUL MR. MONTAGUE

Montague has devoted his life to managing the wealth of London's elite, but at a huge cost: a family of his own. Then the enticing Miss Violet Matcham seeks his help, and in the puzzle she presents him, he finds an intriguing new challenge professionally...and personally.

Violet, devoted lady-companion to the aging Lady Halstead, turns to Montague to reassure her ladyship that her affairs are in order. But the famous Montague is not at all what she'd expected—this man is compelling, decisive, supportive, and strong—everything Violet needs in a champion, a position to which Montague rapidly lays claim.

But then Lady Halstead is murdered and Violet and Montague, aided by Barnaby Adair, Inspector Stokes, Penelope, and Griselda, race to expose a cunning and cold-blooded killer...who stalks closer and closer. Will Montague and Violet learn the shocking truth too late to seize their chance at enduring love?

A pre-Victorian tale of romance and mystery in the classic historical romance style. A novel of 120,000 words.

The fourth volume in
The Casebook of Barnaby Adair mystery-romances
THE CURIOUS CASE OF LADY LATIMER'S SHOES

#1 New York Times *bestselling author Stephanie Laurens brings you a tale of mysterious death, feuding families, star-crossed lovers—and shoes to die for.*

With her husband, amateur-sleuth the Honorable Barnaby Adair, decidedly eccentric fashionable matron Penelope Adair is attending the premier event opening the haut ton's Season when a body is discovered in the gardens. A lady has been struck down with a finial from the terrace balustrade. Her family is present, as are the cream of the haut ton—the shocked hosts turn to Barnaby and Penelope for help.

Barnaby calls in Inspector Basil Stokes and they begin their investigation. Penelope assists by learning all she can about the victim's family, and uncovers a feud between them and the Latimers over the fabulous shoes known as Lady Latimer's shoes, currently exclusive to the Latimers.

The deeper Penelope delves, the more convinced she becomes that the murder is somehow connected to the shoes. She conscripts Griselda, Stokes's wife, and Violet Montague, now Penelope's secretary, and the trio set out to learn all they can about the people involved and most importantly the shoes, a direction vindicated when unexpected witnesses report seeing a lady fleeing the scene—wearing Lady Latimer's shoes.

But nothing is as it seems, and the more Penelope and her friends learn about the shoes, conundrums abound, compounded by a Romeo-and-Juliet romance and escalating social pressure...until at last, the pieces fall into place, and finally understanding what has occurred, the six intrepid investigators race to prevent an even worse tragedy.

A pre-Victorian mystery with strong elements of romance. A novel of 76,000 words.

The fifth volume in
The Casebook of Barnaby Adair mystery-romances
LOVING ROSE: THE REDEMPTION OF MALCOLM SINCLAIR

#1 New York Times bestselling author Stephanie Laurens returns with another thrilling story from the Casebook of Barnaby Adair...

Miraculously spared from death, Malcolm Sinclair erases the notorious man he once was. Reinventing himself as Thomas Glendower, he strives to make amends for his past, yet he never imagines penance might come via a secretive lady he discovers living in his secluded manor.

Rose has a plausible explanation for why she and her children are residing in Thomas's house, but she quickly realizes he's far too intelligent to fool. Revealing the truth is impossibly dangerous, yet day by day, he wins her trust, and then her heart.

But then her enemy closes in, and Rose turns to Thomas as the only man who can protect her and the children. And when she asks for his help, Thomas finally understands his true purpose, and with unwavering commitment, he seeks his redemption in the only way he can—through living the reality of loving Rose.

A pre-Victorian tale of romance and mystery in the classic historical romance style. A novel of 105,000 words.

ABOUT THE AUTHOR

#1 *New York Times* bestselling author Stephanie Laurens began writing romances as an escape from the dry world of professional science. Her hobby quickly became a career when her first novel was accepted for publication, and with entirely becoming alacrity, she gave up writing about facts in favor of writing fiction.

All Laurens's works to date are historical romances, ranging from medieval times to the mid-1800s, and her settings range from Scotland to India. The majority of her works are set in the period of the British Regency. Laurens has published more than 70 works of historical romance, including 39 *New York Times* bestsellers. Laurens has sold more than 20 million print, audio, and e-books globally. All her works are continuously available in print and e-book formats in English worldwide, and have been translated into many other languages. An international bestseller, among other accolades, Laurens has received the Romance Writers of America® prestigious RITA® Award for Best Romance Novella 2008 for *The Fall of Rogue Gerrard*.

Laurens's continuing novels featuring the Cynster family are widely regarded as classics of the historical romance genre. Other series include the *Bastion Club Novels*, the *Black Cobra Quartet*, and the *Casebook of Barnaby Adair Novels*. All her previous works remain available in print and all e-book formats.

For information on all published novels and on upcoming releases and updates on novels yet to come, visit Stephanie's website: www.stephanielaurens.com

To sign up for Stephanie's Email Newsletter (a private list) for heads-up alerts as new books are released, exclusive sneak peeks into upcoming books, and exclusive sweepstakes contests, follow the prompts at Stephanie's Email Newsletter Sign-up Page

Stephanie lives with her husband and a goofy black labradoodle in the hills outside Melbourne, Australia. When she isn't writing, she's reading, and if she isn't reading, she'll be tending her garden.

www.stephanielaurens.com
stephanie@stephanielaurens.com

CPSIA information can be obtained
at www.ICGtesting.com
Printed in the USA
LVHW03s0350270818
588229LV00021BA/1001/P